A RIGHT
HOPE

MICHAEL CAL BROOKS

A RIGHT HOPE

TATE PUBLISHING
AND ENTERPRISES, LLC

Published by Tate Publishing & Enterprises, LLC
127 E. Trade Center Terrace | Mustang, Oklahoma 73064 USA
1.888.361.9473 | www.tatepublishing.com

Tate Publishing is committed to excellence in the publishing industry. The company reflects the philosophy established by the founders, based on Psalm 68:11,
"The Lord gave the word and great was the company of those who published it."

Published in the United States of America

ISBN: 978-1-63063-812-2
1. Fiction / Political
2. Fiction / Romance / General
14.04.07

ACKNOWLEDGEMENTS

I have to thank my Lord and savior Jesus Christ first and foremost, for what he did on the cross for me. His inspiration has guided my journey.

My thanks go out to family and friends for their support and unconditional love. Being a person that usually has much to say, I finally found an avenue in which to channel some of my excess philosophical energy, through my writing. My family and friends endured every single one of my many episodes of "too much to say" if you will, that I have to thank them for being such good sports all these years.

I had no idea what to expect with regard to getting a novel published, so I have to say, that I was blown away by the entire staff at Tate Publishing, who took care of everything pertaining to me and my book, with the utmost professionalism and care. I was a contractor for twenty years, and if I learned one thing in that experience, it was how to treat people, and Tate Publishing knocked it out of the park. Thank you so much.

I would also like to thank Wayne State University, for trimming away my rough edges as a writer, and always encouraging me to express myself with my own thoughts.

INTRODUCTION

M any decades have passed in America, and I still get an unsatisfied feeling every four years while watching a presidential debate. Unsatisfied because I feel like the conservative candidate that is representing the Republican Party always seems to be someone that just fell into that opportunity, or rather is up there just because everyone else is a bad choice. What I have been waiting for, is a politician that was born to be president— one that has the very values that made this country what it has become since it was founded. Washington DC is a very different place than it was a decade or so ago, and this country has slowly but surely been losing some of the values that it once possessed… values that made America what it became when our founding father's built it more than two-hundred years ago.

My purpose for this book, was to bring attention to the things that have caused America to drift away from God. In particular, the institution of marriage and how it has fallen apart for most of society, and the forgotten blessing that comes to a man and woman who put God first and foremost in their lives. I needed a character that would fit, in terms of the type of political candidate that our country has failed to produce over the last thirty years. I created that very candidate in James Ryan Roberts. I did this in the hopes that his willingness to achieve big, would create a willingness in others to also be inspired to be better. I tried not to go overboard, and create someone that was impossible for a young man today to follow. My only intention was to inspire this country to reach down and search for what it has lost over the last years, which has caused Washington to spiral out of control.

I had many things over the past years that inspired me to write this story. I was always inspired by the aura of young royalty that surrounded the late John F. Kennedy Jr. and his wife, Carolyn Bessette-Kennedy. I have always felt that the advantages that the young Kennedy would have had in politics someday, would have been immense had he not died. So I included the prestige which he and Carolyn Bessette-Kennedy created with the popularity they had as America's darling couple. I also included the World Trade Center attacks on September 11, 2001, because I needed something to symbolize how imperative it is that America be led by someone that knows what he is doing, and not by someone that is only seeking power. In addition, for years, I have had this desire to write a story about a grandfather mentoring his grandson, but I never had a story to put together with it until now. The love and admiration that James has for his grandfather, is the motivation that pushes him, to the places that few young men are blessed to go.

I wanted this book to be the creation of something I so desperately wanted to experience in my real life—an experience of a right-wing hope in Washington DC. What I never intended from the beginning—and what I most fortunately discovered while writing this—was the realization of my own desire to experience a real and true romance with someone special. For me, writing about James and Josie had a greater impact on me than I could have ever imagined…it opened my heart as a man, which ultimately led me to the woman I fell in love with; it led me to my darling, Louise.

CHAPTER 1

In the early dim of dawn, while sitting along the Hudson River, James Ryan Roberts leans back on a park bench on campus. He ponders all that has happened, and imagines all that is to come. There are very few opportunities while in New York City to truly experience a moment where time slows down long enough to hear oneself think. A few minutes before 6:00 a.m. in a big city, is not a moment easily taken for granted, that is, if you're an avid listener of silence. It truly is one of very few moments where late owls and early risers are on the same page. Not only is it too early for the noise of societal agendas and commerce, the time is just perfect for the rhythmic singing of birds as they roam the wet grass, pecking for the "early bird's" worm. It is like a seasoned orchestra of harmonious bliss.

As species, birds are very perceptive of the fact that they are considerably safer high up in a tree, than they are lurking on the ground, especially with people around. However, they are even more perceptive at sensing the harmlessness of a single human spirit. So they whistle and frolic in the grass, totally unconcerned with this noticeably familiar gentleman with a look of deep thought in his eyes, sitting on a park bench near the Hudson.

A Columbia University professor notices James sitting there every day at about 5:45 a.m. with the birds. It's quite entertaining for him to witness the trust the birds have with the solitary figure while they search for their morning feed. The professor had been meaning to walk over there but has always decided against it, as James looks as if he's experiencing a state of solace, and also for fear of disrupting the peaceful wildlife.

Thus, James drinks his morning coffee alone near the Hudson, while looking up at the trees and the tops of buildings. When you're elevated enough to see the peaks of metallic mountains in the near distance at Columbia University, and you look in the direction of Lower Manhattan, your memory induces a case of mild despair. The Lower Manhattan skyline today is missing its throne; it is missing its watchtowers of hope and might. Like a number eleven written on a wall, this wall has been stripped of that number.

That early September day in 2001 was a day that will not be forgotten in this country for hundreds of years, and for the people of New York, it will always be stamped in their minds as the thing that is most identifiable about her existence from that day forward. Four years pass, and still, no shocking details of September 11 ever seem to fade from the memory of millions. For the people of New York City, it will always seem like yesterday, especially for the loved ones of the victims.

James whispers, "God, may you grant peace to the people of New York as well as provide strength to move on. In the spirit of those that lost their lives on that day and in the name of our Lord and Savior. Amen."

As a Columbia University graduate student, James sits and ponders where he was the morning of September 11, 2001. He didn't experience that horrible day firsthand, but it had a great influence on where he wanted his life's path to lead. One must understand that from a very early age—due in large part to the influence of his loving grandfather, Michael, who was his mentor growing up without a father in the picture—James has always had his sights set far beyond Macomb, Indiana. So when he experienced the terrorist attacks on a little television monitor just outside the principal's office at Crenshaw High School in

Indiana, all he could think about was what the people of New York were going through while they were running frantically in the streets of Lower Manhattan, trying to get to safety.

James was emotionally captured during his senior year in Indiana, with all that was going on in New York during and after 9/11. You could say that his abundant level of patriotism was instilled in him at a very early age with the mentoring of his grandfather, who was a Vietnam War hero. Also, with the immense belief that James has in himself as a person, the attacks were what gave birth to this unrelenting desire to get out of this small Indiana town, and make a difference in a world that was changing fast following September 11. No moments in recent history have induced changes in America more than the events that transpired on that fateful day. It truly was the commencement of a dark time in America, and it's only the beginning.

The biggest shock on September 11, 2001, was not the planes actually flying into the buildings, even though that would be very hard to understand while the events were unfolding. How could so many people, with all that was happening at that moment, have the wherewithal to even ponder the thought of the implosion of those towers? Most people are usually pretty observant when it comes to things anticipated, but that was the last thing that was going through the minds of Americans at that moment. I'm sure there were structural engineers and architects all over the world on that early Tuesday morning in 2001, who had a slight moment of concern while those buildings were still standing—the concern of what all that burning hot jet fuel would do to the steel frame of the World Trade Center in the event that the crash might have scraped heat-protection insulation away from the steel.

The World Trade Center was built, using a unique weight-bearing technique on the exterior of the towers that ultimately led to its implosion as the wingspan of the planes took out large sections of those supports. If there was just a slight exposure of steel, with the buildings burning that hot, all that would be needed for implosion was a structural weakness, and the weight would be too heavy to bear. Nevertheless, it was an entirely different experience when the buildings came down, than it was with the planes crashing into them. The attacks were like the wound of a soldier in battle, while the implosion was the unfortunate amputation.

Even though James is only twenty-one years old, there were events over the last thirty-some years that ultimately lead to him being a student at Columbia University. No matter what the situation brings, James has never questioned his abilities, nor has he ever felt shaky on his own two feet. However, to be that secure, there had to be moments of frustration in order for him to acquire this immense strength within himself. James leans his head back on the park bench on this late summer morning, and once again ponders things of the past that allowed him to have this opportunity. When his grandfather, Michael, built the pole barn in Indiana, he poured a slab of concrete in the back half of the barn. The area that he used was roughly thirty feet by thirty feet. Then he placed gym mats down to cover the concrete so that he and James had a gymnasium for their own training.

Needless to say, past experiences on those mats can be understood today as benefits of his molding, but at the time they were unfolding, they were confusing moments for James. During those years, James was learning a discipline that he couldn't truly understand the benefits of until he got older. He enjoyed the advancement of his talent through the aikido karate that he was being taught, but discipline was the great benefit of those moments of frustration. However, during those moments, James wasn't exactly old enough to know whether the motivations of his grandfather were completely on the level or not. Nonetheless, he went along with it, and he has benefited greatly for persevering through those rough moments as a boy—being taught discipline and self-defense by his war hero grandfather, and all that in a generation that has truly lost touch with discipline.

Grandfather Michael witnessed some pitiful moments in Vietnam with some of the young kids that the US Military sent over there to defend South Vietnam from the communism of North Vietnam. One of the first things to come to mind for him, as James was growing from an infant into being a little boy, was how he wanted to prepare his grandson for a world that could be cruel at times. When he was getting to know some of those young American soldiers and realizing some of them had no business being in Vietnam, he couldn't help but think of the mothers of those kids, and wonder if they knew their sons probably wouldn't be making it home alive. Consequently, the last thing Grandfather Michael wanted for his daughter Charlotte to experience in this life, was to have to bury her own son. So he taught James everything he knew in the hopes that in the event he was put in a dangerous situation, he would have the necessary survival instincts to make it home alive to his mother.

It wasn't easy because there were times when James ran out of the pole barn and into the house, crying his eyes out. However, because his mother, Charlotte, was aware of what her father was trying to accomplish with James, she provided a soft place for James to land at times. Knowing full well that, if James was ever going to adjust to the discipline before he gave up, he would need a sensitive sanctuary. So for a short while, back when James was six or seven years old, Grandfather Michael was the teacher, and Charlotte was the sensitive landing place for recuperation. Fortunately for them, those moments of James getting upset became few and far between, so it wasn't a long time that Charlotte had to see her boy go through this. She witnessed a subtle change in her boy as the weeks went by.

After a short while, James got really good with karate and eventually graduated to stick fighting as well. He got so good at martial arts that Grandfather Michael had to get him involved in an aikido karate dojo in Indianapolis. James became a black belt in karate at the early age of eight and reached 4th degree black belt before he left for New York. He hasn't had time to join a dojo in New York, but he will once his PhD is finished and he can settle down somewhere. It is very important to him to reach his 5th Dan ranking, but that will have to wait until later.

As James ponders the moments he had with his grandfather at about the age of seven, he remembers that it was a significant moment in his life when grandfather was trying to get him to the point, where he would be able to endure anything physically or mentally. Aikido karate is a discipline that pushes the flexible limits of your opponent's joints and tendons, and in order to be well-skilled, one needs to stretch his own limitations with regard to pain. Needless to say, he and his grandfather had a few heated moments when James was about seven and eight years old. But, it didn't take long for James to realize the benefits of his experience. Physical pain was going to be something that James could now endure a lot of. Later on, when he got into his teens, he started to sense the command which he had around people, and he felt absolutely no fear in situations that would cause most people to tremble.

The mental toughness alone that James received from this training was enough to get him to Columbia University, but he is also pretty talented physically in the art of defense. He once made the joke that Bruce Lee never made it to a 4th Dan ranking. His friends at the dojo in Indianapolis always got a laugh out of that. However, he also made the point that had Bruce Lee been in a ranking system such as that, he probably would have been a 10th Dan, and maybe even better than that.

Those memories for James were the beginning of building him up to achieve all the dreams he had built up in his head over the last ten years. There would be many plateaus to get over in New York, as well as down the road, but if his training is any indication as to the rate at which he would succeed, getting to the top in politics someday wasn't out of the realm of possibility for him.

Columbia University is no ordinary school in the world today. Amani, who is a neighbor that lives in James's apartment building on campus, asked him a question the other day, and James still can't seem to get it off his mind as he continues to take in the early morning silence of Manhattan.

The question Amani asked was, "How did a kid from a small Midwest town in Indiana with no money and without a former alumnus to speak of in the family, ever end up with this opportunity? I know grade point average alone can't get one to Columbia University, so what gives?"

James responded with, "Come by the apartment tonight, and I'll tell you over a cold beer."

"I'll be there."

Amani was a smart Iranian kid, and James really liked him because he could practice speaking Persian—the predominant language of Iran—which was a language James was still in the process of learning. James's grandfather was always telling him to know his Middle East languages, especially the language of Iran, because his grandpa was positive that this country was going to grow into a big concern for the United States. His theory was that if James had the ability to speak Middle East languages, it would give him a greater chance of making a difference in a world that needed brave and talented souls working for its safety. Also, Grandfather Michael was fully aware that if his grandson wanted to go deep into politics someday, he would need to serve his country somewhere along the way in order to acquire respect from his peers as well as from the American people.

The question Amani had for him regarding how he got to Columbia wasn't a tough question for James because he has no hesitations at all as to where he belongs in the world and who he is as a person. Those convictions were more than well-established deep in the western sticks of Indiana. However, there is a considerable amount of modesty in his nature, so revealing this story to Amani wasn't going to be a breeze, even with the pride he holds for his grandfather, and all that he did while serving his country in Vietnam. James just simply has personal memories that are more comfortable remaining in their secrecy. Nevertheless, Amani comes by, and James gives him a cold beer. They find a comfortable spot outside the apartment on a picnic table.

"It's a long story, Amani, so I'll keep it to an abbreviated version. It goes all the way back to 1970, deep in the jungles of Vietnam. To make a long story short, it had to do with a United States senator from New Hampshire, who was a colonel at the time, but I'll get to that shortly. My grandfather, Michael, who was a Captain at the time, didn't like to talk about his experience in Vietnam, as he has always said that his voice regarding those events are deeply buried with the soldiers who died under his command. I mean, he'd say bits and pieces here and there, but this story about Senator John Purcell had to go on paper. It was just the only way he could explain it. I can say I understand your curiosity regarding this, Amani, because I too believe I'm very fortunate to be here at Columbia, and I am extremely grateful to all who've paved my way. It is the reason I work so hard, because it is the least I can do to appreciate the magnitude of my opportunity. Furthermore, everyone has someone who influenced them the most, and for me, my maternal grandfather is my hero and the spirit with which I harbor the determination to succeed. He was the greatest man I'll ever know," James turns his head to conceal a tear, without Amani noticing.

It is 7:00 p.m. on a Thursday in 2005, the first week of the fall semester, Amani and James continue to discuss his grandfather's legacy. James pauses for a moment to gather his thoughts before he decides to return to his grandfather's folder. When you look at James, one notices deepness in his look that cannot be confused with boredom. James is just marching to a completely different drummer if you will. He is six-feet-three-inches tall, with black hair and blue eyes. You won't hear him speak much of it, but aikido karate is very important to him. It is something he doesn't want people to know about, as he prefers to keep things like that more on the down low. James is more interested in being a spirit of compassion and love, rather than a spirit of intimidation or aggression. It was not only his grandfather's instruction to learn the arts of self-defense, but it was also his suggestion to keep it concealed.

Many that are familiar with James know, that he has always said that the Republican Party in America has been missing its tall, young, and distinguished conservative candidate for decades. He once referred to it as a young modern day Teddy Roosevelt. This isn't to say that he was referring to himself. He was only explaining his heart's desire as a young conservative American voter. There have been excellent conservative candidates over the last hundred years or so, but something was just lacking in them. With the exception of Ronald Reagan, there always seemed to have been a feeling that something was missing in Republican candidates. There may have been better Right-Wing prospects from the early half of the twentieth century, but nothing like Teddy Roosevelt. The Democratic Party has produced many promising candidates over the last hundred years. However, James just feels it's time for America to be blessed with a conservative that is right for the job—a man that commands the American public. His thinking to himself is that if he can't be that man, he will help bring that man forward and encourage his success.

James isn't an athlete in terms of sport, but he has a much chiseled body due to his dedication to karate, from which he receives a healthy volume of his immense focus and discipline. Also, James has a considerable long distance running regiment which explains, despite not being an athlete, the great shape he keeps. The remainder of his physical training in terms of muscle is strictly resistance training, along with pull-ups and push-ups as well as abdominals. In addition, his physical condition is accompanied by an even more impressive mental makeup. One of James's favorite reads in philosophy was the mentor-student relationship between eastern transcendentalist Jiddu Krishnamurti and his student, Bruce Lee. And judging by James's discipline, one can tell the influence the writer had on him. However, that isn't to say that he is influenced by the religion, only their mental disciplines, as James is a devout Christian. Again, he was intrigued by his writings, as well as fascinated with the effects it had on Bruce Lee's talent and focus.

James was also moved by many other writers, as his grandfather instilled in him at a very early age, the benefits of a reader's journey as well as writing and the virtually ascending spirit with which it provides. His grandfather felt it would be truly great for James to transcend a young boy's fatherless world through the essence of literature. One cannot say that James was influenced by anyone in particular, but, what can be said, is that the combination of all of them, contributed greatly to what he is today in terms of a thinker, as well as a writer. There are way too many to list, but a short list of his favorites would include Erasmus, Thomas More, Saint Augustine, Thomas Aquinas, Shakespeare, James Baldwin, D.H. Lawrence, William Faulkner, and Cervantes, to name few of what is a larger collection that sits on his book shelf in the apartment at Columbia. However, James would tell you the greatest influence of his life, and what has brought him to be what he is today is the constant sculpture work of God on his life. James has always been a Christian, but his deep devotion to God was greatly influenced by his friendship with Ben Wilson in Macomb, Indiana.

James and Ben spent a lot of time together in Macomb over the years. They are avid hunters and fishermen. Their families, dating back decades, have been very tight through the farming industry, so they kind of grew up together like cousins. They both have this ongoing dream that Ben would one day be James's campaign manager in politics, and Ben would study political science in college. Ben and James are years away from them both being in a position for that, so they will have to wait and see how the next ten to fifteen years unfold. Besides, with regard to experience in politics, one can be sure that James is going to need a heck of a lot more on his resume than his experience as an employee at the local Macomb movie theater in Indiana.

James always went to church even as a child, but Ben went through this transformation spiritually about eight years ago, and ever since, both have had a deep faith in the Lord. Luckily for both of them, it happened before either one of them went through puberty, because if there is a time when a boy pulls away from spirituality, it is definitely around the age of thirteen. For either one of them to carry virginity as far as they have, it was quite beneficial not being introduced to sex until after the good Lord had his protection over them. You could say James and Ben are both in the same boat in terms of conservative politics. Although Ben is not exactly interested all that much, he does have the values and opinions of a definite right-winger though.

James and Ben both have identical faiths with two very different experiences. Both attend church on most Sundays, and both get on their knees three or four times a day and pray. James has mentioned that one of the intriguing aspects of other religions, when he was researching them, was how many times a day other faiths have time to kneel and pray. One of the conclusive results of his research on the matter was that Christians are the least faithful of all the religions, and that is in terms of getting on the knees and praying. James isn't envious of Islam, but he was very moved by how dedicated they are at not missing prayer time, so he incorporated that discipline into his own faith in Jesus Christ. Needless to say, it has made a difference. Anything that would increase the discipline of submitting to God's authority, like prayer, only ensures a person with a deeper faith. It certainly can't have adverse effects, attempting to get closer to the Lord.

James and Ben will make a great team in the next few years because they share a deep faith in God, and that is pretty rare. Putting two people like them together to accomplish something is bound to have its good fortune, especially with how much they draw on God's good graces in all that they do. The last few years since being away from Indiana, it has been difficult for James to show consistency with attending church regularly. However, his involvement with Apostolos Campus Ministry at Columbia University has kept him plenty busy in terms of a church family. Just last Sunday, James was asked to fill in, and give a sermon in place of a pastor friend that had to go out of town for a family emergency. The sermon that he gave wasn't the main word for that particular service because the assistant pastor handled that. James just had to fill in for the assistant pastor and his usual message, which is only about ten minutes long. He can still remember every single word that he said on that day. When you visualize standing in front of people and preaching, it seems to be much easier, but when you actually get up there, you're nervous the first couple of times. After doing it once, James couldn't wait to get back up there some day.

———⬦———

"Everyone, bow your heads and let's pray.

Dear heavenly Father,
we humbly come before you today to attempt
to draw your love
closer and closer to us so that we may see
your will more clearly in us.
We thank you for sending your son, our Lord and
Savior, Jesus Christ, into the world to pay for our sins
so that we can have a close relationship with you.

Give us strength, wisdom, and a spirit of kindness
so that we can go into the world today and be a
lamp of your great love.
We ask these things in Jesus's name. Amen.

James begins his sermon, "I'm not going to ask you to open your Bibles today, but I do want to touch on a subject that I was dwelling on recently. The question of which Christians are saved and which ones are not saved."

As a picture of a muddy sheep appears on the PowerPoint screen, James continues, "It isn't difficult to figure out whether or not we are in God's good graces or not. When a sheep falls down in the mud and gets dirty, it instantly goes into survival mode in order to get out of the mud and get clean."

A picture of a pig lying in the mud now appears on the screen. "A pig doesn't know that being in the mud is anything wrong, and therefore, has no desire to get clean. Christians are very much divided in the same way as the nature of these two species of animals. God chose sheep as an analogy for his saved people for a reason, and James was also, in the back of His mind, thinking of a pig as well with respect to unrepentant Christians. I'm not referencing a pig as a symbolization of a Christian, but a symbolization of a dirty one that is running from God and doesn't know that it needs to be clean."

A picture of Jesus carrying a cross appears on the PowerPoint screen. "What can we say about being dirty? Lighten His load a little, and drop some baggage. The Bible speaks of unsaved people displaying a false faith in the Lord, and I believe that with all the baggage Christians carry around, and the busy agenda that they have, that they can't see clear enough spiritually, to where they would know that they need to get out of the mud and get clean. Though hard to believe, there are those willing to have Christ as their Savior on the outside, yet they are most reluctant to submit to Him as their Lord—to be at His command and to be governed by His unchanging laws. When he said, 'Pick up your cross, and follow me,' he meant drop all the baggage that interferes with the presence of goodness in your heart. Those that can't drop things will perish. Those that turn from those things, even while looking back and missing those things now and then, will eventually seize to desire those things and will be set free of them for eternity in return for that sacrifice. Bow your heads in prayer."

Dear heavenly Father,
thank you for this beautiful day of worship in
your house. Grant us wisdom and strength to be
humble and gentle lights of proof of your
existence and love. As we go into the world for the
remainder of this Sabbath Day, don't let us stray
from the work that you have assigned to us
through our conscience. I ask all these things in
Jesus's name. Amen.

It was a glorious moment for James to get to stand in front of a congregation and speak as a minister of God. One can administer to individuals or small groups, but getting up there in front of many people is quite an experience, and James won't soon forget it. Nor will the desire to get back up there ever subside within him.

We return back to the picnic table with Amani and James out in front of the apartment. After giving Amani a brief introduction a few moments ago, they are now sitting with their beers outside of the apartment building, and once again, James reveals that most of the material within his grandfather's military folder will not be revealed in its entirety. He only wants to explain some of the key details in Vietnam that pertain ultimately to his acceptance at Columbia. Three grueling days in the jungles of Vietnam in 1970 between Captain Michael Stapleton and Colonel John Purcell—these were the events and the ship with which this opportunity traveled from a small town in Indiana, all the way to the University of Columbia in New York.

James lights a cigar and opens the folder to remember. He looks at Amani, "As I said before, my grandfather, Captain Michael Stapleton, didn't talk much of Vietnam, but he did write a lot about his experience with Senator John Purcell of New Hampshire."

"Did he die in Vietnam?"

"No, he made it home, Amani."

"Okay," Amani says, patiently waiting for James to continue.

James pauses for a moment, to gather his memory of his grandfather, and begins to remember his grandfather's voice from years ago.

In 1970, the senator was a colonel and a pilot that flew on special missions in the war. It was a hairy time in this particular region of Vietnam where I crossed paths with the colonel. He was on a mission, and his plane was shot down by anti-aircraft defenses. I had nothing at all to do with this mission that he was on, but our company happened to be in the general vicinity, and a few of us got the assignment to find the colonel and get him back to safety. Fortunately for me, and for the two wet-behind-the-ears soldiers they gave me, we weren't that far from the area where the colonel was. Unfortunately however, they only allowed us to be a small team of three. I prayed every minute we were out there that we didn't run into anything hairy because if it was up to the two that I was with, and the inexperience that they had in the bush, we'd be coming home in body bags. We found the colonel after fifteen hours of humping, but when we did, we also realized because of the accident, he had an injured leg that wasn't going to allow us to get back in the same fifteen hours that it took us to find him. We got on the radio once and asked for airmobile (Air Cavalry) to lift us out, but the army had all of its resources geared towards a big offensive that was kicking off that day. Due to the mobilization of the local forces in the area from the offensive, things began to get a little uneasy. The closer and closer we got toward base, the more uneasy it got, because when one side mobilized, it also caused the enemy to move. The thing is, we wanted the American troops to head our way, but that was unfortunately met with the unenviable experience of retreating Viet Cong forces toward us as well.

At one point during the night while they rested, the colonel looked at the Captain and with a friendly sarcasm, "what mean son of a gun chose you for this mission, Captain?"

Michael laughed, "It must have been someone that didn't like me, and there are many of those. Expendable I guess." The Captain slightly shakes his head with a look of bewilderment.

The Colonel didn't say anything, but chuckled over the Captain's sense of humor in such difficult circumstances. They couldn't see more than two feet in front of their faces, and they were soaking wet from the rain, and they were hearing peculiar noises all night as if there were patrols passing close by. It was a difficult night for the nerves.

James continues to hear the voice of his grandfather reciting his memory of the war.

We talked for about an hour in the jungle that night, the colonel and I, and it was somewhat pleasant because I now had a spirit to put with a name and a face. Sometimes on these missions, you don't want to know anyone personally due to the fact that they usually don't last very long, and after all the young men that died, I didn't want to know anyone else. Consequently, you'll find out soon enough why I haven't mentioned the names of the two boys that were with us. However, it was tough with the Colonel, because he had a certain way about him that was anything but military. Maybe it was an Air Force thing. I don't know. I couldn't quite put my finger on it. All I know is he started to remind me of home, and the more I got to know him, the more he reminded me of the solace of Macomb, Indiana. Anyway, we had to put a halt to our conversation and relieve the boys of watch duty that night, so we split up. Needless to say, to make a long story short, we ran into a lot of crap that night, and the two young men we had with us didn't make it out alive.

James is so deeply involved in this transcript of his grandfather's experience in Vietnam that he did not realize up until that moment, that Amani had taken off. He must have gotten really bored or decided that he'd ask for the punch line later. *Funny thing about young people these days,* James thinks, *they just don't know how to slow down enough to listen.* Anyways, James walks in to the apartment and sits down with a new beer and continues to remember his grandfather. He hadn't thought of this since being accepted to Columbia, so he was kind of getting into it again. James is also thinking, as he did the first time he heard it, that he noticed his grandpa calling the soldiers boys the time before they died, yet he referred to them as men following their death. Consequently, as he did the first time he read it back in high school, it caused his mind to ask the question again. *What was the difference in calling them men, as opposed to boys?* In the last couple of years of his grandfather's life, he had a chance to respond to that question.

Well James, I guess when they're vulnerable, they're boys or kids, and when they die, they have to be men. Anyone that dies for their country deserves the status of a man. That's just the way that is. Those poor boys were scared to death, and that doesn't make them any less of men, it just makes them human. They are brave men though, and there is nothing that can be taken away from them. Only those that didn't serve can take anything away from someone who died for his country, or so they think. I quote my favorite political figure in history. Theodore Roosevelt said,

It is not the critic who counts; not the man who points out how the strong man stumbles, or where the doer of deeds could have done them better. The credit belongs to the man who is actually in the arena, whose face is marred by dust and sweat and blood; who strives valiantly; who errs, who comes short again and again, because there is no effort without error and shortcoming; but who does actually strive to do the deeds; who knows great enthusiasms, the great devotions; who spends himself in a worthy cause; who at the best knows in the end the triumph of high achievement, and who at the worst, if he fails, at least fails while daring greatly, so that his place shall never be with those cold and timid souls who neither know victory nor defeat.

Teddy Roosevelt (TR) was Grandfather Michael's favorite president in history. He became a presidential historian in the years after the war back home in Indiana. He loved reading about the great ones, and TR was one of those. You could say that the seeds were planted in James at an early age. He used to sit on Grandfather Michael's lap when he was a boy, and he would constantly ask questions about Presidents. Those moments back then were the beginning stages of his dream to be President, and it hasn't faded one bit, in fact, his desire has grown since then.

No man will ever see me take a stance on war that would ever dishonor these men that gave their life in the fight for democracy. People don't realize when they whine about this war that they are basically using a dead soldier's voice to argue something that soldiers would never say, even if they were alive. It is a complete and utter dishonoring of those graves at every military cemetery, and it's what I can't stand most about liberal critics. Educated men that never fought have a tendency to let their mouth run out of control while fighting for the logic of peace. However, all they do is discredit the credentials they earned, those which say they are educated, because for years after, ironically, they partake in conversations of ignorance. That is, first and foremost, why we are Republicans, James. Liberalism is the liberty to be increasingly more and more liberal every single day. A Republican's values, however, are to never change their principles because their law, which is the Word of God, never changes. Furthermore, Republicans do grow and adapt as time moves on; however, the true unadulterated essence of conservatism is to never dishonor God's wishes, and those are the same wishes that God had for us thousands of years ago. The law never changes, but people do, and their values do as well.

James leans back at his desk in the apartment, and closes his eyes with his hands behind his head. He just finished his second beer, which he rarely does, and is very relaxed, and begins to remember more of his grandfather.

I tell you this, James, because I've seen from an early age that you are going somewhere special. And someday, when you ask yourself how you got this opportunity, this will be plenty for you to know the answer to that question. To expedite a long story and avoid some of the more painful events in my memory of Vietnam, the Colonel and I went through hell in a meat grinder during the final hours of that rescue mission. I tore all the tendons in my shoulder and broke bones in my hand holding on to the colonel for twenty minutes while hanging out of an airmobile helicopter. A couple of hours later, I found myself in a hospital. The doctor said I had to stay a couple days to hydrate and get a cast on my hand.

Colonel John Purcell walked into the hospital with a staff member. He handed me the address and phone number to where he lives back home, and asked me to visit him when I return to the States. He also told me he knew what the two dead soldiers and I did to get him to safety. He said he'd never forget it, that he owed me for what I did, and for keeping him in that helicopter. I told him not to worry about it though, and he said for me to promise that I would come see him in the States. I returned with a yes, that I would come to see him, and I promised. I had heard rumors while in rehab, when I was pushing a pencil that Colonel John Purcell had reviewed my military record and put in a request for my promotion. I was shocked because I knew that would mean being a major. Nevertheless, I was presented with the rank of major (Oak Leafs). In addition, due in large part with the Colonel's request, I received a Purple Heart and a Silver Star. I would arrive in Macomb, Indiana, sometime later. When I got off the bus, the smells, sounds, and entire ambiance of Macomb was the sweetest moment I had in years. I had made a promise to myself that if I made it back there, I would never leave again. I did, however, have one trip left to make to the northeast to see the colonel, and I was definitely taking a bus. It took longer, but due to the events in Vietnam, I wasn't ever going to fly again. The Colonel treated me with respect and didn't want our visit to be polluted by a bureaucratic political agenda, so he invited me to his home on a Sunday, which wasn't a day he'd be busy at the office. To make a long story short, James, he said he was forever indebted to me, and he wanted to offer me a job somewhere in Washington. Colonel John Purcell wanted me to know that he was going into politics and that because I saved his life as he claims, he wanted to return the favor in some way. I told him how much I appreciated that but also said it was unnecessary. However, he forcefully insisted, and I didn't want to disrespect him in his home, so I indulged him this one time. I wasn't as much on board at the time about him offering me a job or offering me a future rain check, because you boys weren't born yet, and I was uninterested in anything other than working the farm back home, so I asked for a while to think about it.

James is thinking this is the moment where the scholarship fund came to life.

After years passed, I appreciated my experience with Colonel John Purcell more and more, because I now see someone that can benefit from that offer he gave me in 1971, and that person is you, James. John Purcell has taken care of a scholarship fund that will cover you no matter where you want to go, and he has assured me, as long as your grades are there, he will do everything he can to push your college acceptance and career. You are going to cash in on that card that I didn't play in Washington in 1971 because you will need it someday. We don't have money, we don't have alumnus in high places, and we certainly don't know anyone other than Colonel John Purcell, so this is your ticket to wherever you want to go. There will also be opportunities for your brother, Jack, but they will not be revealed to him until graduation.

At this point, James is remembering some emotional words between him and his grandfather. Not everything that he once told James was emotional at the moment that he said it, but now that he doesn't get to speak to his grandfather anymore, everything is emotional, especially the ones where he was acting as his mentor. James remembers more.

Those three days in Vietnam were unforgettable, and the pain I felt with the colonel hanging from my arm for his life was the most honest thing I have ever done in my life, so I ask that you handle everything with the utmost honesty as you head out into the world to start your career. Don't forget anything I taught you over the years. It was all meant for a purpose, and you will see that someday. I love you, and good luck.

Your grandfather,
Major Michael Stapleton.

James can remember the first time he heard these words... they really moved him. He and his grandfather had many great talks over the years, but the ones about Vietnam were few.

When James was finished revisiting his voice, he was inspired to write a poem about the growing liberal concern in Washington. He wrote a fictional short story the other day, and it was about the next president of the United States. In the story, the next president is a liberal, and gets in trouble involving himself with the Internal Revenue Service, and the scandal leads all the way back to the White House. Nevertheless, James wrote a poem about it.

TRAIL OF FALLACY

A liberal deep from within,
has infiltrated that which is us.
Her majority has assured it not sin,
and implores not that we fuss.

Four long years lest honesty pass,
the web begins to unravel.
Buries his head in surrounding brass,
and bluffs that verity not travel.

Three rough years ahead,
of spying, cheating and stealing.
Lord, please rescue this beautiful land,
and bless it with loving and healing.

COINTELPRO he tried to revive,
yet fell to a stumbling connive.
Lord, please place your hand on this strife,
and bless it so we can survive.

Nobody knows just yet what kind of career James will head into when he's done at Columbia, but when talking about the education or the opportunity of a talented young conservative man, it never hurts to have Republican friends in DC. James had to be Columbia material, and he had to honestly meet all the necessary criteria that all Columbia students have to meet, and he did that in the top one percent of admittance.

Grandfather Michael couldn't have imagined the caliber of help that Senator John Purcell of New Hampshire would provide for James. However, had he been alive to witness it, he would have been impressed with how much what he did in Vietnam meant to the senator and what the career of his grandson James meant to the senator as well. He went above and beyond paying one back for the saving of a life, and he was not even close to being done. James ended up with a tuition-paid deal from a fund that the senator started decades ago when James was a baby. So the bottom of the well of academic finances, as well as opportunity, will not be dry as long as James says otherwise.

Major Michael Stapleton and Senator John Purcell stayed in touch for years. A few times, they got together for the holidays, but this last decade was hard when James's grandfather, Michael, got sick. The senator came to see him once in the hospital a few weeks before he passed and later returned for the funeral. In fact, he gave the eulogy in a full military service. James is forever indebted to his Grandfather Michael, and is determined to honor that by carrying on all the values and wishes he bestowed upon him. He knows that even in his grandfather's death, he can still express a true love for him by honoring the opportunity with which his grandfather provided. When James's mother revealed to him at his grandfather's funeral that he had a scholarship to literally any school in America, he set his sights high.

One honorable three-day mission in Vietnam created a friendship that would last a lifetime, and from which would stem the fruit of the potential of James Ryan Roberts and maybe the future of conservative politics in Washington as well.

CHAPTER 2

Macomb, Indiana, is captivating at dawn, when the sun begins to show itself beyond the horizon. One would never believe, that the odors of a farm and the silence of an early hour, would be attached with such magnificence. For those who grew up in this town and have gone away, when they return, they never leave again; it is just that intoxicating. When you try the fast-paced way of life elsewhere, you can never adjust because you were once a resident of Macomb, and there's no place like it. A few minutes from now, one will be blinded by the sun in the direction of the east. The weather is clear, and an airplane passes overhead. It leaves a trail of its exhaust streaking through the bright blue sky. It is a couple of minutes past 6:00 a.m. on a Sunday at the west edge of town. The first day of school is tomorrow, and for many kids, their agendas will be changing quickly, due in large part to school relieving them of their seasonal farming chores.

Most people in Macomb, Indiana, don't go too far academically after high school. It is quite uncommon when one makes it to the junior college thirty miles away, much less to the university an hour away. It's not that they aren't smart enough, but folks in this part of Indiana have their priorities so far away from the mainland, that they look back in astonishment after forty years of agriculture and pastoralism, and they humbly realize it went by in the blink of an eye. However, there are a dozen or so people each year that do have their sights set beyond Macomb all the way to a local university. Nevertheless, it is quite rare for someone to venture as far as James has—all the way to Columbia University in New York City.

The Wilson property is exquisite in the early daylight hours, and with the surrounding trees hanging over their property, it makes it very cool despite the high humidity this time of year. The trees block out the sun very well for a good part of the morning, but once the sun gets overhead, there is no escaping it. As for the best aspect of the Wilson property—well, that would be the best aspect of Macomb, and maybe even all of Indiana—that place is where the stream travels through the Wilson property. The way the trees hang over the stream from both sides—it makes it feel like you are in another world. The sounds and the ambiance that is created by it is quite rapturous. When you are sitting on a log or sitting on a rock at the edge of the stream with your feet dipped in the cold water, you can't help but close your eyes, and thank the heavens for such a moment.

The stream is definitely best experienced with someone special. It's not that coming down here alone isn't particularly sweet, but the romantic atmosphere makes it that much more rewarding with someone. The purr of the sounds of insects and birds from nearby and from afar, add to the tranquility of this cathedral of the wild. Experiencing this for the very first time, or even the second time for that matter, leaves you with nothing other than a sigh of contentment to speak of. This is due in large part to the hypnotic attributes of all that is filtered through the perception of your mind. Ben Wilson, who lives on this property where he can truly appreciate from a cerebral nature the essence of its indulgence on an everyday basis, has to be the luckiest kid in the world.

Ben Wilson has been friends with James Ryan Roberts for a long time. Their moms were close, so you could say they've been like family all these years. Ben is going to be a senior at Crenshaw High School tomorrow. He's a pretty good student, but he isn't going to get offers from any of the big schools in America. You could say he's the hardworking type and gets about all his results from that hard work. Consequently, he will probably go to the local junior college for a couple of years before his mind ever ventures beyond home. However, it is still early enough in Ben's life, where the existence of cerebral mediocrity is attributed to his efforts, and not his mind. So often in life, kids don't blossom until after high school, especially in recent generations around the country. Some could just be bored by the curriculum or even disinterested with the lack of encouragement coming from the front of a classroom.

Some social philosophers believe that the caliber of teaching today at the junior college level could reveal the answers to why students blossom later. We went through a period of time in recent history, where many people were going to college to be a teacher, and it made it crowded to find a teaching job at a university. Consequently, there are more teachers at junior colleges today that graduated from prestigious universities in America, thereby resulting in a considerable upgrade in teaching talent at two-year schools. In addition, the passion of a modern day K-12 teacher has declined in today's society, where it has become more likely for them to go on strike than it is to stay after school to give special attention to a struggling student. Moreover, in the K-12 system, it has truly become what we can do for the teacher, and less about what they can do for their students.

James's younger brother, Jack, also attends Crenshaw High School in Macomb. He is in tenth grade and is also friends with Ben. He is more of a cousin-like friend, rather than a best-friend type. Ben and James, however, are best friends. Even though James is away at school, both of them are very secure in the fact that they are lifelong friends and someday soon will be back in each other's life every day. James and Jack's father left town when Jack was too young to remember, but James has a clear memory of the experience. The fatherly presence while James and Jack were boys came from their grandfather, Michael, on their mother's side. If that isn't a contrast of opposite extremes, one wouldn't know what is—a fatherly grandfather who served his country to the fullest, and an absent father who was allergic to every known natural essence of responsibility a man feels in life. Little Jack has never been afforded the enriching experience of having his grandfather as a mentor; he was old enough to have him up until he was nine or ten years old. However, James got everything that a boy could get out of a mentor in the years before his Grandfather Michael passed away. Moreover, all the great qualities that a man can possess in life, their grandfather had, and James turned out just like him. Grandpa Michael was a regular ole John Wayne in the truest sense.

The boys have their father's last name, Roberts, while their mother reestablished herself with her maiden name, Stapleton. At birth, James's got his middle name, which was Kevin, from his paternal grandfather, but since he never met him, and his father left so long ago, James wanted to change his middle name to something that meant more to him. So on his fourteenth birthday, he changed it from Kevin to Ryan, making him James Ryan Roberts. It probably didn't have as much to do with the lack of paternal influence in his life as much as it most likely had to do with James's liking that name from a character in a book that he read years ago. Although James would never admit something like that. Nevertheless, his middle name was changed to Ryan. In addition to reading, James has written an extraordinary amount of literature, and he is an avid poet. In fact, has written three books and says that he is going to try and get them published one day.

James has read something by just about every great writer in history. Even though some series of books were fictional, they still added to his desire and fantasy for the political aspirations that developed over the years that followed. You could say that those stories for James were similar to another kid going to Yankee

Stadium for the very first time, and that experience fueling that kid's desire to play baseball one day, likewise for James with reading giving him the desire to write.

Obviously, James really couldn't understand too much of the political world as a kid, but as he got older, when he was able to understand the basic principles of government, conservatism took its course to say the least. James stated on a number of occasions that the modern Republican Party was missing its Great Right Hope or A Right Hope—meaning, a right-wing hope. For decades, the party has been deprived of a candidate that is extremely qualified, as well as stable enough in Washington, to confidently push the values of a conservative in such an epidemically liberal society. There have been candidates, but for whatever reason, James believes they don't really have the aspirations to run, or they don't really have the qualities of leadership to save this nation from falling into a state of complete disarray. Furthermore, James has, at times, playfully joked with the idea of being this country's right-wing hope. He is well aware of the arduous nature of what it is he is speaking about, so one can assume that it is something that isn't entirely out of the realm of possibility in his mind. However, this isn't a dream that James is going out of his way to annunciate to the entire world, and he would just assume accomplish the necessary intangibles that will be greatly needed in order to have a successful political career, or any kind of a career for that matter.

James and Jack's mom, Charlotte, works as a registered nurse at the local hospital in Romeo, Indiana. It's about ten miles from downtown Macomb. She has been working lots of overtime to help James with expenses at school, to add to what he saved over the years. From all that her boys know, she has had no romantic encounters for the entire time since their father left. However, there are some nights where she is out with her friends after work, and judging by the smile on her face the next day, it wasn't just the entertainment of her girlfriends that made her feel good.

Her romantic endeavors remained a matter of secrecy over the years. It was assumed that the boys appreciated her happiness. In later years, James understood that she just didn't want their lives to be bothered by an unnecessary masculine influence. God knows the first one didn't work out; she didn't want to attempt to make a right out of two wrongs.

The boys had their role models in town. James worked a lot of evenings at the Macomb Theater, and he and the owner, Mr. Johnson, really hit it off. Mr. Johnson was a Korean War veteran, so James really enjoyed his elderly friendship, especially after Grandfather Michael had passed away. It was likewise for Mr. Johnson, as his wife had been dead for twenty years. He enjoyed closing the theater with James on Friday and Saturday nights as well. In fact, just a few weeks ago, Mr. Johnson told Charlotte Stapleton that he had received an e-mail from James, and James had said that he missed closing the old theater on weekends with him. Mr. Johnson was full of warmth when he read this message from James and there was pride in his voice whenever he spoke of the boy to his mother. It was as if he was one of his own sons. It was nice for James to have him for a friend.

Also, Jack had plenty of mentors with all the baseball coaches he had, but James is his true mentor. Jack worships him as way more than just an older brother. Jack also misses him greatly. It hasn't been easy for him with his mom working all the time and James half the country away in New York City.

Ben Wilson's parents are still together and are very happily married after twenty strong years. So Ben has had a very loving and wholesome upbringing. His family life is a little more of a contrast from Jack's; however, both families have managed to bring up good kids, and instill a strong value system. Ben and his mother are very close and can talk about anything. They tease each other a lot, almost like a brother would with his older sister.

Ben and James go way back to birth, and even though James spent a lot of time by himself with all the reading, when he was out and about and not working, the two were always together. They were only two years apart, even though James is four years ahead in school since he skipped two grades. Ben would love to read more but just doesn't seem to have the patience just yet. James encouraged him to be persistent with his reading and told him that it would come in time. The context of persistence which he meant wasn't an hour every day. Nor did he mean every day. What he meant was regular bouts of reading for two straight hours or even four or five hours, with only five-minute breaks. He told Ben to trust him, that he had to work at it and not give up. James did have one warning for him with regard to reading. He said that if he was going to read that much, he would eventually need glasses. Ironically, James wears contacts.

James and Ben have remained in touch during the years that James was away at Columbia. They have discussed now and then through e-mail about James future in politics and how he would need Ben's help one day. James has, now and then, told him to take history and political science courses when he gets to school. You could say that the friendly nature at which this conversation takes place is a little less serious from Ben's perspective than it is from James's perspective. James is a private person and is looking ahead to his political aspirations and trying to keep it on the down-low as much as possible. Furthermore, he is also keeping the seriousness of it on the down-low to protect Ben from unnecessary pressure. In addition, James wants it to remain a secret because he can foresee years in advance how important it will be to have someone he can trust running his campaigns and political advisement. For that, Ben fits the mold perfectly—the future campaign manager of James Ryan Roberts.

———◆———

Jack walks up to the home of Ben Wilson on Sunday in early September 2005. It is exactly five days from the fourth anniversary of the terrorist attacks on America. Anyone that knows James will never forget that day. That incident in American history is the event that caused James to attend school in New York rather than anywhere else. The national healing of that horrible day had a special place in James heart, but it didn't get in the way of his desires to find out the true answers to the questions the Americans were asking on that terrible September day in 2001.

Anyway, James was an interesting character all around, especially for his age. Some of the things he's said absolutely defy the common thoughts of modern man. Nevertheless, Ben and Jack hangout in the Wilson backyard and reminisce about old times with James.

Jack says, "James has said some off-the-wall things before, and most of them make so much sense, it begins to make you wonder sometimes why we can't see things two inches in front of our face. Truly, James seems to have such a vision for the unseen. For example, he always told me that having someone at your side can be the loneliest moments of one's life. In fact, he has said that the last couple years that he can remember dad being home sort of felt to him like, he really wasn't there emotionally. I guess that kind of prepared him for years without him. James has said that there isn't much value in togetherness, if ninety-five percent of that person is emotionally absent or checked out. He always said true loneliness comes in a crowded room, or even lying next to one person. When there is no one there, you're not investing in anyone. Therefore you can't be left out in the cold so to speak. James always assumed that I got more without a father than most have with. That isn't to say that I don't respect the value of a good fatherly upbringing, but I have had an older brother that well made up for the loss of a father. Not to mention, I have felt like I didn't miss any time without my grandfather these last few years, because James has virtually recited just about everything my Grandpa had ever said. James was real fond of my mother's father, and Grandpa did everything he could to make up for the loss of our father not being around."

"Jack, do you want to stay for supper since your mom is working late at the hospital tonight?"

"Sure! It would be nice to have a family to hang with today," Jack says. "I'm sure my mom would appreciate it, so thanks."

"Oh, it's nothing, Jack."

"I really thank you, Ben. You have been there a lot for me this summer, with my mom working so much now. Ever since James went away to school three years ago, she has had to work extra. You know, James gave her his entire paycheck every week when he lived here. He meant for it to be helpful with groceries, which was noble, but it's probably the money my mom has been sending him to New York. She's too proud to let her son support her. She had to tell him she never spent the money he gave her. Otherwise, James would have mailed the checks back to her."

"No, I didn't know. That's pretty great of him, Jack."

"That's my brother!"

"Your brother thinks the world of you. My mom was shocked when your dad left years ago, but my mom is also pretty envious of the perseverance your mom displayed these ten or so years—getting James to college and all. I'm sure she has a plan for you too."

"I hope she don't get her hopes up too much for me with school. It has never been my strong point." Jack says. "I wish I could get noticed by a baseball scout. Now that would be my ticket—major league baseball!" Jack had a dreamy look on his face.

"You sure hit the ball good, Jack. Maybe you'll get noticed by scouts."

"Next spring will be my chance to get noticed. I'll be a sophomore, and scouts usually start their charts on high school players in that year." Jack knows a ton about baseball. "*Baseball America* usually publishes separate lists every year of the best high school sophomores, juniors, and seniors, so maybe. It depends on how well I hit the ball."

Jack and Ben went down toward the stream that passes the back of Ben Wilson's property. To get there, they have to jump over this huge log that was left by a lightning bolt that destroyed a tree last April. As the path to the stream continues, you walk by a huge tree over hanging the water. Years ago, Mr. Wilson set up a large truck tire hanging over the stream, and many kids in Macomb think it's the coolest place in town. As you approach the stream, and you notice the trees hanging over the stream from the surrounding watershed, it makes this place feel like it's where God created man. It feels completely detached from the reality of the outside world. The sounds of whistling birds echo in the distance, as if when you close your eyes, you are in a prehistoric jungle. The experience definitely challenges the limits of one's ability to ever find the strength to leave. When James is lying in bed in New York, he misses everyone, but if there's a single place he misses most, it's definitely this spot on the Wilson property.

Maybe the most engaging characteristic of this place is the constant sound of running water. When you close your eyes, you can imagine a waterfall in the rain forest. With it being midday, it is kind of unearthly to walk out of the bright overhead sunlight of the back of the Wilson property and into the forest that surrounds the stream. The stream is lit up well, but the sun overhead disappearing makes for a considerable contrast in lighting, and therefore adds to the surrealistic experience.

"Ben, you ever swing from that tire?"

"Oh yes." Ben says. "I have many stories to tell you about summers down here and the many firsts that fail to escape my memory. James used to bring his girl down here, and they would sometimes play until dark," Jack has a peculiar look on his face following this bit of information that Ben just revealed.

"What did my brother do when he would come down here?" Ben subtly laughs at the curiosity of a fifteen year old Jack.

"They played, went swimming, read, and wrote poetry," Ben says. "I left them alone a lot so they wouldn't be bothered."

"Which girl did he come down here with?" Jack asks with an intense interest.

"Oh, he came down here with many different girls at different times," Ben casually says.

"I didn't know James had so many girlfriends." Jack mumbles out of the corner of his mouth while having a confused look on his face.

This is an area of James's life, that Ben is probably a little more knowledgeable about than Jack. "James had a lot of friends he probably never brought home." Ben informs him. "But make no mistake, he found ways to socialize. Many friends would come up to the theater where he worked."

"Yeah, I hear that, Ben."

"Jack, you have to understand that your brother is coming from a place that is quite rare. I remember James telling me once that he had to break up with this girl because she couldn't respect his values on premarital sex. He had said it got to the point of sleaziness, and he no longer could respect her, so he ended the relationship. She heckled him about it for a few weeks but eventually realized their differences, and finally let it rest. He has said modern liberal women today have these assumptions during their relationships with men; as if they can consecrate these relationships themselves as a union of marriage, which they naively don't have the authority, only God does. He just had a different viewpoint on marriage. He has also said once before in a half-joking manner, that two thousand years ago, God gave man free will, and nineteen-hundred and seventy years later, liberal man, gave the liberal woman free will, and look what we have today to show for it. He also said there was a purpose for Paul's letters to Timothy in the New Testament. They weren't put there for supremacy reasons. They were put there for leadership purposes, and that God made man and women with their own distinct qualities physically as well as mentally and emotionally. God knew thousands of years ago that a woman was more likely to have a meltdown after a long day's work than men were. Also, it is entirely unhealthy for a republic of any kind to have a leader that is trying to impress from an inferior point of view or the 'big dog, little dog' analogy, where the little dog is out of control in order to compensate for his insecurity as a physically inferior entity. Now I'm exhausted, Jack" With how much Ben had to say, Jack was kind of losing concentration, and how could anyone blame him.

"You said a lot, Ben. Sounds like James shared much with you."

"He did. Not a lot of people will agree with him, and he has stated that he doesn't want that information getting out. Nor does he advise me reciting it for any reason. But he did say it's all true. Our society today encourages us to lie to people, as well as lie to ourselves. We are similar to a modern Babylonian society. Why do you think it's difficult to recognize America or identify with who she is in the book of Revelation? It is more than likely because it is possible that America doesn't exist at the end of times—as it may have already been conquered by another country or union. With all the recent events in the world and the situations that are escalating, it really makes you think that it is possible to take for granted that America will always be on top of the world." Jack can't help but think of what Ben said earlier about James coming down to the stream with his girlfriends. He's a curious fifteen year old kid, as boys naturally are at this age regarding girls. As he gets a little older, he'll most definitely come to the realization why James kept those things on the down-low. Furthermore, there's much more that Jack doesn't know about his brother that Ben does know, but that will just have to wait until he gets a little older than fifteen. Ben and Jack, over the next few minutes, just meditate on the reality of being in such an exquisite place down at the stream. However, Jack still has this stare of curiosity regarding the subject they just spoke of, and Jack asks, "Do you think James has a girlfriend in New York?"

"I have no idea," Ben says. "He's not mentioned anything in any e-mails. I'm sure he's been dating since he's been gone."

"When he finished his freshman year that summer in New York, he said he ran into a couple models when he was at Metropolitan Museum of Art (the Met). He said they were taken by his knowledge of art. When I spoke to him weeks later, he mentioned nothing of it again. When I asked what happened, he was short and sweet and said that they are just friends," Jack reveals.

"Supermodels! Wow!" Ben says excitedly. "He really hit the big time. I'd have a hard time believing that in a big city like that, James hasn't already broken a few hearts, you know what I mean."

"Yeah, my mom and I were there. It's nothing like Indianapolis. Not even close."

"I'm fascinated with the big city, Jack." Ben has this deep look on his face as if he'd love to go to New York one day.

"Me too." Jack says. "Although I'm not sure how much James sees of the big city with how busy he's been. He doesn't take the summers off and goes nonstop with courses all year round. His only real break has been Christmas each year, but he doesn't get to come home because he and my mom are trying to keep his expenses down. His winter semester overlaps the spring semester, which is then overlapped by the summer courses. Also, the summer curriculum doesn't end until like ten days before the fall, so as you can see, there isn't much time to get a bus ride back to Indiana. Although, he has recently said he may come home for Christmas this year. We'll wait and see. He misses us, and we miss him."

At birth, James was named after his father, but nobody calls him James Jr. because his father left town avoiding the responsibilities of being their dad. Jack dreams about what his father might be like, but that is as close as he's ever been to his father, at least from what he can remember. On the other hand, James spent enough time with his father to have a decent idea of what he was like. James mentions a little at a time in his e-mails, but it's easy to see it is not a subject he is very open to revealing. It must have been hard for him to experience being left for good like that. Anyway, James was a man taking on the fatherly duties of his absent dad, and to have Jack turn out the way he did and also find himself getting an education from an Ivy League school at the same time is pretty impressive.

James was the high school valedictorian in his senior year, and he was the one who was chosen to speak at graduation. He was accepted to just about every school in America, including Georgetown and Duke, which he gave consideration to, but he decided on Columbia. The only thing Jack remembers from its significance was that it is in New York City. September 11, 2001 happened early in James's senior year in high school. With his passion, it was something he couldn't let go of, and you could say the events that year are what led James to New York, all the way from Macomb, Indiana. You know how teenagers are when they get gung ho about something like 9/11. When we're young, we have the adrenaline and the ignorance of putting ourselves in harm's way and for a cause we can't truly understand just yet. Thank goodness James chose to accept an education rather than do something else. You never know where that would have led. Of course, serving your country is an honorable thing to do, and it is important to James as well, but when you get to know James, it's difficult to discard how much good he can do serving his country in Washington DC instead.

"I have a lot that I know about James that maybe you don't, Jack."

"Tell me, tell me, Ben!" Jack enthusiastically expresses himself while nudging Ben on the arm. "I wanna know, please. Please?"

"James is a very complex person in relation to many things, but it's important to be thorough when explaining him, so you can't misunderstand his interpretation of things because they can be controversial, as they are real close to the line of criticism.

Also, along with the extraordinary nature of your brother also comes a heavy dose of modesty, so I'm pretty sure it is difficult for you to learn about James from himself. It's not in his nature to be self-revealing. So if you don't hear this from me, it will most likely end up in a permanent vault that doesn't have a key."

"Okay Ben, I'm looking forward to it. I get the idea from all that you're saying that you're not going to say anything bad?"

"No, Jack! No! If it were something of a sensitive nature, I would respect that James would want to be the one to tell you those things himself. Besides, he may have already told you, or you may already have a decent idea of some aspects of it, so it's nothing to lose sleep over. You can tell by some of the stuff he's read over the years."

"I couldn't keep up with everything he read. He had a different book in his hand every other day," Jack reveals.

"I remember, Jack."

Since Jack was already over Ben's on Sunday afternoon, Ben's mom, Lois, asked him to stay for supper. With Mr. Wilson working until 11:00 p.m., they would have an empty spot at the table, which conveniently made room for Jack. Lois has trouble sometimes avoiding treating Jack as her own, as she was very hospitable to James over the years as well. Lois Wilson adores Charlotte Stapleton and all that she has accomplished since the two met years ago. The Stapleton's and the Wilson's have been friends for generations, as the grandparents used to be in the farming business, and the children grew up together. So Charlotte and Lois, as well as their brothers and sisters, have been friends since they were two or three years old. That's why it seems like they are all cousins, even though they are friends. After dinner, Ben and Jack finish up the dishes and head down by the stream, while Lois heads up to the hospital to see a friend.

"Supper was great, Ben. Your mom's stew is good, thanks."

"No problem," Ben says. "She'll be pleased to hear that when she returns this evening."

Jack smiles. "Are we heading down to the stream, Ben?"

"Yeah!"

"Cool. It's unbelievable down there." Jack also innovatively suggests, "we should set up tents and sleep down there."

"That's a great idea, Jack, I never thought of that."

Jack has this proud look on his face as if he just invented something. "That would be fun, Ben."

"Yes it would."

"Maybe we can try something like that before the weather gets too bad this fall?" Jack asks.

"I'll ask my mom." Ben says. "We'll see what she thinks about it. It can't be all that different from camping in the back yard, which we've done a million times before."

"Okay. Tell me more about my brother."

"Jack, you have to understand, James has always had an unconventional approach to life, especially in our society today. When it is all said and done at graduation, he won't have half the education that he has managed to give himself, or the education that he has managed to give to those who he has encountered. Even some of the teachers that we have both had at Crenshaw High School have said to me, that they learned more from James than James learned from them. While most Americans believe what is convenient for their own agenda, James had the ability to answer a lot of his own questions without naive assumptions, but by just researching the facts on his own. I'll never forget that summer when he carried around the Quran. He carried it everywhere he went until he was done reading it. I know James is Christian, which makes reading the Quran all the more out there, or rather out of the reach of the understanding of the majority. I think even when he was done reading it, he continued to study the places in the book that he had highlighted. Your brother caught a lot of criticism that summer, and some of his classmates were tough on him. All James wanted was to confirm what Americans were saying about Muslims, and that they were put on this planet to kill Americans. James wanted to believe the truth so he read it, and he found that it wasn't completely true—well, it wasn't true for a lot of Muslims. In fact, he found that when a Muslim kills a person, it is according to the Quran, like he has killed all of mankind, and if a Muslim loves his neighbor, it is as if he loves all of mankind. How many opinions do you hear weekly about people spouting off about something they know absolutely nothing about? I hear it all the time from every other Tom, Dick, and Harry in town. Your brother changed me for the rest of my life. I have never known anyone that is as educated as he is, and if he wants to know something, he'll find it, and he would never talk about something he knows nothing about. Most people's opinions are as annoying to him as an insecure poodle. You just know in their tone that if someone called them out, they wouldn't know crap about what they were saying, nor could they defend a debate regarding what they were saying."

Ben rests and reaches down to tie his shoes then sits up and looks into the forest in front of him, "From James's point of view, the attacks on September 11 were terrible, and the men that were responsible should be hunted and brought to justice. But that was not exactly how it went. People wanted to take it out on small Muslim communities in America. There were small riots, where Muslim men and women on campuses and in communities all over America, were attacked by Christians. James wrote in one of his essays, "that nothing good can ever be accomplished by reacting to human ignorance, with more human ignorance."

Ben rests for a moment and continues, "James said that the answers to the questions Americans were asking could only be answered by our own government. His question was what goes on overseas while we are asleep? And what are the secrets our government keeps from us? Our government is for the people, by the people, and of the people. What goes on? And what are we unaware of that would cause a group of people to want to kill me and my family? Every time I hear a Muslim extremist talk about

Americans, I can't help but think what someone is not telling us. Were there unrecorded incidents in the world the last forty years, that American military or intelligence were involved in, that has been kept secret by our government?"

Ben takes a deep breath and lies down on a rock, and pauses for a few moments. "With regards to his interest in improving his knowledge of the Quran, he was also very intrigued by the idea of what a Muslim is willing to do for his God. Don't get me wrong, he wasn't at all envious of what they did on September 11, but what they are willing to do. He would ask, 'Why is a Muslim so willing to fly airplanes into a building for their God, yet a high percentage of Americans aren't willing to give up anything of a minute's nature or even an hour a week for their God? For a Muslim, it is a way of life not to be gluttonous, and it is completely the opposite for many Christians. When is the last time you saw a Muslim stumbling out of a local bar, falling all over the place drunk? When is the last time you saw a half-naked Muslim woman standing on the street corner?' He said, 'Why are the righteous so disobedient and the unrighteous so obedient?' James told me Krishnamurti, one of his favorite writers, said, 'It is no measure of health to be well adjusted to a profoundly sick society.' I never thought of things this way until I met your brother, but the more and more I think this way, the more I think the world is beginning to make sense to me. For so long, subconsciously, I had this feeling that things just weren't right and people weren't either. Little did I know, after listening to James, I begin to realize too that it's like a plague, and the only reason we don't realize it, is because everyone has it. The symptoms have become an accepted way of life and an accepted philosophy. Nobody realizes there is anything wrong because when everyone has something, you no longer realize that something to be an individual's distinctive characteristic. If we were all wearing the same uniform, there would not be one person that had their own style, therefore an alternative style would be nonexistent, and after time, no one would recognize any longer the desire to be fashionable. That too can be the case with morality, as well as political ideology. When a Party and its voters believe in a lie long enough, they all become brainwashed by the ideology of that Party. If one voter or member of that Party was saying the opposite, voters of that Party would start to analyze the lie. Therefore, it would weaken the stability of that lie. All it takes is one to buck the system in order to reveal the truth."

Ben stops, and meditates on the atmosphere down at the stream. Even Ben, who lives on this property, never forgets to realize its extraordinary beauty, he continues, "The gradual escalation of liberalism goes unnoticed over a hundred years. However, if a hundred years of evolution changed in one day, we would have had an epidemic of immorality. I mean yesteryear's left wing would make today's right wing look like cesspool swimmers, which is sadly the case. In fact, the left wing from just as little as thirty years ago was more conservative than today's right wing. It's ironic now because it almost looks like there are Democrats posing as Republicans with the purpose of bringing down the GOP once and for all. You can't tell anymore what side these devious politicians are on. Furthermore, today's liberal didn't even exist a hundred years ago. The only place it did exist is in the Bible, when John the Divine is describing the end of times, and the way man becomes an abomination at the end. It was clear to James that the Republican Party is becoming lost, and has been since Ronald Reagan. He's told me on a number of occasions that the modern right wing is way more immoral than they were ten or twelve years ago. There are some Republicans that should just quit wearing the disguise and call themselves Democrats."

Ben rests as he has never spoken this much in all of his life, but Jack and he haven't had much time to talk, and Jack needs to know some things about his brother. He's surprised at himself though, and amazed he remembers all of this, and then continues, "The summer before your brother started college back in 2002, you have to remember that he was becoming wise to the lies of the world. A few times, some of the boys from school would mess with him verbally, but they knew not to push him, as they were aware of James's black belt in aikido. James kept in mind Nietzsche's words, 'What doesn't kill you only makes you stronger.' One of the guys from school had a father that was wounded in Desert Storm back in 1991, and he was at the center of the heckling, but James actually felt compassion for him and his father and handled it very kindly. It was quite impressive."

Jack begins to smile with pride over this revelation of his brother. "That's my bro!"

Ben reveals more to Jack, "The year 1991 wasn't a time where Americans were as anti-Muslim as they are today. However, there were still many incidents in the world regarding Muslim extremists. Let's just say that emotions could get wild with James's classmates from school if the moment was ripe. No matter what happened though, James showed compassion and kindness regarding the boy and his father. Things have just become unsettling in the world. If it wasn't for how involved America has been in the Muslim world the last twenty years, 9/11 probably wouldn't have happened, but that wasn't the case."

Ben walks over to the water, grabs a branch that was floating down stream, and puts his feet in the water. The water can start feeling a little cold this time of year, but with how hot it has been for September, it is quite warm. After a brief rest, Ben begins to conclude, "There is another thing you have to understand about James. He wasn't a loner. He was very comfortable standing on his own and defending himself rhetorically, and, if need be, physically as well. He always would tell me stories about your Grandfather Michael, from whom he received a substantial education from all of those years.

"Oh yeah, my grandpa was a great dude," Jack is presently wearing this expression of pride on his face after speaking of his grandfather.

"I know," Ben says. "James told me all about him being a war hero."

Jack says, "Yeah, my mom mentioned it on a number of occasions when we'd see something that reminded her of the war, but she never revealed any details of Vietnam."

"Anyway, James always seemed to have time for people, which is probably why he was so well-liked in town. I have spoken to many adults in town and at school, who always seem to ask about him and how he is doing. He made more than just you and your mom proud. He made all of us proud.

Jack is old enough to understand more and more about his brother; however, some of it will have to come in time. The Roberts brothers are very different, yet they are very similar. Jack has a heart like James, and they both get it from their mother. However, Jack, who is a terror on a baseball diamond, is more physically gifted in sports than James. On the other hand, James is more cerebral than Jack, at least at this stage—meaning Jack does have a few more years before the jury begins to deliberate on his intellectual capacities. James is physically talented in karate, but a lot of that is because of how psychologically and spiritually demanding karate is. As good as Jack is at baseball, it is very probable that, wherever he ends up going, he will get to go to college for free, regardless of a scholarship fund. Scouts are already impressed with the fact that he is already one of the best players in Indiana.

"Until what time does your mom work, Jack?"

"Until 11:00 p.m. She was pleased when I called her, and I told her your mom invited me over for dinner. She's been so busy with work since James went away. My mom has done so much to make sure James receives the best of everything. He wanted to come home after graduation to help with money, so my mother asked him what he wanted. After she asked a few hundred times, he came down from his stubborn horse and told her. She returned to him an order to get his Ph.D. I guess she figured something as difficult as that probably had a better chance of being accomplished without a trip home. Maybe it was a fear that he would never return if he got that far away from the institution. He didn't say another word, in fact started it that summer. My mother isn't going to be making a donation to Columbia for a million dollars anytime soon, but that doesn't mean James can't leave his mark there and make that school proud. I guess what I mean is, she helped James kick the door in, but he's going to have to keep the candles lit himself, because in this country, unless you're sharp as a whip, money talks. Columbia has educated the most United States presidents," Jack says passionately.

Ben has a look of being impressed with that bit of information. "I didn't know that, Jack."

Jack continues with his bit of knowledge, "Columbia also has the most Nobel Prizes, Academy awards, and they administer the Pulitzer Prize themselves. Harvard, Yale, and Princeton get all the hype, but Columbia has quite a history."

"Where did you get all that from, Jack?"

"Looked it up when James was choosing Columbia."

"Jack, I bet a government agency is sitting across the street from his apartment as we speak, waiting for him to finish school. Probably get a six-figure salary and a sweet car to boot. Hell, I wouldn't be surprised to see James working in Washington someday. This country desperately needs a thinker on Capitol Hill like James."

"You sure can say that again, Ben. James has mentioned a number of times that he could see himself in Washington. The way he described it was, *the best place in this country for change is right there in the heart of DC.* He has never been just a critic of what is going wrong in this nation, and I don't think he could ever be truly happy unless he was right in the center of an evolution of change."

"You're telling me, Jack. Where is your brother in school now?"

"He graduated in May with a degree in political science, with a minor in history. But I believe he is going the other way in graduate school, with a PhD. in history. We went to his commencements in New York City. My mom and I had a blast. We had never been out of the Midwest. When he finishes, we are going back, and I want you to come with us, Ben. James wants you to as well."

"Oh, that would be great," Ben says. "I can't wait. I would love that."

"I think, ultimately, his graduate school is going to be as long as his undergraduate was. Maybe even longer," Jack says.

"I always knew we'd be talking about this, Jack. James talked about it five years ago as if it was happening then. Exactly the way he described it then is the way it is actually happening. He is the most focused person I have ever met, and it's inspiring. He was like a bright light that stayed lit all year round."

"You know a lot more than I do, Ben."

"No way, he's your brother. I only remember everything about him that I experienced, Jack."

"Which was a hell of a lot more than I experienced here living in the same house with him."

"I only felt privileged, Jack, that he wanted to be friends."

"Privileged? He considered you his dearest friend." Jack says.

"Really, Jack?"

"Oh yeah." Jack says. "You need to believe something, you had no less of an impact on him than he had on you and don't forget it. It was important for him to have a friend like you. It's not just my mother that kept him on the straight and narrow—it was you too, and it was this town as well—that made it so easy for him to feel like he could be himself. We owe you more than you know, Ben, and we owe this town."

"That's great to hear, Jack. I guess people really never know how much they mean to others. I guess it's an insecurity that comes with being human."

"Your faith in Christ, Ben, was very important to James."

"Thank you. Your brother was always like the big brother I always wanted." Ben turns his head while inconspicuously shedding a tear without Jack seeing.

Jack with a look of pride, "We're brothers too, Ben, always."

As Ben and Jack finish their conversation down at the stream, they head up to the house for the night. When Ben's mom returns from the hospital, she tells Jack that she spoke to his mom, and if he wanted to, he could spend the night. Jack returned with an excitement like he wouldn't be alone at home again tonight, and that he and Ben could hang together. With all of the crazy shifts that Jack's mother has been working, he has had to spend a lot of time at home alone these last couple of years. The Wilson's are the only friends that he is close enough to spend the night at. Most of his other friends are on the other side of town, and it's too far to walk. He's excited tonight, because he gets to stay with Ben.

"This is going to be excellent, Ben. Tonight will be fun, and I will write James tomorrow. He will love to hear that I spent the night at your house."

"Tell him I said hello."

"I will," Jack says positively. "He'll be pleased."

Ben and Jack get ready for bed on this Sunday night, the day before the first day of school. They continue to talk and reminisce well into the late stages of the evening. Most people in these parts are asleep by 10:00 p.m., but Ben and Jack continue to chat until midnight.

CHAPTER 3

———◆———

James returns from Sunday church and makes himself breakfast while listening to "Days Like This" by Van Morrison. Usually, on Sundays, James will just grab a takeout on the way home, but lately, he has been getting into the cooking thing. This is not a research day. Nor is it a day of work. It's a day of rest, and that is exactly what James has planned for the day. The only thing better than a day of rest for a Sunday afternoon agenda, would be to have someone to do that with. James hasn't been without opportunity to meet girls at Columbia, but he has made a vow to God not to date anyone again that he doesn't see as a potential wife. He's had enough relationships with people who don't see eye to eye with him or can't understand his value system. He has always been a man of prayer, but not until recently has he been praying specifically for a woman that God wants for him.

On Sundays, Professor King usually makes his way by the apartment for a conversation with James. Many times, they'll just sit outside on a couple of chairs and smoke a cigar. Other times, they'll walk to the pub for a couple of beers and a long chat. It wasn't until recently that James was able to buy a beer at the pub, and ever since his twenty-first birthday, he and the professor have made it a regular meeting place. They are quite fond of each other's friendship. The professor has been at Columbia for fifteen years and can't remember the last time he had a student with more potential. He is one of the reasons James made the choice of a PhD in history. So, he stops by on this Sunday night to pass some time. Later on Sunday, he and James light up a couple of cigars and talk about immigration. James responds to a question from the professor.

James says, "In my opinion, something as great as being a United States citizen should be a privilege, or even a pleasure to a certain extent. It's not about Mexico, or whatever country you come from. To the system, it's all about upper and lower class and nothing at all about Mexican and American or nationality for that matter. It's about rich and poor and education and no education—meaning, the doctor can stay because he's a contributing member of society, but the construction worker can't because he's a construction worker. Why isn't he a contributing member of society? This will be a very unpopular question among Americans with regard to contributing members of society, but here it goes—how many American citizens aren't taking advantage of the opportunity that being an American citizen brings with it? I have never met a noncitizen that was collecting unemployment checks for years or playing video games all night on the electricity that an unemployment check provides or that welfare provides. Also, I've never met a Mexican or any other immigrant that wasn't working hard or at least trying to make ends meet on their own and without government assistance. Furthermore, the Mexican culture, for one thing, is the most hardworking culture I have ever encountered in my life. They work for sixteen straight hours with very few breaks. That makes the work ethic in this country look less than admirable. The people in this country that are doing all the crying, are those that are sitting around and reaping the benefits of a broken system. It's the foreigner that is on our side of the border that gets all the blame. But it is the lazy American citizen that has been in this country, slothfully existing like a rock on a beach, who has taken for granted the opportunity that comes with the privilege of being born in this nation. Our parents need to kick their twenty-seven-year-old kids out of the house if they don't want to work or go to school."

The professor says, "You're in rare form this evening, James, but very interesting."

"Some of those things have no solutions." James says. "I was only making an assessment of the problems. Like I said earlier, the sociological plague that this country has had for decades is very contagious and undetectable—even by the average intelligent American. The other day, I spoke to a kid who used to install kitchen linoleum in the New York area, and he said when he'd do a job in an urban community, he was surprised with how many families had a thirty-some year old son living in their basement. He also said it wasn't just the shock of an unemployed thirty-year-old kid living in the basement, it was also discovering them sleeping in until one in the afternoon. There is a degenerate epidemic in our society, and liberals are going to bankrupt this country with their never-ending desire to financially help these people that don't have ambition. John F. Kennedy was a smart liberal and said, 'Ask not what your country can do for you; ask what you can do for your country." I'm sorry, but we need to light a fire under the butts of Americans and get them educated, or get them into a vocational school."

"The greatest problem with society today, Professor, is the separation of church and state. How can we sit with a straight face and deny the escalation of immorality isn't attributed to removing God from schools and public places? How can I tell a ten-year-old girl that God is going to protect her in school from a crazy gunman when God isn't even allowed in school?

"Well, I guess I asked for it, James, therefore I deserve a mouthful," the Professor says with a chuckle.

"I know," James confesses in a bashful tone. "I have to clean it up too."

"It's okay. What do you think of the separation of church and state?" the professor asks.

"I think it's one of the failed moments in human civilization, but to me personally, I don't need the two to be together for me to live a faithful life," James says. "It doesn't really bother me, it's more of a loss for those that believe in that separation, as far as I'm concerned."

Professor King asks curiously, "What do you mean?"

"Well, I don't need the inspiration of my neighbor to understand that God deserves all the praise and glory in one's life. I don't need it to be approved by a member of society. It's an individual thing. Most people think it's a collective thing, but it is an individual thing. I can't save you, nor can I do anything to save you. You can't save me, nor can you do anything to save me. It's between us and God individually," James reveals with passion.

"You have mentioned a number of times regarding the post–World War II era, and you have mentioned the separation of church and state in the same breath." Professor says. "What exactly do you mean?"

"All I was saying is, since World War II, our society has managed to produce the separation of church and state, women's liberation, a congratulatory attitude with regard to a homosexual coming out of the closet then same-sex marriage. We have legalized killing babies in the womb so a teenage girl can dispose of a mistake that was produced by promiscuity. We have just made a mess of society and all in the name of liberalism. If God didn't say that He was allowing the devil to have his way on earth in the end, I would be confused, but seeing that he did, we are in the last days, my friend," James regretfully says.

"Wow!" Professor King says with a chuckle. "That's about all I can take in for an evening." The professor holds his hand over his mouth with a smile, as if he's trying to hold in what he wants to say, but he doesn't.

"I'm sorry, I went on and on," James apologizes.

"Don't you say that, I enjoy all of our talks and wouldn't change a thing." The professor warmly says. "You truly stretch my brain in terms of stimulation. It's a pleasure. I have to run though. I will see you in school this week, my brother, keep in touch."

"I will, and thanks for the advice. See you Friday, Professor,"

"You too, my friend," Professor says before leaving for home. "Goodbye."

"Talk to you later," James says. "Don't forget to bring the cigars next time." James chuckles as the professor walks away smiling.

James sits on a park bench outside the building where he lives and finishes his cigar. He is considering how beautiful it is outside on this September evening. His emotions shift to extremely curious as he ponders thoughts of Josie Weathers from Friday's philosophy class. James has never seen her in Morningside Heights, but there's a first for everything, and what a great night it would be to see her pretty face. He has seen her at Low Plaza before and begins to think what a great night to take a stroll over to Low Steps. She seems to be the one thing on campus that gets school off of his mind. He couldn't miss her on the first day of school—she was spectacular, and she is every bit that much more spectacular every time he sees her. The way the slightest of breezes blows her golden blonde hair is paralyzing to him. James never knew before he saw her *that* the most subtle of human movements could be so gracefully beautiful. These images are forever embedded in his thoughts. Sometimes, he's terrified she'll turn and look right at him because of the stupid look that must be on his face while he's in awe of her. She truly is to him nothing short of a lone white flower in a bed of ferns.

James isn't sure quite yet if she even knows he exists. The first time they were dismissed from class on Friday, they somehow ended up at the door at just the same time, and James immediately stopped to allow her to go first. With a giggle, she insisted that he go first. Then he returned with another invitation for her to go first, and then she accepted by proceeding into the hallway.

The doors at the end of the hall on that hot day were propped open, and as soon as he turned to walk in the same direction as her, the entire essence of her floral aroma intoxicated him. That was the single moment in which she was truly baptized into his good graces. As they both headed out the doors, she glanced at him while he was looking at her, and she gave him this innocent smile that he hadn't seen before. He smiled back but was hopeless in hesitation by her immense beauty, and she walked off.

I wouldn't say based on James's history with girls that he is as self-assertive with girls, as he is in his other endeavors, but he holds his own. However, the immense beauty of Josie Weathers is enough to cause any man a healthy case of brain freeze. This one will take some time to say the least, which is something James has plenty of. He looks around and realizes that she had vacated the scene, not that he wouldn't prefer another vision of her over anything else in the world. James sits on a bench and begins to write a sonnet.

What is it said of Grace,
of man's spirit behold?
Harbors of a darkened pain,
yet forevermore unsold.

What is it said of Grace,
my loving Rock lest die alone?
Forevermore we have told,
let a Rock be forever known.

What is it said of Grace,
with which the weakest sore?
Upon thy Rock His face,
fill us with, which we adore.

Lonely child of silent lore,
Forsake us not, forevermore.

James misses his mom, as it has been quite a while since they've had a good hug. She was an affectionate mom. She tried to do everything she could to make the loss of their father insignificant. Charlotte Stapleton is somewhat grateful to her ex-husband for leaving, because if he hadn't, she would have never finished school and become a registered nurse. It is probably the reason she isn't as broken up about losing him as you might think. She was allowed to achieve all of her dreams while her husband was gone—dreams that she wouldn't otherwise have been able to pursue had he not left. So, in a way, she feels she owes everything she has to her ex-husband and blames him for absolutely nothing. She is the one who James gets his philosophy from. Her logic is that there is no loss if the loss is thirty years with someone that wants to be elsewhere. People can't make someone want someone, or make someone want a life that they don't want. He saved her from decades of misery and despair by leaving. Nevertheless, James and his mom are quite close and very similar, as she is very much like her father, Michael, whom James also takes many traits from.

Later on Sunday evening, James is winding down on campus. It had been relatively difficult falling asleep at 11:00 p.m. on campus the past few years; however, now that James is in an apartment, there is much more peace of mind in the evening. Sunday nights aren't as loud around there as they had been in the undergraduate housing the previous years. James grabs a German Weiss beer from the fridge and heads back to his office area. That should take the edge off the first week of school. Before he cracks open his beer, he sits down to write Jack an e-mail. He leans back in his black leather reclining office chair and has a moment of thought then begins to write. After he's done, and because he misses his mother so much, he usually goes back and reads e-mails he's shared with her. It temporarily soothes him and refreshes his memory as to the things they have shared since getting to Columbia. James goes way back in his e-mail history to find the first one he sent his mom after arriving at Columbia for the first time.

Dear Mom,   September 7, 2002

The journey that has led me to Columbia is anything but fortuitous, so I am forever indebted to you and Grandpa for making this opportunity so possible. We've talked at length of all the things that were always going on in my life over the years, but never really spent much time talking about you, and I want to apologize for that. You deserve to be happy, and I pray that you will let down the guard that you have had up for so long in order to protect Jack and I. It is my utmost wish for you to find someone that appreciates you and that will treat you the way a woman deserves to be treated. Maybe you and I both could pray for each other to find someone special. I have never really prayed to God for Him to send someone into my life, so maybe it is about time for me to start.

There isn't a son anywhere on this planet, nor is there a son anywhere in the history of the world, that is more proud than I am of you, mom. You have truly been one of God's angels to me all these years, and I will never forget or take for granted all that you did. I've always been so proud and fortunate to have such a close relationship with you and hope that it not only continues, but I truly hope that it even evolves into us being even closer as the years go by. I am the luckiest man in the world to have had you for a mother.

The transition from Macomb, Indiana, to Manhattan is quite overwhelming, and I am still, after three weeks, trying to adjust to the speed of life here in New York. I do not regret for one second the choice I made to attend Columbia. Manhattan has got to be the most diverse mixture of cultures of any place on earth, and I can already tell that I am going to enjoy this. I have already found a campus ministry to become a part of, and there is also a club for young Republicans that I believe I will join. There are also some pretty cool places to eat close by the dormitory, and there is a market in walking distance in case I need something.

I really miss you and Jack and can't wait to see you again. Maybe I can take a bus home for the holidays this year—I'll have to look into that. Tell Jack I said I love him, and I'll see him soon. I love you, Mom. Thank you once again for everything you and Grandpa provided for us. I couldn't have been sitting here writing this without you. I love you more than words can express.

Have a great week at work.

Love,
James.

After reading the first one James ever sent to his mother, he reads her reply to him from that September 7, 2002 e-mail.

Dear James, September 8, 2002

I so appreciate your e-mail; it was so heartwarming. I am so lucky to have a son that articulates his thoughts and feelings the way that you do. You are going to melt one lucky woman's heart someday, James. As for helping you get to where you are, you are the most intelligent and talented young man on this planet, and you owe your opportunity to yourself, and I know if your Grandfather Michael was here, he would second that.

Jack and I both miss you greatly, but we also know that you have work to do in this world. Every great man is on a mission of some kind, and I expect nothing different from where you are going, my dearest son. The people of this country someday will be so lucky to have such an honest and wholesome person such as you to represent it in whatever capacity you choose.

I have always prayed for you and Jack to be happy but never really prayed for a woman to come into your lives. Maybe I have been a little less encouraging in that department than I should have been as a mother. You know, with dad leaving years ago, it kind of left me with too much of an independent attitude on things. I should have chalked your father up as just an individual case of failure. Maybe I haven't been open enough to the possibility of romance. I promise I'll start opening my heart a little bit more. I'll start praying for a woman for you as well.

Thank you for the warm e-mail, James, and good luck at school.

Love,
Mom.

———— ✦ ————

Ben and Jack rise on Monday in Macomb for the first day of the new school year, and Jack looks up from where he was sleeping on the floor and says, "Why don't I see Lisa over your house anymore, Ben? You guys seem to be a great match."

"She went away for the summer with her parents and didn't return until yesterday," Ben says.

"I guess she just hasn't had a chance to call or come by." He reveals a look of sadness. "I left a message on their machine Friday because I forgot they weren't coming home until Saturday, and I haven't received a call back yet."

"It sounds to me, Ben, like you miss her a lot?"

"Perhaps," Ben adds. "I wonder if she enjoyed the vacation."

"Ben, it's a little difficult in Macomb to forget about anything such as missing Lisa, especially with how boring it is around here."

"You mentioned that more than once this weekend," Ben says with curiosity. "What is there to do at home for fun?"

"Not a lot, Ben. I have books up the you-know-what, but I've never really been the reading type. My grandfather built a pole barn out back many years ago. He originally built it for shelter for the farm equipment. Until James built a loft inside, it was mostly for storage and working, but he wanted to have a place away from civilization to read and write. I really haven't gone in the loft since, darn…a year or two before James left for school. It's been about five years."

"Wow. I never knew that, Jack. Sounds like it would be interesting to check that out."

"Ben, I wonder if there are things growing from the ceiling in there—just kidding." Jack humorously says. "You should come home with me after school today, and we can check it out."

"Sounds good, Jack."

"I have a baseball meeting after school, Ben, but I should be out of there in less than an hour."

"Okay, Jack, I'll find something to do. Maybe Lisa is back from vacation because she has band practice after school usually, and there are always cool places for me to hide in the auditorium." Ben reminisces about some of the funnier moments he's had with Lisa after band practice. "I get a kick out of messing with her while she's trying to be so serious with her instrument."

"I'll bet." Jack says with a chuckle. "That sounds like fun."

"She's one in a million, Jack. I guess I fear that someday she'll meet someone else and like him more."

"You crazy, Ben." Jack gets all up in his face. "That girl ain't goin' nowhere."

"For me, Jack, the sun rises and sets with her. Anyways, I'll think of something to do for an hour during your baseball meeting. I'm curious to see what James has in that loft." Ben confesses a level of curiosity as he and Jack get ready for school.

"Ben, does Lisa ride this bus?"

"No, she's from the other side of town. Her parents drive her, and I take her home—that is, if they don't."

It didn't take long for the bus to arrive at the school for the first time this year in Macomb, Indiana. That bus ride on the first day of school always seems to be the fastest one of the year. Most people would just like that bus driver to drive around the block a few times before taking kids to school. Ben usually has his car, but his father needs to look at it before he can drive it, and his dad has been so busy with work lately. He was hoping his father would have made it home in time last night to fix it, but it'll have to wait another day. Nevertheless, the bus pulls up, and immediately, Jack notices Ben's girl, Lisa, saying good-bye to her father in the parking lot. He nudges Ben on the arm and points to her.

"Wow, Jack," Ben says. "She made it home from vacation."

"Yes she did, Ben. It seems like she's been gone for a year."

Ben reveals, "I have butterflies, like I had on the second day that we were going together." Ben's in a mild state of confusion. "This is really weird."

"I'd have butterflies every day as well, if my girl looked like Lisa. Trust me on that," Jack says with a laugh. "I'm not joking one bit."

"I think what makes me nervous is every year that passes, she looks better and better," Ben reveals.

"I can see what you mean." Well, see you after school, Ben."

"You too, Jack. I'll find you near the gym an hour after the last bell rings."

"Okay, sounds good."

Ben's girlfriend, Lisa, immediately went into the school after getting out of her father's car. She must not have noticed that it was Ben's bus that had just arrived. Ben walks in the door to a crowded hall and tries to look for her in as subtle of a manner as possible—without, of course, making it look as though he's looking for his long lost love. It's funny; men want their love to know how much they mean to them, but isn't it difficult to be so vulnerable so voluntarily? It seems as though Lisa wanted to tease him, as she comes out from behind the pillar next to the door and comes up from behind him and playfully blindfolds him with her hands. Just the touch of her hands brought an uncontrollable smile to Ben's face, as though he knew exactly who the perpetrator was. There is this electricity that takes place when a passionate love touches your skin with theirs. It is as if two high-voltage wires were connected for the very first time. Every inch of Lisa's body is pressed against Ben as she pulls her hands away from over his eyes. At the moment, Ben is lost in her touch, as if he is in a temporary state of paralysis and befuddlement.

"Guess who, Ben?" Lisa most energetically says.

"Lisa, when did you get home from vacation?"

"Oh, not until after 11:00 p.m. It was way too late to call you. I was hoping we'd get home earlier because I missed you so much and wanted to see you, but we ran into some bad weather on Saturday night."

"I missed you too," Ben confesses. "The days were long and boring without you this summer." He's also thinking that, "maybe we shouldn't do that next summer. Maybe we should go somewhere together."

As the first school bell goes off, Lisa takes a step toward Ben, leans in, and gives him a slow kiss. Up until this moment in their relationship, a kiss like this has never been experienced in exactly this manner. Ben is mesmerized for the moment, and Lisa notices. She giggles as girls do when they notice they have left their man speechless and disoriented. Lisa runs off to homeroom, and leaves Ben wandering slowly in the hall, still looking like he forgot exactly where he was, and what day it was. Ben gathers himself and his bag and heads upstairs for first hour. The hallways quickly empty as Ben ponders the different vibe he felt from Lisa. It's not like he hasn't seen Lisa before, but a lot of time has passed since she left for her summer trip, and when girls get around seventeen years old, they are becoming something else entirely as time passes. If you asked Ben, he would probably tell you that something also seemed quite different in Lisa as well. She felt more like a woman than she did when she left, not that she wasn't a woman four months ago, but there was a noticeable maturity in her. He couldn't quite put his finger on it.

———————

On Monday morning, back at Columbia, James sits on a stone wall waiting for class. To pass the time, he scribbles the rough draft of a poem he's been working on. It's still really raw, but he's been adding and subtracting with it all weekend. James had thought about graduate school in literature but thought that with all he has read in his life, he has already in a way given himself a graduate degree in literature. Nevertheless, he returns to write,

> The sighs from fears and cries of tears,
> nurtured and mended, through thoughts of heaven,
> while into the night, we persevere,
> Weathered by time, September Eleven.
>
> Years have passed, without much mention,
> of those that lost so many years,
> as well as them, that gave so much.
> We honor them, who still have tears.
>
> Bright blue sky, still missing its throne,
> on ole New Amsterdam, we must remember,
> while a sweet sad child carries us home.
> So we remember that day in September.
>
> Remember them from September Eleven,
> may we rejoice once more, one day in heaven.

James looks up to the New York skyline and notices what a bright sunny day it will be as he finishes a quick scribbled poem while waiting. He gets up and heads into the building for his 8:00 a.m. class. These classes aren't exactly like they are in the undergraduate curriculum. Sometimes, James could go to that class and only see two or three students at one time. Graduate courses do not have many people in them, so the teacher can work with everyone individually. It really benefits the student being well prepared for the next level, as well as preparing the student for their thesis.

"Good morning, Professor."

"Morning, James. How was your weekend?"

"It was busy, thank you. And you?"

"Did nothing all weekend but relax at home." The professor reveals. "I usually don't like to do much on weekends at the beginning of the semester because I want to focus, and plus, I am usually exhausted by how active I was all summer. So it's kind of a time for relaxation for me every school year."

"I like that," James enthusiastically says. "The days are getting shorter as well."

As the time expires in class, James leaves and takes a seat out in front of the building again and notices what a nice day it turned out to be. He looks up at the sun shining at him and notices the building that is in his peripheral vision. He can't help that it reminds him of the way the video showed the second plane flying into the second tower almost four years ago. Being in New York on this Monday and having a clear sky and a tall building in your peripheral as you look up, only brings back nightmarish memories for anyone in this town. It doesn't help when the fourth anniversary of that day is only a few days away. That would be Thursday, and James is to speak at the 9/11 tribute right here on campus. Even though he is terribly nervous, he has an immense excitement about him regarding the event. For once in his life, he gets to speak in front of hundreds regarding a topic of importance. This is the beginning. It has been three fast years since he started at Columbia, and things are already beginning to evolve the way he had dreamed.

Later, James takes a walk over and grabs a quick bite of chicken and rice from Halal Cart. He's done with everything for the day on campus and decided to get dinner a little early on this Monday because he is swamped with research tonight. He'll most likely be up until the wee hours of Tuesday morning. James doesn't have school on Tuesday, so it doesn't matter when he sleeps, as long as his research is done before Wednesday. He also needs to find time to work on what he'll say on Thursday at the 9/11 tribute, even though most of it should just be from the heart. Naturally, he is more concerned with what not to say than he is with what to say. He doesn't have much time to mess around this week, with all that is on his plate. James grabs his takeout and heads home for the night. The Colts are on *Monday Night Football* tonight, so he most definitely wants to get home and see what Peyton Manning does.

———— ◆ ————

Back in Macomb, Ben enters his second class, which is literature. He will have to, unfortunately, read a couple of novels in this course, which is something he's not very fond of. However, the last couple years, he has been inspired to read more than he has ever in his life, thanks to his best friend. James told him that reading would get easier and more enjoyable so long as he didn't neglect it, and that the brain connections for reading are like muscles that needed to be worked every day. This class should push Ben even more and give him a wonderful opportunity to see where he is regarding school beyond Crenshaw High School. He had always figured that Lisa was for sure going to school somewhere, and Ben hates the idea of being at home while she is meeting new guys away at school. So, for the time being, the unmentioned plan is for Ben to work hard and improve his application profile. If his grades improve greatly in his senior year, there is a chance that a school would give him a semester to prove himself, as long as he does okay on the entrance exams.

Ben arrives with Jack at his house to check out the pole barn. They had to leave the school before Ben was ready because Lisa was still in her band practice. Ben did walk by her room and did get to wave good-bye to her and say, "I'll call you." She had responded with a silent lip read gesture that answered, "Okay, Ben." She wasn't disappointed in her reaction, although she did have a little touch of confusion. It didn't dawn on Ben until later that she may have been counting on him for a ride home, and he hadn't mentioned to her that his car wasn't ready to drive yet.

Most of the times that Ben has visited James's house was for birthday parties. He's never seen the pole barn out back. Jack vaguely remembers when he was really young, playing around at Grandpa's feet while he was working on the cars out in the barn. Never has he had a recollection though, of the loft that James had built years after the barn was built. In fact, with the automotive aspect of the shop being in the very back of the barn, they had just always entered back there when he was a kid because that is precisely where Grandpa was at all of the time. Besides, the way James built the loft, the stairway, and the little hall that he built to the stairway looks like it was designed to keep the working area of the barn from disturbing the peace of mind of anyone studying in the loft.

Ben is thinking that this loft was strictly for the privacy and peace of mind of a young man that has a little brother six years behind him in age. They seem to have an understanding relationship for brothers, but with all the reading and writing James did, you'd like to think that would have been difficult without the loft. Charlotte's take on the whole loft thing was that it allowed Jack to be a kid, without bugging his brother, and it allowed James to be a young man that needed peace of mind with his studies. It was kind of her idea of a compensatory justification for the wake that a man leaves when walking out on his wife and two sons. Charlotte always felt that for the greatness that James was headed for, he was going to need an atmosphere to encourage creativity. Because all men can do those things, but great men create great works, and it was just the only way to get the best out of James, considering the circumstances that he was in as a young man all those years.

"Are you sure this is okay to enter the loft?" Ben asks.

"Sure thing. Otherwise, James would have left something saying he didn't want visitors up here."

"Well, that's good to hear," Ben says. "Last thing I want is the feeling of intruding on someone's space, especially James's."

"Oh, it's okay, Ben. I will let James know that we came up here. I know most of his things he took with him to New York, but once he hears that we came up, he may even want us to send him something he may have forgotten when he left."

"Sounds good, Jack."

Jack unlocks the loft door, and he turns on the light, and they enter. The first thing they notice is an entire wall of bookcases filled to the max with books. The loft is ten feet wide and fifteen feet long, and that long bookcase literally stretched almost the entire fifteen feet on one side of the room. On the other side of the room is a black leather couch that is long enough for someone to stretch their feet out on and catch a nap if needed. Ben is thinking, *What a great setup this must have been to just get lost in an entire weekend and study without any distractions.*

James built the loft so that all of the entertainment connected to the speakers is mounted up near the ceiling in two opposite corners of the loft, giving it surround sound. Ben and Jack stumble on James's box of music CDs. James is into classical music and a wide range of contemporary artists. However, his favorite was the Verve, which was an alternative rock band. He loved Beethoven and couldn't get enough of his music. In fact, they couldn't find any in the box because James took all the good ones to New York. There must have been a folded-up photo of Ludwig Van Beethoven in one of the CD cases because he has one of the walls of the loft decorated with two things—a huge poster of ole Ludwig Van himself, and a poster from the film production of the 1999 Johnny Depp film *The Ninth Gate*. When James worked at the theater, and it was time for a new movie to come to the theater, they just threw out the posters from the previous movies. One weekend, James asked where the posters go, and Mr. Johnson asked him if he wanted it, and he said sure.

Ben takes a deep breath, and he leans back in James's reclining office chair and pauses for a moment in deep thought.

"Jack, do you think he read all these books?"

"Not sure, but does James seem like the type to have a book he didn't or wouldn't read?" Jack asks.

"You're right. Hard to believe because there are so many, but you're right. There is a purpose for every one of these books and every page that is in them. He must have a hundred of the best American literature classics alone. I see Hemingway, Hawthorne, Melville, Stevenson, Dickens, and Arthur Miller, to name a few. I even see Thoreau and Emerson." Ben counts with a sigh. "There are too many books for me to read."

"And that is only one single section of James's bookcase, Ben. There are like fifteen other sections of various subjects. From Krishnamurti and Machiavelli to Milton and Erasmus, you name it—he's got all that one would want to read. Here's an entire section on civil rights."

"Jack, he must have read a thousand books," Ben says with amazement. "There's no way I could do that."

"He's read at least that many." There are five hundred books right here in front of us. He probably took two hundred with him and has probably read hundreds since he left for school."

"Wow!" Ben, with amazement in his voice. "I have only read like twenty books in my life. I feel like a dope."

"Join the party, Ben. Why do you think I play baseball? There is no way I could keep up with this. I'd be worried my eyes would fall out reading this much."

"I want to start reading more, but this is intimidating, Jack."

"Don't let this bother you." Think on the bright side, you got some time to catch up to him on reading, because you just know he's reading things now that he would have never chose to read on his own. So pick one, Ben. Read one a week. You're more than welcome to use these, as long as you return them as you finish them."

"Thanks, Jack. I will not let you guys down."

"Let's make a point of coming up here once a week. That will give you a chance to exchange books."

"Okay, Jack."

"Next week, when we come up here, we'll grab a pizza and watch a movie," Jacks suggests as he's going through the movies. "He's got some pretty good ones here. I know his favorite one is *Nobody's Fool* with Paul Newman. He loves that movie. He said it reminds him of our family."

"I have never seen it."

"Well, there's a bunch of good ones," Jack says. "We'll check them out when you come over next week."

"Sounds great, Jack, I look forward to it."

Ben heads down the steps and out the door of the pole barn and notices that his dad picked him up in the GTO. Ben is as happy as he has ever been to see his car fixed, and he gives his dad a big hug. After supper, Ben calls Lisa and asks if it's okay to stop by on this evening, and she answers with a big yes.

CHAPTER 4

B en pulls the GTO into Lisa's driveway on Monday evening at the end of the first day of school. The evening is warm, as the sun is disappearing into the tree-line that stretches the length of the property. She lives at the end of a dirt road about a mile from the main highway that runs directly through downtown Macomb. The tree line that runs down the side of the property is perpendicular to the road that they live on. They have an aboveground swimming pool in the back of the house that has a wood deck that surrounds the perimeter of the pool and is attached to the back of the home. It's been a few months since Ben and Lisa have had an opportunity to swim together, but sometimes, they just sit on the edge of the deck and put their feet in the water.

When Ben gets out of his car, he can't help but notice how nervous he is coming to her house this evening. It is as if he is relearning her all over again, and it seems as though it is like when they first met.

Lisa lives with both of her parents, and they both work in town—her father at the local hardware store that they have owned for decades, and her mother part-time at the local diner. Lisa's father is really into birds, so there is a birdbath and a bird feeder on the side of the house closest to the trees. So when you are approaching the home, you become overwhelmed with sights and sounds, as if you were walking straight into the deep wild. With birds flying to and fro, from the tree line then back to the feeder to bathe, it's quite an experience, especially coupled with the beautiful background color of the forest. Although the Wilson property lays claim to the best place in town, and maybe even all of Indiana, Lisa's home is also quite indicative of the fact that all of Indiana is an exceptional experience in itself. It truly is a sanctuary in its own right.

Lisa's home is a white house of many gables, with an old classic look. The front porch spans the entire width of the front of the home and is enclosed. It is so nice when the sun goes down, and you are completely surrounded by screen windows inside of the enclosure. It truly makes it seem as if you are sitting right in the middle of the forest and enjoying the sights and sounds of the wilderness, and all without bugs crawling all over you. The enclosure is, of the opinion of many, the best feature of Lisa's home.

This home has been in Lisa's family for sixty-five years. Her late grandparents bought the home right before her grandfather left for Normandy in 1944. Lisa and the folks have done a lot of improvements to the interior over the years to maintain that contemporary look. However, they have done very little to the exterior, with the exception of painting and such, and that is in order to maintain an old classic look to the outside of the home. The soffits and windows are white, and the walls are also painted white board. The gables are all gray-painted old wood cedar shake. The fascias and window trims are also gray, which leaves a nice gray and white contrast of course, with the home appearing from afar as completely white.

After Ben shakes off the butterflies and gets over a little anxiety about the anticipation of Lisa's immense beauty, he closes the door to his car. When he gets to the door, he has to go through the front door to the enclosed front porch first before reaching the front door to the home. When the enclosure door shuts, it slams loudly and the noise acts as a doorbell. So, before Ben has a chance to press it, he notices Lisa walking from the kitchen to the front door. When she comes to the door to greet him, it was so like the moment earlier, where it felt as though he hadn't seen her in a year. She was wearing a white summer dress that only dropped inches below her knees and her skin was as brown as he had ever remembered it. Her bare feet only added to the essence of her beauty and innocence. Ben looks at her as if this is as good as she has ever looked to him, and Lisa returns with a blushing turn of the head, as if she knows exactly what's on Ben's mind.

Lisa exits the home, they sit down on a swing on the front porch, and Ben makes sure he sits first, so it will be up to her as to the appropriate closeness with her parents' home and all. But ironically, Lisa's mom whispers out the front window, "Hi there, Ben, how's your parents?"

"They're great," he says. "My dad has been working a lot."

"Well, tell them I said hello."

"I will do that." Ben says to Lisa's mother.

"You kids enjoy yourself."

As her Mom leaves, Lisa giggles at the brief conversation between Ben and her mother, and as she teases him, he begins to blush and turn bright red. He turns his head in embarrassment, and all it does is fuel her fire even more to play with him, so he straightens up and begins tickling her, and then she begins to put a reluctant end to her playful fury. During all the giggling and heckling, it seems as though she used the playfulness to have an excuse to inconspicuously sit real close to Ben. Ben's heart begins to race, as he can't help but notice her smooth bare leg touching his, and as she turns to lean into him, he can feel and smell her warm, sensuous breath. It is driving Ben nutty on the inside, and he does his best to make it unnoticeable. One experience with Lisa though, can cause you to beg to differ, because she is so playful with Ben's vulnerability, and that makes her like him even more that she has that control.

Her mother finishes her work in the kitchen, which you can see well from the porch, and she goes into the family room on the other side of the house to join her husband, who was watching television. Ben notices a lot more lights are turned off inside, than there were when he sat down, and as Lisa notices the same, she puts her legs on Ben's lap and begins to kiss him all over his neck. Ben missed her so much, and he just wants so bad to let go of the imaginary chains that hold him, but he has too much respect for her parents to lose control. Ben's parents and Lisa's parents know each other very well. It would be mighty embarrassing for Ben to let Lisa's parents down. So he just sits and lets Lisa tease him out of his mind. She mauls him like the wife of a Roman soldier whose husband has just returned home after five years in battle. Her smell is intoxicatingly indulgent. Her warm, smooth, lovely skin touching his is almost unbearable for Ben, who is trying to hold every desire from being let out of a cage. Ben can hardly remember her being this sexy before, which leaves him with the probability that she must have missed him just as much as he did her.

"Are you okay, my darling Ben?"

"Doing fine," he says. "How about you?"

"Great. You just look a little tense sitting there," Lisa says while teasing him.

"You're driving me nuts with how sexy you are tonight." She has this deviously playful look on her face as she looks away in embarrassment that Ben just said those words. "You are so beautiful."

"That's a nice thing to say, Ben, and thank you."

Under the circumstances of the day, Ben can barely help himself from thinking of a great reason to have a loft in a pole barn, as he wishes, at the moment, that he was upstairs with her right now on that black couch. Finding privacy such as that will have to wait a few more days until the weekend, but for now, Ben must remain in control because he wouldn't want to ruin the opportunity to freely visit Lisa at home in the future. If her parents respect him, then he will be welcome to visit as if he was one of their own, and Ben doesn't want to ruin that in their senior year.

Lisa turns around and points her feet in the other direction on the bench and leans back into Ben's lap. He runs his hand through her shiny blond hair in the moonlight, and she looks right into his eyes as if he was her everything. She gets closer to his face and continues to stare into the abyss of his eyes. He notices that she closes her eyes as her lips touch his for one slow wet kiss and then another one that lasts even longer. Ben begins to grow nervous about her parents seeing them, so he playfully starts to tickle her to cease her momentary passion.

"Stop it Ben!" Lisa shouts while laughing. "I'm the one that does all the tickling."

"Not until you stop trying to get me in trouble with your parents." Ben says with laughter.

"I just like to see you get all up in a bunch," Lisa reveals. "It's so cute."

"Ha-ha-ha," Ben sarcastically says with a playful tone.

Ben stops Lisa and puts his arms around her and gives her the hug that he has been waiting to give her since he arrived this evening. He whispers in her ear that he has to be home at 10:00 p.m. She returns with a frustrated moan, like she doesn't want him to ever go, and he returns to her that he still has ninety minutes to visit her. She leans into Ben's arms for a while, and she tells him all about the vacation. She tells him what a cool place Myrtle Beach is and all the cool colleges they passed along the way. It was not exactly the thing Ben wanted to talk about this evening, so he gives her a look, and she gives him a hug and says she's sorry. Lisa likes to joke with Ben, but she is serious about being sensitive about college next year. It will more than likely work itself out. Lisa has a grin on her face, as if she knows something Ben doesn't know, but she doesn't want to talk about it until next year.

Lisa wants Ben to do well in his senior year, and doesn't want to tell him just yet that she would never go away to school where she couldn't see him every night. She has always felt that commuting to Purdue in West Lafayette or Indiana University in Bloomington was something she would seriously consider—at least until Ben got accepted to one of them. It would be easy to gear a college schedule toward not having to commute more than twice a week. It would be quite doable in her eyes. She's not committing to anything because she would go with him wherever he got accepted—if he gets accepted at a university. Anyway, it's almost 10:00 p.m., and she comes to the realization that this will have to pick back up tomorrow at school, so she begins to walk him to his car.

"Jack mentioned to me in the hall at school that your car wasn't running," Lisa says. "Did you get it fixed tonight?"

"Yeah, my Dad worked on it while I was at school today. I had no idea, and he came to pick me up at Jack's after school in it and surprised me to say the least."

"Oh, that was a sweet thing to do, Ben. Your parents are so cool. I miss them and want to see them soon, so our next meeting can be at your place with you teasing me."

"Sounds like a plan, Lisa. I can't wait to see you again."

"Ah, you're sweet." She snuggles up to him and becomes goofy. "I'm the luckiest girl in Macomb."

"You were driving me absolutely nuts on the porch tonight. You're lucky we weren't anywhere else." Ben warns Lisa with a grin.

"Hmmm, I can't wait to see you tomorrow, Ben. You're driving me crazy just telling me this."

"Okay," he says while realizing this is getting dangerous. "I'm going now."

"Kiss me, Ben. Kiss me! Kiss me!" Lisa playfully shouts.

As Ben notices that there are no windows or openings on this side of the house that would allow her parents to see him kiss her good-bye, he reaches over to her, as he has his back to his car. He pulls her in close to him, puts one hand on the small of her back and the other hand behind her neck, and gives her the longest kiss he has ever given her. She rubs her leg up against his legs, and she takes her mouth up to his ear and whispers into his ear with that sexy breathy voice of hers. "Oh Ben, I missed you all summer and couldn't wait to see you."

"I missed you too, Lisa. Maybe next time we can go together."

"Are you serious?" She asks. "Would you go next time?"

"I would for sure, Lisa. I don't see how I could ever spend four months away from you again. I have no idea what I'm going to do if the college thing doesn't work out in my favor."

"Don't worry yourself," she says. "I love you. I'll always love you. It would take Armageddon to separate my love from you. Okay?" This really made Ben feel much better, as he looks at her with a smile.

"I love you too, Lisa. We'll see what happens when it happens."

"That's the spirit, my Ben."

They finally separate at 9:45 p.m., and Ben heads home. As he's pulling away, he watches Lisa walking up to the house and notices the wind blowing her white dress around, enough to reveal how amazing her legs are. As she is no longer in sight, he turns toward the road, and lets out a sigh and ponders the idea of how he must be the luckiest guy on the planet, for that girl to have chosen him over all the other boys in the world. If he doesn't have the motivation to improve enough as a student to go to college with her, he has it now. Falling asleep right away for Ben tonight is going to have its challenges. You see, for men, there are moments in one's life that, no matter how many years and decades pass, they never forget, and tonight was just one of those times for Ben. Lisa's behavior this evening will most definitely have him tossing and turning all night. It's what you could call the heartbeat of passion, and there is no way his pulse will drop anytime soon. They've been together for a long time, but this was a first. Lisa was a woman this time, instead of a teenager. She obviously went through changes while she was away.

The first book that he grabbed from James's loft earlier today was *The Life You Imagine*, which is about the Yankee shortstop, Derek Jeter. That will be his first book to read on his relentless quest to become the best student that he can be, and it will greatly improve his chances of getting accepted to a university in the spring. Ben sets the book down on the nightstand before lying down. It will come in handy tonight, with how long it will take him to fall asleep because Lisa put that love spell on him that all boys get put on them at some point. However, after lying in bed for ten minutes with a smile as wide as the Missouri river, he falls asleep.

On Tuesday morning, with Ben still disoriented by the passion Lisa dished out on Monday evening, he comes down the stairs for breakfast.

"Good morning, Mom."

"Morning," Lois says. "How was your sleep?"

"Oh, best sleep ever."

"Wow Ben! What brought on this sudden burst of enthusiasm over a night of sleep?"

"Oh, because," He says. "Lisa was so beautiful last night."

"Oh boy, had fun did you?" Mom says with a giggle.

"Yeah, we sure did." Ben has this look on his face like he's still curious about why Lisa seems so different. "She seems to have changed since the spring, but I can't put my finger on it."

Suddenly, Ben is entering back into another state of romantic mush brain that he was in just before dozing off Monday night. His Mom walks away from the conversation, giggling just like she had when Ben first walked in the house yesterday for dinner. The relationship that Ben has with his Mom is very playful as you might have already noticed. She has a tendency, as Lisa does, to really try and make light of his serious nature. Ben just has those moments where he seems like he has too serious of a look on his face, and it must be just like throwing red meat at the wolves when it comes to Lisa and his Mom's playful manner. Ben gets into his car and fires it up for the first time for school.

Ben's car is black and in great condition, with no rust at all. His father helped him get it from a farmer down south a couple of years ago, and it was already in great condition, so Ben has never had to do any bodywork. There are different styles of GTOs, and Ben's is the 1972 version of the LeMans body style. Lisa loves Ben's car. She gets excited when she hears the sound of the engine, especially when she is in it and he presses the gas pedal down.

Ben arrives at the school a little after the time that Lisa usually gets dropped off by her father. She is outside, and she hears his car, and just as Ben was hoping, she skips her way quickly out to where he is parking. It puts an instant smile of joy on Ben's face. She is like a lightning rod for him. It was more painful than he was comfortable sharing when she dropped the bomb on him that her and her family were going to be gone all summer. It was the longest summer of his life.

Lisa arrives at his car, and Ben hasn't gotten out yet, so Lisa gets into the passenger seat. They have ten minutes before first bell, so there is no real hurry to sprint into the building. Lisa is wearing tight faded blue jeans today, which more than show how beautiful she is. She is also wearing tennis shoes and a white cotton button-up with light blue pinstripes. She playfully teased Ben by showing him the lingerie top she had on underneath. She had mentioned once before on the phone that she had matching lingerie top and bottoms, but Ben didn't believe her, as he thought it was her teasing him again. The pink color goes perfect with the summer tan that she received on her vacation, and Ben is going to be wondering all day if she has the matching bottoms on as well. The image of this in school all day will make it virtually impossible to pay attention to any lecture.

She leans over to him in his car and says thank you for coming over last night, and he leans over to meet her in between the two bucket seats and says he would come over every night if it was up to him, and gives her a huge long kiss. They both get out and head to their first class. However, before they part ways, Ben grabs the buttons on her shirt and buttons a couple of them up as if he was buttoning up a package that he is the rightful owner of. Lisa smiles at him. In any event, they separate from each other as their first classes are on opposite sides of the high school. But she asks, before he gets too far from her, if he would meet her for lunch, and he says for sure as the warning bell rings for first hour. She turns the corner and is now out of sight, so Ben heads into the building for his first class.

As Ben sits down and leans back in his chair, he takes a deep breath from the roller coaster of hormonal shifts he has been through in the last twenty-four hours. He can't help but see Lisa walking around in his mind with just the pink lingerie on. Needless to say, Ben will never in a million years ever forget the last fifteen hours that has transpired. Ben has this feeling that she all up and became a woman while she was gone this summer, and wonders if she was really gone all that long for that to happen. She had her birthday during the trip, so one would assume when a sixteen-year-old girl becomes a seventeen-year-old girl, she becomes a woman. That would explain everything that happened the last two days—both his immense attraction to her, and even more so, her most obvious desire for him.

———— • ————

"What do you say, Steve? Ben asks. "You up for a Saturday in Terre Haute?"

"That sounds great to me, Ben. How long has it been?"

"I think the last time we went, was before Lisa left town with her parents." Ben says with a distant look due to him mentioning something he doesn't want to think of. "That must have been four months ago."

"Yeah, sure seems like that long ago, Ben. I haven't seen Lisa's friend, Amy, much this summer. I hope I see her this weekend when we go."

"I'll make sure she's there, Steve. Let me talk to Lisa about it later."

"Sounds good," Steve concurs. "See you at lunch."

"Later."

Steve is another one of Ben's really good friends, as they have been in the same classes since grade school. They sometimes go to Terre Haute on Saturdays because there's more to do there. Many times, Lisa and her friend, Amy, will tag along, which is exactly what is happening this weekend, as Ben wants to have time to be alone with Lisa for the first time in four months.

Monday night in New York is winding down for James also. He has fallen asleep in his chair with one book opened in his lap and a handful of notes lying on his chest. With the lights and the television still on from watching the game earlier, he apparently didn't finish his work before nodding off. But with not having school tomorrow, he'll have plenty of time to catch up. James is a little nervous about the speech on Thursday, even though it's not really a speech. They just wanted an academic speaker for the late stages of the tribute, and James was at the top of a very short list. With regard to his nervousness, on the other hand, there is going to be a lot of emotional people in the crowd when he does speak, so it won't be hard to get cheers out of people, and that can go a long way in smoothing over the anxiety of a speaker.

James awakens in his chair and realizes it is the middle of the night. Well, it's closer to getting up than it is to bedtime. It is 3:10 a.m. in New York. James fell asleep about 10:00 p.m., so he might as well stay up and finish his research. He figures if he doesn't get enough sleep, he can doze off at any point again because he doesn't have class on Tuesday. While drinking a cup of coffee, James opens the curtains wide enough to see the lighted Manhattan skyline in the wee hours of Tuesday morning. He has made a few friends over the first few years at Columbia, and one of them pulled some strings to get him an apartment with a view of the Manhattan skyline. How can anyone ever again look into that skyline and not feel like there is something substantial missing from it? The anniversary for 9/11 isn't until Thursday, but with today being the Tuesday of the week of the anniversary, one can't help but think that this morning is the anniversary of that terrible Tuesday in Lower Manhattan in 2001. He closes the curtains and gets back to work on his research, preparing something to say for Thursday.

James leans back in his recliner and ponders in a deep gaze while staring at the wall of his apartment, as he desires to snatch from out of thin air, a substantial direction in what to say at the podium on Thursday. The walls to James's apartment are desperately missing the touch of a woman to say the least. It is most obviously decorated by a twenty-one-year-old bachelor. James was lucky to have a friend that could get him this place. It is a corner apartment and has windows on both sides of the building facing Lower Manhattan as well as a window on the back of the building facing the Hudson River.

Momentarily returning back to what Jack and Ben were discussing earlier, James was able to acquire a lot of movie posters from the downtown Macomb movie theater. One unique thing about the theater was that it was always showing a double feature. Most of the time, it was showing two modern movies that had been released that year. However, on several occasions, due in large part to the availability of films, Mr. Johnson would sometimes make the second film an old movie. Many of the older folks in Macomb would get a kick out of that because many times, the second movie would be from their generation. Consequently, James had his apartment in Morningside Heights partially decorated with old film posters.

When you first walk into the apartment, you can't help but instantly notice the movie production poster of the film *West Side Story* on the wall across from the door. As you proceed toward the couch area, you see a picture of James and his mother on the wall that is bookended by the poster of the movie *Ghostbusters* with Bill Murray and a poster of the movie *Marathon Man* with Dustin Hoffman. Other than that, the rest of the apartment is filled with overloaded bookcases on every wall. There must be enough books in this place to start the beginning stages of another Manhattan library, and he has read just about all of them. Also, in the corner of the living room area is an artist easel of a sketch that James has been working on for some time. It is a landscape of a beautiful countryside, and from the details, one would assume that it is from somewhere in Europe. It will eventually become a painting of a French countryside that is viewed from the vines of a vineyard. James isn't even close to being done with it, as he only gets to work on it like once a month if he's lucky.

As James leans back forward in his chair, he begins to write down some notes for his speaking moment at Thursday's 9/11 tribute on Columbia University's campus. After he jotted down a few things, it occurred to him to search the internet for an old poem that might be appropriate for the occasion. Lo and behold, he found exactly that from an early 20th century medical corps soldier in the English army in the Great War (World War I). James wanted to say something relevant that wasn't written by him, and he found exactly that in Laurence Binyon's poem "For the Fallen."

James is more of a self-taught poet, and would never consider his poetry good enough to reveal in front of a thousand people at a September 11 speaking event. Those that have read his poetry, however, beg to differ. Despite his modest attitude on the subject, he has a very sensitive and romantic way with words. He does, however, consider himself a writer but definitely not of the poetic nature, although he has thought very much about writing in prose. The writing aspects of James's aspirations will most definitely come as he finishes his degree, but for now, it is nothing more than a hobby. Besides, school is keeping him busy enough at the moment.

Even though James is slightly hesitant at revealing his poetry to people, reading the Binyon poem did prompt him to start writing a poem of his own. He stares at his sketch of a French countryside and begins to ponder an abyss of words that would convey the appropriate feelings of this great event of remembrance. He has had many courses on American history, so he tries to draw in some of that knowledge that he learned in his undergraduate degree…the knowledge that will allow him to express a unique gesture of grace, that would be most deserving for this great city.

Not only does James include unique aspects of this great city's history, but he also includes one single word (*sore* instead of *so*) in a line in the middle of the poem that represents the accent of this great city by the sea. A few of James's close friends have read some of his work and have stated that there is some great stuff there. Even though some of it is quite raw and needs a little revision, he does have a knack for un-juggling words and incorporating them into a meaning that greatly compliments the knowledge that he has acquired in college.

Without much further ado, James begins to write.

HER SWEET APPLE

Her love's heroic of alarm's endless,
To the other side via one door,
For one fight of a hopeless might,
On zero ground of rest once more.

Image branded of her adorn,
Yet dolor's of a morning plight,
And solace not of soldier's roar,
To Ismail's fight of an evil smite.

Hold us dear for but one night,
Endless morn of silent lore,
Anoint us Grace for one last rite,
And into the light, so're she could soar.

Fallen child of a morning plunder,
see the apple of her sweet wonder.

One of the reasons James feels that so much of his poetry is unworthy of an unsheltered publicity is because he is such an unrelenting perfectionist. The reason the painting on the easel in his living room has taken just about his entire three years at Columbia is because he is so picky about not going off in a contrary direction to the vision he has in his mind of that particular countryside. He'd rather not work on it, as opposed to getting off track with his vision of the painting. Had he not made the Renaissance painters a big part of his education, he might not have inherited this restless quality of precision and craftsmanship. However, that is precisely the quality of a classic artist that is most endearing to James. In fact, one of the manuscripts that he has worked on since beginning to write years ago is a book that is about Raphael, who was the great Italian Renaissance painter.

James has always thought, even though Michelangelo is the greatest artist of all time, that Raphael did not get the credit he was due, at least in terms of contemporary popularity. He was fascinated by the competitive nature between the two artists and started writing a book about it years ago.

James finished his research for Tuesday and took a nap to finish up on his rest from waking up in the middle of the night on Monday night. James heads out on Tuesday evening after dinner to meet up with the bible study group that he met with in his undergraduate years. Many of those people keep in close touch with James because he was such a leader in Apostolos Ministry for those three years. Many of these people whom he mentored, still draw on him every day for his nonstop wisdom.

CHAPTER 5

On Wednesday afternoon, before James went down to Low Steps, he got caught up on the e-mails from back home. In response to the e-mail he sent to his mother earlier in the week, he received a response from her.

Dear James,   September 9, 2005

I'm so glad you and I decided a couple years ago to pray for each other with regard to us meeting people. I met a couple people in that time, and for whatever reason, they just didn't seem to work out. However, I am writing this e-mail to tell you that I met someone a few months ago, and so far, it has been amazing. Had we never started to pray for romantic encounters, I don't think I would have ever met these people, and found out whether or not I was interested in a relationship. Furthermore, I don't think I would have ever come out of my shell again had we not done this. I want you to know that not only has it been a pleasure to be your mother, but it has been an even greater pleasure to have you for a friend. I had gotten to a point in my life that surely my best days romantically were behind me, but in the last three months, I have found that my best days are still ahead.

The people that you have touched in your life have learned as much from you James as you have learned from them. I don't know what the future would have held if I had never gotten out of the hole I was in with respect to meeting men. Your father closed a book in my life that I never thought I would reopen, but thanks to you as an inspiration, I have something to get excited about every day. Everyone deserves to have someone that makes them excited every night about the next day ahead. I have begun to step up the praying for you, James. I am praying that you find a woman that is right for you and is compatible to all the things that encompass you as a man.

It is so hilarious being in love after years and years of thinking it would never happen again. I actually feel like I am pinching myself every day, making sure that this isn't just a dream. Even though it is kind of scary putting yourself out there again, it isn't as scary as it was at one time in my life. I think I spent so many years alone that I don't think it is as scary worrying about being alone, not after being alone for so long. Now that I know it is possible to feel something again, I think I will be fine because I truly believe now that there is someone for everyone.

I am praying so hard for you to find someone, James. I am also praying that if there is someone, that you would find the strength and assertiveness to make the move. I believe if you haven't met that special someone yet, that you will meet her shortly.

I hope you have a great rest of the week and a great weekend. I love you so much and can't wait to see you again.

Love,
Mom.

The night before the September 11 tribute, on Wednesday evening, James had organized his own rally on campus at Low Steps. He has casually passed out leaflets all week in an attempt to get Columbia students in the mood for Thursday, September 11, 2005. Many of James's brothers and sisters from Model Congress, as well as Columbia College Republicans came out.

Also, the Apostolos Campus Ministry and friends from Riverside Church and Calvary Baptist Church made an appearance. They mingle for an hour before James gives an address to them. About forty people were there initially, but by the time James was done speaking, there must have been a hundred strong. James has this charm about him and a voice that makes people gravitate toward him. He begins,

Fellow Columbia students, and friends from Manhattan and of all different backgrounds, religions, and experiences, we gather here for a moment to establish a spirit of benevolence the night before an important day in our university's history. This campus, on Thursday, will be crowded with many of the families of New Yorkers that were directly affected by the World Trade Center attacks four years ago. As young students, we are filled with passion and opinion, so I ask that each and every one of you be a little more empathetic in your approach to strangers on campus tomorrow, as many of them will have either lost a mother, father, child, or even a friend on 9/11. If you encounter someone tomorrow that your heart tells you to befriend, please allow your actions to be led by your spirit, instead of your mind being led by your hesitance. There is no greater task on Thursday for a Columbia student, than to embrace pain and suffering with a spirit of warmth and compassion. Thank you for your cooperation, and I would like to end this in a prayer. Please extend your hands out to someone near you. Let this be a prayer of where two or three are gathered in His name.

Dear Lord, we gather here tonight to draw on your
magnificent grace,
so that we may be at our best tomorrow in our attempts
of a collective
hospitality. I ask you to bless each and every one of us
here at Low Steps and instill in us your
spirit of compassion,

understanding, and patience. We aren't perfect,
my Lord, so I ask
that you bless each and every one of us,
especially anyone here that might
be going through something individually.
Give us strength to be ministers
of your instruction and grace to be your lamp.
I ask that you place
your hand on someone here this evening and
fill them with your
love and wisdom, that they too may begin a lifelong
journey. With all due praise, my heavenly Father,
in the name of our Lord and Savior, Jesus Christ. Amen.

As James walks down the steps, he's wiping a tear from his eye. He shakes hands with many of his classmates, and he begins to work his way through the crowd, receiving appreciation for the words he spoke. There seemed to be a cloud of grace hovering over the people at Low Steps at this moment, and one student makes a reference to James regarding how surprisingly peaceful she feels at the moment—that it feels like the prayer filled her with something powerful. James reached over to her and grabbed her hand and said Matthew 18:20 says, "For where two or three are gathered together in my name, there I am in the midst of them" (KJV).

"How does that come to be so easy for you?" the woman asks. "To just retrieve scripture just like that?" She stares into his eyes with her baby blues.

"I had an incredible teacher, he was an angel on my shoulders for most of my life," James says. "He's passed away now."

"Who are you referring to?" She asks with growing curiosity.

"My grandfather, whose name was Michael."

"He must have been one heck of a guy," She says.

"He sure was. He was the best mentor anyone could have as a father, or any teacher for that matter. I miss him greatly."

"My name is Josie." Reaching for his hand, somewhat pretending she's never seen him before.

"The funny thing is, Josie, I already knew who you were," he confesses. "I've seen you around, and you're in my class on Friday's."

"You're kidding me, James?" Josie asks with a grin. "I have sociology on Friday's." She slides her hair behind an ear with her hand, trying to conceal her guilt. "Hmmm."

"Nope, I'm not kidding you." James says short and sweet with a half grin as if he's onto her every move now.

Josie maintained a look of playful concealment. "What do you think of professor King from our class?" She plays with a strand of her hair, as women do when their running out of small talk or becoming anxious.

"He's a dear friend of mine," James reveals. "I met him in my undergraduate, and we have become good friends outside of school."

She was impressed.

Both Josie and James are beginning to blush regarding the conversation they are having. It is as if they both knew each other, but neither one was going out of their way to let the other know, with the exception, of course, of his declaration of his knowledge of her as a classmate on Fridays. James is getting embarrassingly bashful and Josie is too. They both begin to act on each other being caught off guard and playfully antagonize one another in a subtle way. For James, there's no person in the world that he would rather talk to, but for a man that has all the right things to say in front of hundreds, he is as speechless and befuddled as any moment he has ever experienced. You could say she is the Kryptonite of his brain, and when it is on the subject of Josie, he can't even hear the question, much less have an answer to it. They continue trading flirtatious jabs back and forth.

"Excuse me, James, I must have missed something. I know I've seen you last week in Philosophy, but how do you know me?"

"I don't know," James confesses bashfully. "I just know who you are by face."

"You're not getting off scot-free on this one, James. I'm going to squeeze this one out of you if it's the last thing I do tonight."

"Sounds like fun."

James is beginning to cave on the whole secret admirer routine. She has torn the cat completely out of the bag and has seen a side of him, that doesn't fit at all with the "have all the right things to say" type of guy that was just standing at the top of Low Steps a few moments ago, speaking endless wisdom to a hundred. If there was something else of great value that Grandfather Michael gave to James, it was also the ability to never let a great love get away on account of the ignorance of hesitation. As he begins to realize that this isn't going to get any more embarrassing than it already has, he begins to remember the advice of his grandpa and acts on it.

"I know this great coffee-and-pie joint down the road," James confidently reveals. "Would you like to accompany me this evening?"

James is hit with a massive case of internal anxiety that every man gets when asking a question such as this. He holds his breath as if he was waiting for a less-than-desirable response. This kind of anxiety seems like it lasts for minutes, even though the question is answered literally two seconds after it was asked. It just seems like things go into slow motion. However, despite all the unnecessary fears and butterflies, the answer wasn't long in coming.

"I would love to," She answers him nervously. "Where is this place?"

"It's just a couple blocks. We can walk."

"Okay, James. You lead the way." She turns to follow him, and slightly glances at him, finding it terribly difficult to take her eyes of him.

Josie seemed pleasantly taken, that James had asked. It was a little more of her being caught off guard than it was her not being sure. After all, while James was trying his best to suppress his premeditated feelings, the truth of the matter is, when James wasn't looking last week, she had peeked over at him a few times as well. Moreover, up until tonight, both had done a pretty good job of being fairly inconspicuous about their interest for each other. As James walks down the street at Josie's side, he has this grin on his face like he knew that the spirit of his grandfather had intervened and didn't let him waste a most wonderful opportunity. It is as if his grandfather's spirit knew more than James even did about Josie's interest in him.

It was almost dark on a Wednesday night in Manhattan's Upper Westside, as James and Josie walk to Tom's Restaurant. Both of them seem to have a sudden case of hesitance as to what to say next, and they bump into each other off and on while bashfully trading looks of puppy love and nervousness. One single look at James brings a more concerning thought. Will he get anything done tonight with regards to research? Playfully speaking, it sure doesn't look like it, but knowing James, he'll find a way to fit all important aspects of the day into his agenda. It is still only about eight on Wednesday night, so any worries of him having time for preparation for tomorrow isn't yet on the urgent list of priorities. How many moments like this do we have in our lifetime? One can only speak for themselves when they say the great ones aren't on the long list of romantic experiences. Needless to say, this particular moment, on this night, pushes all previous events to the bottom of the list—with Josie at the top, just for now.

Verbal communication takes a backseat to body language and the looks of passion between James and Josie. However, after a few more minutes pass, he looks in her direction and begins talking again.

"Where are you from?" he asks.

"I'm from many places, but before I started school here, I lived near Virginia Beach. We moved around a lot when I was growing up because my father works for the government. How about you?"

"I'm from Macomb, Indiana," he says. "I've lived there my entire life."

"Where about is that?" Josie has an intense focus on his every word.

"It's on the western side of the state, close to Illinois, and about halfway between Terre Haute and Lafayette."

"Wow! That's interesting," she mentions with an increase in energy. "One of the schools I almost went to was Purdue in West Lafayette."

"That's very close to home, Josie. I think some people back home were hoping I would choose Purdue, but for the longest time, I have had my eyes set on the East Coast for school. So you live in Virginia Beach?"

"Well…kind of. I technically live here in New York with you." Time freezes to ponder how so cute she was in saying those words.

There are so many of those moments you never forget when looking back at a great romance. The first time you ask her out is difficult, because that is like the threshold of thresholds to get past. Not long after that great moment, of which will never be forgotten, another one blurts out of her mouth when she playfully mentioned that she lives here in New York with him. It looked like James had swallowed an apple at first, but that one single sentence eventually took things to another level in terms of comfort. There are many great moments that are unforgettable, but those first acknowledgements of approval are priceless and cannot be acted out. They are as pure as the love itself.

The night is still young for them as they arrive at Tom's Restaurant, so there may be another moment or two that make the list before the evening runs out. You can rest assured that the first moment of mutual contact will be a moment that leapfrogs all other events. That will move to the top of the list of milestones that are significant in the life of a romance. Nothing has been said since she blurted it out, and both have spent about two minutes just witnessing the expressional aftereffects of that playful comment. How cute it truly was, and how significant it was as well. There are twenty-five or thirty people in the restaurant, but with what is going on between Josie and James at the moment, they might as well be on a deserted island together because they have no idea that, they are not alone. Ah, the power of love and passion—it will trump any force in the world. It truly is the treasure of this world, and that won't change even at the end of time, because it is precisely the essence of it, that truly carries us to New Jerusalem.

The moment has come. A moment James has been thinking about since they started to talk at Low Steps this evening. This is one of those moments that go at the top of the list of unforgettable ones. The first instance James was really tempted to do it, was right after she said she'd walk to Tom's Restaurant with him. It literally occupied his thoughts the entire walk to the restaurant. For some reason, it is just one of the most difficult barriers to get past when with someone for the first time. However, once that moment is past, things really begin to relax. What is it for a man about the touch of a woman? It is truly the Kryptonite of the masculine nature of a man. We just melt when it is with the right person. Nothing else in the world matters. The sun rises and sets under it. To be deprived of this is to be deprived of life. Nevertheless, the moment has arrived for James. Not much time has passed since she said the cute words of her living in New York with him. James wipes the smile off his face, leans into the table, and reaches for her hand. This time, it looks like her heart melted, and she looks right into his eyes and says, "What took you so long, James? I've been waiting for you to do that. I was agonizing all the way down the street when our hands were inches from each other."

"You're okay, aren't you, Josie?"

"I'm very much okay. I am just so glad we had a chance to talk tonight. There's so much I'd like to know, but I don't want to pressure you. I think this is nice," Josie reveals with a look of contentment on her face.

"Go ahead and pressure me. What would you like to know?" He surrenders his walls.

"Well, I look forward to finding out all about you," she says with an optimistic tone. "I can't wait."

So little has been said tonight, because they've both been so giggly nervous and have traded so many flirtatious looks just like two sixteen-year-olds, that neither one them really knows much about the other. They just finish up their snack and head out the door back to school. As they both get out to the sidewalk, she grabs James by the hand and pulls him close to her and then gives him a slow wet kiss on his cheek. To him, this was the best moment all night because instead of just a face and a voice, he could feel the warmth and wetness of her breath, and when her lips touched his face, his eyes shut, and the proverbial lights went out. She playfully smacks him on the cheek and says in a laughing voice, "Wake up, James."

"Wow! I'm speechless, Josie."

Josie is cracking up, and James is playfully telling her to stop, but she keeps going. She's making fun of him because she's attempting to hide the fact of how much that moment meant to her as well. She eases up on him finally, for his sake. She grabs his hand again and pulls herself close to him. They begin to walk, as she leans her head against his arm.

"So your father is in government, and you live in Virginia Beach. That must mean he works in Richmond or Langley?" James asks while in a state of curiosity.

"There's more there than just—" *Josie says but is interrupted by him.*

"I know that, Josie. I was just being mildly facetious. My question was quite rhetorical and was meant more or less for conversation, rather than for informative purposes."

"You're funny," she says with excitement. "You make me laugh. Even when you're not being funny, you have expressions so full of meaning." She giggles. "Yet I don't know you well enough to know half of what those looks mean, but I aim to accomplish that in due time…in due time."

"I look forward to it, Josie. Is this your apartment?"

"Yes," she says. "I had a wonderful time." James has a look on his face that he hasn't sported since leaving home after high school. "Don't be a stranger, James."

"I won't, Josie. I promise."

"I'm holding you to that," she says, going out of her way to tell James that she wants to continue getting to know him.

"You got it, girl," he says with a look of assurance that he too wants to see her again. "I can't wait until the next time.

Josie is slowly drifting toward her door to the dorm, and she's doing it in a way as if she's expecting something more. James is bashfully drifting nowhere, and can't seem to put himself in a coherent state. He begins to walk very slowly toward her, and of every step that he takes, there's a growing state of contentment on the face of Josie, which would lead you only to believe that the one single thing missing from this night was one more kiss. James gets to her and pulls her to him—one hand on the small of her back and one playing with her hair. He is once again in a fully immersed state of disorientation, but that is because this is another one of those unforgettable moments. As he gathers her close, he notices that the look on her face is as serious as it has been tonight. He leans in very slowly, almost stopping at moments, and after what seems like an eternity, his lips finally meet hers. He pulls back to see where she is, and this time, it is her who has her eyes closed, so he kisses her. She doesn't seem to want to go anywhere now. He pulls back and plays with her this time, as she did with him in front of Tom's Restaurant.

"Josie, I'm only joking. I'm only teasing because I so owed you the return treatment." James has a look of "I told you so" on his face.

"I guess you did," she says, while chuckling. "I can live with that."

This time it is Josie who seems disoriented by the events, and she can't seem to get this frozen smile off her face. Instead of using it to play and tease her more, James decides to give her a break. It is entertaining enough for him to witness the happiness that he has caused her this evening. He can't believe how beautiful she is. Sometimes, it's just difficult not to wonder what someone that beautiful sees in you, and for the moment, it just feels good to James that she has been made happy on his account. All the times he has seen her in school, she was serious and not laughing, so the smile has drawn him in even more. The mysteries that are between these two will have to be revealed another day, as it is time for them to head in, and it is time for James to get back to his research.

"Bye, Josie."

"Good-bye, James."

She is about to grab the door, but as James is back out by the sidewalk with his back to her, she sneaks up to him and puts her arms around him. He turns his head to her, and she gives him the biggest, most sensual kiss yet. It is as if all kisses before it were just hesitant pecks. She wanted to lay her head down on the pillow tonight, thinking of something far more memorable and passionate. This is one of those kisses that required them to part ways soon, or someone could forget their studies for the evening. They stop, and she skips back to the door like a happy little girl and enters. James drifts down the sidewalk and heads to his building. They didn't trade e-mail addresses or phone numbers, but they do have class together on Friday. It just seemed as though there was this mutually unspoken understanding between them, like they didn't need sources of communication just yet. Neither one could deny that they each had not felt this way before after only knowing someone for hours. They knew this was just the beginning. They just have a feeling that they both started something tonight that has changed their lives forever.

When you see someone in school or at work that you would love to meet, there is only this hope that you would one day get to meet them. The rest of it is just secluded to a dream or a delusion of some kind. Both felt the same way last Friday when school started, and both were brought together by a prayer at Low Steps. He hopes to see here tomorrow, of course, but Thursday is a busy day in the morning. Besides, he doesn't even know if she has a class on Thursday or not. There was so much unsaid tonight that it is surprising that they spent three hours together and know so little about each other. That reminds James that she was pretty secretive about where her father worked. That curiosity is going to build in the meantime. So much to talk to her about, and he'll just have to wait.

James arrives back at the place and gets the mail on his way up. As he's approaching the top step, he sees that Jack has sent him something from Macomb. They correspond sometimes through e-mail but are still very old school with their choice of using the mailing system. You could say it reminds them of their grandfather, who was never willing to adapt to the changing technology in the world and never passed up a condescending word toward it. You could say this style of correspondence could be a thing between James and Jack for the duration of their lives, only out of unspoken respect for their grandfather. He grabs a seat on the couch and opens the letter.

Dear James,

It's been a while since I spoke to you. I know Mom talked to you today (Sunday), but I wasn't home. Sorry I missed you. Hope everything is going well in New York, as we are very proud of you. I spent the night over Ben's on Sunday night because Mom was working until 11:00, and Mrs. Wilson invited me to stay for dinner, and it was great. They wanted me to say hello to you for them. We had a blast. Ben told me some things I never knew about you—things that made me even more proud of you. I hope we see each other soon. Can you send me an e-mail and give me a time this weekend to be by the phone so I can talk to you? I don't care what day or time. I'll make myself available.

I was thinking of getting a job this winter, as it's going to be a long wait until baseball season. I'm not sure who took over for you at the theater after you left, but I was thinking of going up there this week to see if he needs any help. I remember how close you and Mr. Johnson were, and every time I see him, he says for me to say hello to you. Anyway, I was just curious what you thought of that idea.

Mom told me not to get my hopes up for seeing you this Christmas, but I have to say, it would be the best Christmas ever if we saw you. I know I've heard Mom mention alternative ways to see each other during the holidays, but I didn't want to pester her about them because she was tired at that time.

Well, I have to go. Send me an e-mail, and let me know what's been going on besides school.

Until next time, my brother.

Love,
Jack.

James leans his head back on the couch and closes his eyes as he ponders all that had happened this evening. He could still smell that beautiful smell that Josie had. For only knowing her for one day, he had emotions and feelings come up in him tonight that were quite rare with respect to anything he felt back in Macomb.

He's beginning to realize that he will need much discipline and strength as they get to know each other, he begins to pray.

Lord, I know I haven't spoken to you
much these last few days
with the exception of my prayer at Low Steps.
I wanted you to know
how much I thank you for what happened tonight.
I know you
have a plan for me, and the last thing
I want to do is get in the
way of your will. I praise you for bringing
her into my life.
I hold you completely responsible for this
opportunity, and I want
you to know that I will never take back the
promise I made about
being your lifelong servant. I don't know
a lot about her yet,
but the fact that she came up to me after my prayer
at Low Steps tells me she isn't afraid of you. In fact,
I can see your light in her blue eyes when
I'm speaking to her. I ask that you
grant us both disciplines and protection from the
clutches of the lion as
we get to know each other in these early days.
I ask for these things in the
name of my Lord and Savior, Jesus Christ. Amen.

James grabs a pen and pad and begins to think about what to say tomorrow. He is thinking that most of what he'll say will be straight from the heart, but he wants to read something that is written by someone else—something that would have great meaning to the occasion. He knows there'll be no prayer in his speaking moment because there will be pastors there that will handle that. He's just there to say something inspiring and appropriate. These are the families and friends of those that lost their lives on September 11, 2001. So it is in his best interest, as well as the best interest of the university, that there is no personal agenda in his words. This is strictly and completely about compassion and encouragement.

James is lying in his bed in Morningside Heights, pondering all of the events that transpired this evening. It was quite eerie meeting Josie at Low Steps, literally minutes removed from reading an e-mail from his mother saying she was praying for him to find someone. He, at the moment, finds some amusement in the irony of the events of this Wednesday night. In his fourth year at Columbia University, it is time that he found someone that finally interested him. With all the strong thoughts he had during the summer, it was most obvious that James was getting tiresome of being alone at home in the evening. He came to New York to get an education and find the woman of his dreams. Lo and behold, that just might be what is transpiring here in James's first year of graduate school.

Josie is unwinding in her apartment on this Wednesday night as well, as she is lying on her bed stretched out with feet folded and her hands behind her head. She is staring at the ceiling while daydreaming of the events that had just unfolded with James. She has this ear-to-ear smile on her face, like someone that has just met the man of her dreams. She feels a little cautious in her premature thoughts, but at the same time, she can't help but be excited about how amazing it had felt with him for just a short time. She has had boyfriends in the past, but the way she felt with him at Tom's Restaurant tonight was something she has never felt before with a boy. She grabs her pillow and hugs it with all her body and turns on her side and gets into the fetal position. She just lays there for an hour with a deep and content look on her face while periodically turning over back and forth to the other side. It would be difficult for her to fall asleep because she can't get him off her mind.

Josie begins to wonder when she'll see James again. He did say that he was participating in the September 11 tribute at Low Steps tomorrow, so she begins to devise a plan to head over there early enough to maybe catch her new friend. Josie finally falls asleep on this forever memorable night where she and James finally meet.

CHAPTER 6

B ack in Macomb, Jack is reminiscing with a picture of him and his brother that usually sits on a nightstand in his room. He is also curious if his brother received his letter yet. Ironically, as his mother knocks on the door to say goodnight, she also tells him she received an e-mail a few minutes ago, telling her that James got his letter. "He said he is really busy tonight and tomorrow morning, but he would e-mail you when he got home tomorrow night and tell you all about the amazing night he had on Wednesday. He also said to be by the phone Saturday at 9:00 p.m. central," his mom added

"Thanks, Mom, and goodnight," Jack says.

"Goodnight, sweetheart. I have to work until 11:00 p.m. on Thursday, so grab something on your way home, or there is stuff in the fridge that you can make for dinner. See you Friday."

"Okay," Jack says. "I love you."

"Love you too, sweetheart. Goodnight."

Charlotte doesn't go to bed until about 3:00 a.m. on evenings where she works an afternoon shift the following day. She's gone to work before after being up for eight hours, and it gets pretty tiring when they ask her to work an extra shift at the end of an afternoon shift. Those are the days where Jack gets himself off to school. It was more enjoyable for him when James was around because he would get Jack up and make him breakfast in the morning, and when Charlotte was working on those days, it was especially nice having a brother at the table. Jack is particularly lonely on those mornings now, because not only is his mother sleeping, but he knows those mornings with James will never happen again unless it's just an occasional visit. Jack isn't naive to the fact that James isn't going to be coming home after New York, at least not to live. He is fully aware that things won't transpire that way because he knows how important James will be when he's done at school.

Nevertheless, Jack lays his head back down on the pillow and holds the picture of him and James above his head and ponders memories. He reminisces of old times with his brother. He remembers the day when James was a junior in high school at Crenshaw, and they ended up with a snow day in January 2001. It was just after they had returned to school after the Christmas break that winter. Their mother was working mornings that year, so she wasn't around to enjoy the day off together. It was just one of those rare days where he and James just sat around and talked.

The sky had dropped so much snow on that day that James and Jack had to shovel the snow more than once. It was a good day to just vegetate and enjoy the midweek break from school. It was something James rarely did, but he indulged Jack this once. They took an inventory of the refrigerator and the cupboards in order to see what they could cook. When you leave kids alone in the kitchen on a snow day, they come up with some pretty creative and wacky dishes. The funny thing is, those are the ones that satisfy the taste buds the most.

The thing Jack remembers most about that day is that James talked a lot about Grandfather Michael. He remembers James talking about the love of Grandpa's life in Vietnam. He said this Vietnamese woman was the most beautiful woman he had ever seen when he first saw her. He also told Jack that this woman was too sweet to be an American. She had a presence of humility about her that doesn't exist in folks that are raised in American society.

After Jack had been told the details of Grandpa Michael's love affair with this woman, he began to understand more about why Grandpa never married back in the States. He did, however, see a woman years later in Macomb that he spent a lot of time with over the years—a woman that had been widowed with children. Her husband had died of cancer when their kids were young, and Grandpa Michael did a lot to make sure her kids were well taken care of.

James then told Jack that Grandpa had been married to this woman in Vietnam and that she was killed accidentally by the explosion of a mine-bomb near the road where she was walking. Jack got upset when he heard this and got even more upset once James had revealed to him how long it took his grandfather to get over it. When Jack was told that Grandpa's wife was killed in Vietnam while she was pregnant with their baby, he lost it. Anymore became too difficult for Jack to bear, so James decided to stop talking. However, Jack began to ask questions. He would ask where his grandmother was buried. At first James was caught off guard, but after a few moments, he had realized that Jack was referring to Grandpa Michael's late Vietnamese wife as Grandmother. Jack also pointed out that the baby that was in her womb was either their aunt or uncle. This means that Jack and James have relatives buried in Vietnam. James promised Jack, at that moment, that someday they would look for and visit her grave in Vietnam.

Those were tough revelations for the ten-year-old Jack on that snow day. Most kids remember bowling or something like that when reminiscing of a snow day. However, Jack's recollection of this snow day was finding out that he had more relatives than he originally thought. Charlotte never speaks of it because it broke her heart when she heard it from her father's broken voice on the phone from Vietnam. Her father was divorced from her mother when he served in Vietnam because Charlotte's mother had an affair in those days, and he wanted a divorce immediately. That is why he remarried in Vietnam. The death of his wife and baby was very hard to take for Charlotte because she always wanted her father to be happy, and she always wanted a brother or a sister as well.

Years later, Charlotte and her father, Michael, would sit on the front porch once a week and drink themselves to sleep. After her father had experienced the sweetness of a Vietnamese woman, he never attempted to find that level of humility in an American woman, so he remained unmarried. Besides, he wasn't interested in getting married for a third time. The first two didn't end on his account, so he figured it was meant to be. Charlotte's mother had an affair behind her father's back, and his next wife passed away. Years later, when Charlotte was told of her mother's affair that had ended her parents' marriage, she decided to choose sides, and she and her mother never communicated closely again. Her mother did come to her father's funeral, but she only had a couple of words with her and hasn't spoken to her since.

It took James most of that snow day to reveal all this to Jack. By the time they were done, Charlotte had come home. And once she realized the boys had eaten everything in the house, she had taken them out for pizza at the bowling alley.

That was a great day for Jack's memory, and every time he gets lonely and misses James, he remembers that day because it seems like the day that James revealed most, plus the pizza and bowling wasn't so bad.

———◆———

Back in Manhattan on Thursday, September 11, 2005, the temperature is warm. The skies are clear on this historical day—the fourth anniversary of the terrorist attacks on New York City in 2001. The weather today is not unlike what it was on that day four years ago. On a day like this, it is difficult to spend more than one minute in this town without thinking about the Twin Towers. Radio and television shows all over New York this morning are gearing their broadcasts toward the theme of September 11, out of respect for those that lost their lives on that day. It is 9:00 a.m., which was ironically just about the time where all hell broke loose on that morning four years ago.

On the side of a hill, near the site of where the September 11 tribute will take place, James Ryan Roberts is lying on his back. He is stretched out on the grass with his hands interlocked behind his head, as if he's taking a nap. He has on jeans, a light blue dress shirt without a tie, a dark blue sport coat and a pair of all black low-cut Dr. Martens. He looks extremely relaxed, almost as if he is lying on a beach, waiting for the surf to come in. However, anyone that knows James is well aware of what he is doing. Most people would be rehearsing their speech in their head and making sure that they had their own performance covered, but that isn't what James is doing. You can sure bet the day is blessed that James is praying for everyone else and attempting to draw from God a collective blessing that would positively affect the victims' families and friends that will be coming here today. That is just James, and that is the way he is, and you can never expect any less than that of him.

James remains there for about an hour and didn't move an inch. You would be hard-pressed to ever find more than a few men of faith that speak to God for as long as James does at any given moment. Most men of cloth would even find it sufficient to end a prayer after a few minutes, but James goes on and on, meditating on the Spirit. Don't get me wrong, James does not let anyone know what he is doing, which is why you'll often see him alone. Anyway, James is a real man of faith, and it is obvious he is working with more strength than a man can acquire without faith.

When you've seen things that can only be explained through faith, you'll never go back to the empty life. Most people never get past the skepticism to find out if there is something greater on the other side, and if they do make an attempt, they kind of get lost after a day or so. When the faith fades in forty-eight hours, I hardly call that an attempt. And if man hardly calls that an attempt, what does God call it? I can give someone a map to the treasure of the history of the world, but they have to completely let go, and nothing short of that will allow you to see it, or experience it for that matter.

A walk with God is a mutual journey and partnership with Him. He meets us halfway on everything and that includes blessing. Metaphorically speaking, if God is in San Diego, California, and I'm in New York, our halfway point is approximately St. Louis, Missouri. Most people get from New York to New Jersey and have this delusion that they have met God halfway and are already expecting the blessing that would come with actually being in St. Louis with God at the halfway point of effort, if you will. However, they never consider the fact that when they stopped only twenty miles away from their starting point, God also stopped twenty miles from his starting point as well. Furthermore, if the blessing is to be received at the halfway point in St. Louis, how can man ever think that he can taste the sweetness of the fruit in St. Louis all the way from New Jersey? So our selfish assumptions that God is going to do 99 percent of the miracle without our effort is about the greatest misconception in the history of man.

If you're in a hospital waiting room all weekend, with a loved one fighting for their life, why is it not a purpose to draw in God's blessing with fasts accompanied with prayer rather than prayer accompanied with gluttony, idolatry, or greed? People have no idea the miracles they can accomplish through fasting— fasting from food, drink, smoke, idols, lusts, and anything that can be thought of as a vice, contrary to meditation. It isn't the occupying of our time that is the vice, but the fast is an act of love for God. This is also one of the great misconceptions of tithing, which people think is greed of the church, but they don't realize that they love money so much that any rationalization on their part is the truth. However, a tithe is an act of love for God, from His perspective, because he knows how much we love wealth and the idea of it. Tithing is a symbolization of God asking us to trust him. What more of an act of love is there for a loved one, than to cut away from themselves, something that they can't do without, solely for the purpose of pleasing their loved one? These are also very pleasing to God. They are instances that he regards as rewarding, and He pours out blessing for partaking in them. People have the access right in front of them, all they have to do is strain just a little bit, but that is too far beyond their agenda. Yet they lose faith because God is not helping them. It's quite ironic.

Anyways, let's go back to James at Low Plaza. The time is 9:45 a.m., which is a symbolic time on September 11, 2001. On her way to class, Josie was able to recognize from afar that it was James lying on the side of the hill over by the stage of the tribute venue. She had thirty minutes before class, so she snuck over behind him but didn't want to interrupt him because she wasn't sure what he was doing. So, out of respect, she just quietly lay down about ten feet away from him and waited for him to say something. Josie was only there ninety seconds or so, when James finally noticed her, but she didn't notice that he peeked yet. So he rolled over real quick, "Good morning, beautiful baby doll. How was your sleep?"

"It was magnificent, James. I had a wonderful time with you last night, as you were a gentleman."

"Well, thank you," he says. "You were sweet as well."

"Do you have school today?" she asks.

"No. No class today. I'm saying something at the tribute today, nothing long—just a word and a poem."

"Wow!" She's impressed. "You must be proud to have been asked to do that," Josie asks. She looks away with this beautiful look of humility that comes over her while learning of this.

"I'm pretty aware of the honor. I just hope I don't say something stupid."

"Oh, I'm sure you won't. You'll do great. I have confidence in you."

"You do?" James asks curiously. "You just met me."

"Yes, James, I do. How did you sleep?"

"I slept okay," he says. "The one problem I had was your beautiful blue eyes." She was stunned by his sweet choice in words. "Every time I closed my eyes, there they were looking at me. And your perfume—I smelled you all night last night. And even this morning when I woke, I rolled over and smelled you on my shirt from last night. You were everywhere in my apartment. Oh, those baby blues, they were unavoidable." She fell back on the grass in amazement.

"I would have loved to be there. That way you could have had the real thing…" Josie says with a flirtatious look, "You could have had the real me." Now James is shocked by her choice in words, and they both lean back cracking up in laughter.

Josie was blushing and blown away by all that James just said and started to look as if she no longer wanted to attend class this morning. But James encouraged her that she had to go to class, and that he wanted nothing to do with her missing anything. She was playfully disappointed and said that she would go, but she also said that she would try to get out early, if the lecture was boring.

James says, "When I first got home last night, I realized how much time we spent together, yet we still didn't know a lot about each other."

"I have nothing to do after our class on Friday," she says. "I am free all evening because my tennis tournament was postponed due to the flooding in Connecticut from the hurricane, so if you have time, I would love to see you." Her expression was bashful, but with a touch of anxiety as she waited for his answer.

"Sounds great, Josie. I have some work to do, but you can help me with it, or you can bring your own studies over."

"So, it is a date Friday?" She asks with a happy go lucky tone.

"Yes, Josie, it's our second date."

"You're so right." Her big smile widens. "That is our second date."

"That is a second date, so does that mean you like me?" James asks cautiously with a touch of humor.

"You are so funny," she says while kissing his cheek. "I'll see you later."

"Okay, beautiful. You have a nice class."

"I will," she says, sporting an even wider smile than before. "Bye, James, my sweetheart."

"Bye, Josie."

James has completely forgotten why he's at Low Steps, as all he can think about at the moment is Friday with Josie. As James watches Josie walk away on her way to class, he can't help but gaze at her beauty, and amazement with how much electricity fills him when she is there. She has this mature way about her movements, and the way she walks—that would have some mistake her for a professor if they didn't know her. Her confidence is way ahead of her peers', and James is thinking that this is one of the reasons that drew him to her. Little does he know what great affect he has had on her mood and confidence. James is so modest that he wouldn't even notice that she is completely different following their meeting at Tom's Restaurant. Neither of them have any clue how much the other has put a pep in each other's step on this Thursday.

James sits on a chair among speakers off to the side of the stage at the 9/11 tribute while waiting for his turn to speak. Without further ado, James steps to the podium to say a few closing words. He keeps his speaking moment brief and ends with a poem.

Josie is walking with her girlfriend after class. It's about 12:45, and she presumes with the tribute starting at noon, that it has already ended. They don't seem to be in much of a hurry as they are getting caught up on the things from the weekend. However, the closer and closer they get to the venue, the louder and louder it gets. This is bringing a curiosity as to whether it is over or not, so they begin to double-time it. As Josie gets around the corner, she grabs Allie on the arm and points to James and says, "That's James speaking right now."

Allie is laughing at Josie's demeanor, "Girl, you gotta crush on him."

"Shut up!" Josie says with exuberance.

"Oh my, you mean that's the James I've been hearing so much about?"

"Yes, Allie, that's him."

James is just finishing up his five minutes of speaking. He touched on what this day meant to him as a young high school student in Indiana four years ago. He also said that the effect it had on him and the fact that he hadn't decided yet where to attend college led him to attend Columbia University. He reads a poem written by an early twentieth century poet that was in the British medical corps in the First World War, and the poem is called "For the Fallen." It is quite ironic that this poem was written in the month of September.

> They went with songs to the battle, they were young.
> Straight of limb, true of eyes, steady and aglow.
> They were staunch to the end against odds uncounted,
> they fell with their faces to the foe.
>
> They shall grow not old, as we that are left grow old:
> Age shall not weary them, nor the years condemn.
> At the going down of the sun and in the morning,
> we will remember them.
>
> (Laurence Binyon, 1914)

"Why are you crying, Josie?" Allie asks with concern.

"I don't know. I guess they're tears of happiness. I've never felt like this before, and he's so passionate about everything he does. It's inspiring."

"Oh my god, Josie! You are in love." Allie says while giggling and playfully punching her on the arm. "You are madly in love, girl. I still can't believe this is the guy you've been babbling about like a hyena. Wow!"

"That's him."

"Boy, you shot for the stars on this one." Allie's playful sarcasm was evident. "Nobody else on campus interest you?"

"Not like him, my dear friend..." Josie states positively. "Not like him."

The tribute is over, yet the place is still crowded with people from on and off campus. When you look up near the stage and see some of those whom James is shaking hands with, you can tell there are very important people here. The one man talking to James now looks awfully familiar to Josie, but she doesn't want to intrude on James just yet, with them only knowing each other for a couple of days. To be fair to her, she doesn't exactly want to go diving in like a hovering wife or anything that seems like that. However, Allie gives her a slight nudge and expresses to her the look like it's time to go and kick some butt.

"Go Josie!" Her friend forcefully encourages. "This is more stressful than getting rejected."

"Where?" Josie asks.

"What do you think, girl? I want to meet him," Eagerly Allie says. "He won't mind."

"Okay. But if he gets uncomfortable, it's your fault," Josie warns with a giggle. "Okay?"

"I can handle that, sister Josie. Let's get it on!"

The two of them head over toward the stage where James is speaking to two very important-looking men. They were both sitting with the president of the university, so they must be important in this town. Josie and Allie are moving very deliberately and cautiously. The two of them are so concerned about who these men are and whether or not they're doing the right thing, that a state of slaphappy giggles relieves part of the stress. However, out of the corner of James's eye, he notices Josie, and immediately and without hesitation, says, "Excuse me one moment, sir," and moves his way toward her and gives her a big hug. He makes her feel more important than she has ever felt before in her life, considering the fact that he just left a group of very important looking men on her account. Allie, off to the side, has a jaw-dropping look on her face as Josie and James separate.

"I see what you mean, Josie. Wow!" Allie says in front of James.

"I want you to meet Allie."

"Hi, Allie, I'm James, very nice to meet you."

"Nice to meet you as well," she says with a big smile. "I heard a lot about you last night, ha-ha."

"It's my pleasure, Allie," James says with a smile and a touch of curiosity over what might have been said last night between two gals in their pajamas.

"Allie is on the tennis team with me, James," Josie reveals.

"The women's tennis team here on campus?" James asks while in amazement that he isn't finding out about this interesting piece of information until now. "Wow!"

"That's the one, Mr. James," Josie playfully says.

"Josie, I need to introduce you to a couple of people," he says professionally. "Come with me." He grabs her by the hand and leads her towards the stage.

"Who are they?"

"Don't worry, sweetie. Trust me," James says with assurance.

"Sweetie?" Josie asks with a chuckle.

"Excuse me, sir, I'd like to introduce you to a friend. This is Josie. This is Senator John Purcell of New Hampshire."

"It's very nice to meet you, sir."

"Nice to meet you as well, Josie." Senator Purcell glances at James while he shakes her hand, and it was as if his eyes were saying "Nice job, James, she's beautiful." James wearing a look of pride.

"Also, Josie," James adds, "this is the senator's son, Secretary Joseph Purcell of Homeland Security." An expressionless gaze of shock comes over her.

"I'm pleased to meet you, sir."

"It's my pleasure, Josie."

As everyone gets a chuckle over Josie being a little overwhelmed with the upper echelon connections of her new friend, Allie and Josie begin to drift toward each other. James is saying good-bye to his friends from Washington DC. When Josie gets to Allie, she is greeted by Allie with a violent hug-like tackle. "You're an ole dog, Josie. Who were those guys? Men in black? Ha-ha."

"You will not believe me, Allie. That was the senator of New Hampshire and the secretary of Homeland Security."

"You have to be kidding me, Josie?" Allie puts her hand on her own head in an expression of amazement.

"No. I'm not, and did you just call me an ole dog?" Josie playfully asks.

"You mean to tell me the same secretary of Homeland Security that is in the president's cabinet?" Allie asks.

"Yes, Allie. I know. I'm blown away as well."

"Who is this guy you met last night?" Allie asks with a look of bewilderment. "He has friends in such high places."

"Yeah, tell me about it. It's been an interesting last twenty-four hours," Josie reveals with emotional exhaustion.

"I'll say," Allie expresses while laughing, "This is getting interesting."

At this point, Josie and Allie find themselves in a hysterical state, laughing at anything. James walks over to them and starts blushing over their slap happiness. They both fall over each other on the side of the hill that James was laying on this morning, and James sits down next to the giggly girls and starts laughing himself. Allie, in a very laughing manner, looks at James and says, "We need a margarita!"

"I have a ton of research to do tonight, otherwise I would," James regretfully states.

"You party pooper," Allie says in a playful manner. "You can't come?"

"I'm sorry."

"It's okay," Allie says. "Josie will drink one for you."

"I'll be done around 11:00 p.m.," he reveals. "If you'll still be out."

"Hmmmmm," Josie says with a look of curiosity as to where she might be at 11:00 p.m.

"You girls have fun, and be careful," James says instead of intruding on them at 11:00 this evening. "Don't forget about tomorrow, Josie. I'm looking forward."

"I can't wait too, James. See you in class tomorrow."

"Okay, girls, have fun."

"It was nice to me you, James."

"It was my pleasure, Allie. Good-bye, girls."

"Good-bye, James."

The girls head back to their apartment to freshen up for happy hour at Amsterdam's. James heads for the Butler Media Center for research until 11:00 p.m. By the time he's done there, he'll be ready to pass out.

After eight hours of studying, James heads home exhausted. First thing he does when he gets home is crack open a German Weiss beer. James doesn't often get into a habit of studying for that many hours in a row, but with his plans tomorrow with Josie, he wanted to study enough for both days. He leans back on the couch, puts his feet up on the table, and takes a long drink from his beer. He begins to wonder about what Josie said earlier about being on the tennis team, so he gets the women's tennis team up on the computer. He is pleasantly surprised with what he discovers. It turns out that his friend, Josie, is a hell of a tennis player. In fact, she is a two-time, first team All-Ivy League. She was also freshman of the year in the Ivy League back in 2003.

He reluctantly digs deeper to find that she has been the most valuable player of her team all three years. Maybe the most impressive thing of all is an article written by a tennis analyst stating that Josie and two other girls from California are the top three candidates for the 2006 player of the year in all of women's college tennis.

James runs to the fridge for another beer and excitingly skips back to the computer as if he can't get enough of the revelation of Josie Weathers. He feels like a thirteen-year-old kid again. In her biographical, it says she led Virginia Beach High School to the state championship in 2001 and 2002. In addition, it says she had scholarship offers to every school in the country, and she chose Columbia for academic reasons. However, it also says that she and her family used to live in Rochester, New York, and that she has always wanted to go to Columbia. James is presently impressed, as Josie seems like a woman who goes after and achieves what she wants. The tennis guru in the article says that choosing a top education over a chance for a national championship didn't bother her because she has aspirations of playing professionally after graduation in spring of 2006.

James is beginning to feel quite dirty for reading all of this about Josie because she knows so little about him, so he stops and goes back to the couch. After only sitting there for sixty seconds, James curiously darts back to the computer and searches for a good picture of her. After looking at the team picture, he types her name into the athletic search box, and an article pops up on Josie. He is stunned when he realizes the article is from the New York Times athletic page. He is in a trance as he notices the beautiful action shot of her, and he is amazed at how muscular her upper legs are. At this point, James is intensely anticipating tomorrow after class. After he settles down, he proceeds to read the article and how the Columbia coach believes she can be the college player of the year in women's tennis. He goes on to state that he knows the other two national candidates from California and that Josie has the greatest upside of anyone in the nation. James is in a frozen gaze and begins once again to realize that he shouldn't be doing this, so he prints her picture out and tries to fall asleep on the couch. He is almost asleep with her picture on his chest, leaving no mystery at all as to the subject matter that will be on his mind when his lights go out.

Before James dozes off, he rolls over and gets on his knees to say a prayer before bed.

Dear heavenly Father, thank you for this beautiful day.
Thank you for your son, Jesus Christ, whom you sent into
this world to save us from our sins, and so we can enjoy
a close relationship with you. I ask that you bless my new
friends, Josie and Allie, as they went out to
drink some alcohol
today, and I want to ask that they return
home safely. Thank you
my Lord for giving me this opportunity
with Josie, and I ask
that you give me the wisdom, patience,
and love that I need to
make our relationship grow. I give you all the
due praise, my Father.
I pray for these things in the name of my
Lord and Savior,
Jesus Christ. Amen.

After James said his prayers, he got up and went to the kitchen to grab a drink of water before bed. As he's looking into the sink to wait for the water to cool, he realizes how long it has been since he got on his knees before bed like that. It begins to dawn on him that he might have so easily found his way to getting on his knees because of his mother praying for him. Maybe she prayed for more than just a beautiful angel to enter into his life. Maybe she prayed for his faith as well. Nevertheless, it made him feel quite peaceful when he was finished praying, and he feels a little more grace than usual while getting ready for bed.

He figures whatever it is that is happening the last couple of days or so is fine by him. This is something that James could get used to. It had been three years of literally spending time by himself because he isn't the party type, so he never really had anyone over the apartment and never really took anyone up on an invitation to a party because he knew he would have ended up leaving the party right away anyway. James isn't kosher with being around a lot of people while they are drinking. Needless to say, he passed up many opportunities of a social nature while at school due to the fact that he not only wanted to stay free from trouble but also because it was difficult to be around people when they are drinking, especially when you're not. And James doesn't really drink with the exception of a beer or two of course.

Nevertheless, the last thing James does before bed is write Josie a letter. He made a little homemade greeting card out of poster board. He printed a colored picture of a single rose and taped it to the cover of the card, and he opened the card and began to write.

Dear Josie,   September 11, 2005

Ever since I saw you a week ago on the first day of school, I have lied down in bed every night, totally excited about the next day ahead…excited for that moment of the day where I would get to see your beautiful face and those eyes. For three years, I have waited patiently for the right person to come along, but the last few months, that patience was beginning to be challenged. I am so glad that you came into my life, and I praise God every hour of the day that he decided to send you to me. I look forward to spending time with you and want you to know that if you ever need anything, please ask me. I know we haven't known each other long, but I have a wonderful feeling about you. I will pray every day for us and ask God to grant us a blessing for our relationship. I ask that he give us strength and discipline to keep the Lord's will as the number one goal in our relationship, and that we please Him in all that we do together.

When I first saw you, I had never had that feeling before in my life—the feeling like my heart was going to bounce out of my chest. I had never experienced a feeling where everything just stopped like that, and the only thing that mattered was you. It was totally unexpected because I was always so comfortable with juggling many priorities at one time. Maybe I shouldn't be telling you these things so early in our relationship, but it has always been the nature of my being, to reveal what is on my mind, so for that I am sorry.

When we were together those few times this last week, I couldn't help but notice how amazing it felt to be in your presence. It really was an intoxicating feeling. When you walked out of the classroom last Friday, and I saw the wind from the door in the hall blow the smell of your shampoo in my direction, it sent shock waves of passion through my body. You literally had me at that moment, and you probably didn't even know it. To make matters even more passionate on that day, you gave me such a big smile when we both walked outside at that moment. Your smile on that day was the most beautiful thing I have ever seen in my entire life.

When we look into the future, I can only hope that we can both see ourselves in each other's life. I will pray to our Father in Heaven every chance I get and ask him to bless us both and protect us from this secular world we live in. I will ask him to put an umbrella over us and protect us from outside criticism and influence.

Thank you so much for spending time with me and allowing me this opportunity to be in your life. You are truly a flower to me, my dearest Josie.

Love,
James

James puts his head down on the pillow late on this Thursday evening and falls asleep instantly. He had a busy week getting to class and researching and preparing for that September 11 tribute. His research is done for the weekend, and now he can just enjoy spending time with Josie on Friday and Saturday. For James, it will be difficult to remain focused, even though he is the most channeled individual on campus. He has just been waiting a long time for someone special, and Josie seems like she is really occupying his heart at the moment, which is great. What is important, is that he remains focused, so if they are at all right for each other, they will each provided the other with encouragement to remain focused with school and tennis.

It is too early in their relationship for James to know everything about her, but he is about to learn in the next few days that she is right out of the mold of a person perfectly designed for his affection. Both of their personalities will mesh together and create one awesome team. His strengths with her weaknesses and her strengths with his weaknesses will make for a perfect couple that can accomplish anything together.

Grandfather Michael always said that to accomplish goals as lofty as James has, he will need to find someone special that perfectly complements him. In addition, he'll need someone to complement his weaknesses as a man as well. You might say, "Well, James doesn't have any weaknesses," and I would say, "Everyone has weaknesses." Even though James and his mother have handled the leaving of their father and husband as well as anyone could have handled it psychologically, they both suffer from abandonment issues. James isn't exactly a loner or a socially meek person. He suffers from a subconscious fear of being abandoned, and for years, it has affected him with settling down with a girlfriend and trusting them. He is so tight with Ben Wilson because he trusts him, and growing up around him, he developed a comfort in the Wilson family. James has, for three years now, slowly developed into a more social man. He has included himself in many on-campus groups that have greatly increased his capacity to trust people and look at them with optimism instead of seeing them with pessimism.

CHAPTER 7

James arrives at the front lawn of his apartment building after his run on Friday morning, and falls over on the grass in exhaustion. His regular morning run hasn't exactly made the priority list in about a week. Usually when that much time passes between runs, it takes a few days for the lungs and legs to get in shape again. It is about three hours until his Friday philosophy class with Josie, and as the hours pass, the excitement continues to build. When James gets nervous about an exam, it's because he doesn't know what to expect, but this romantic nervousness is entirely different. It's more crippling, similar to when he used to get nervous before speeches. Needless to say, this nervousness was more about not being speechless with her, when it is time to speak or not speak, when it's time to be quiet. Romantic conversation is like a classical music piece—the sounds need time to breathe as well as time to play. Then there are those moments where it's time to do neither—a pause or caesura if you will. One would consider that moment a good time for a kiss. I suppose some of these things are unnecessary to worry about for James, as it seems as though Josie herself is nervous about him as well. There seems to be quite a sweet balance between the two of them, and it becomes ever so exciting to consider their future together.

James admires Josie as an athlete as he has always admired the talents of his brother, Jack. James is quite pleased that she is the leadership type, as he puts a considerable amount of importance in the capabilities of the type of woman that he would marry. He has always felt that it would take much more than just him alone, for him to achieve the things he wants to achieve. It will also take a spouse that is smarter than him at things he can't possible know. Also, it requires a woman to stand up and be forceful with encouragement in the face of hopeless discouragement. Josie is a great match for his weaknesses. She is much more social and more optimistic with regard to people. James is more pessimistic about people, but he can hardly be blamed for that with his father abandoning his family as a little boy. James has learned to stand on his own two feet, and that has been quite beneficial at times, but it does need a balance, especially if you are getting into the people business of politics.

Grandpa Michael gave James quite an education while he was growing up, but the one thing his grandpa couldn't teach him was with regard to trusting people. Grandpa was one who had reasons as well not to trust the better judgment of humanity, so he left that one alone with regard to teaching James the finer things in life. Besides, his grandfather lost the love of his life to a roadside bomb, and that can also cause a person to feel abandoned. James is, however, very trustworthy, and in politics, that will matter more than trusting people. That is, of course, as long as you have a campaign manager that you trust. Also, he would have to be very thorough with choosing his cabinet in the event that he does ever get to the White House. Josie is one that can help James in the area of being a people person. James isn't completely ready for Capitol Hill just yet, but if Josie has anything to say about it, it won't be long before he is.

James will need her strength and encouragement, and Josie will need his smarts and competitive guidance with regard to her tennis career. She can really get a benefit from his depth and understanding of the human mind and getting on top of her opponent within the battles of competition. She has the talent to be a great player but lacks a little with confidence and competitive spirit on the tennis court. Anyway, James finishes up with his morning feeding of the birds on the park bench by the Hudson River on this Friday morning.

James suddenly has an expression of guilt on his face due to the shame of his own curious investigation of Josie's tennis career last night. He's not going to forgive himself anytime soon for acting like a weirdo with her biography info online or falling asleep with her photo on his chest. That is of course because she didn't have a say about the revelation of those secrets, especially with it being early in their relationship. To ease the pain and suffering of his guilt, and rather than harbor secrets from Josie, he decides to put everything out in the open. Therefore, it's highly probable that she will see the inside of his apartment today, so he puts the printed picture of her in her sexy tennis outfit right on the table where she'll be sitting today. That way, she'll be able to respond, and that response will dictate whether James reveals to her all that he shamefully read last night regarding her career. On the contrary, however, you'd highly doubt something such as this would break the romantic momentum that these two have started. Moreover, Josie and James both seem to be so excitingly intrigued by each other that something of a mild nature can't possibly be important enough to stop something this strong.

James takes a shower and heads toward class two hours early. This time of morning is great for having a nice read for a couple of hours in the shade of a big tree right outside the building of Friday's class. The solace he feels from reading there, is quite indicative as to where he will be just before this class every Friday. Last Friday, James saw Josie from afar, on her way to this class, as he was here reading then as well. At that moment, he could have sworn when she walked by that she was looking right at him through her sunglasses, but he wasn't quite sure. If she was staring right at him, then there was no mistaking from her perspective what James was looking at. Nevertheless, the insecurity of whether or not she was looking at him remained in him for the time being. That is, however, until this past Wednesday evening. She did have this slight grin, like she was lightly amused by something. Until this day, he still isn't sure whether she was looking at him on that sunny Friday last week. He wonders if she will mention that at any point, which would confirm for him, that it was her romantic interest in him that ultimately caused that beautiful grin on her face. It would sure go a long way in explaining to him the mystery of where she came from out of the blue on Wednesday night at Low Steps right after his group prayer. That moment actually shocked James, but he did a wonderful job of not showing it.

James finds a nice tree to lean up against and opens a book that is for his research for his graduate thesis. Theology within military regimes is the subject, and the book is *The Holy Reich* (Steigmann-Gall), which is about the interpretation of Christianity within Nazi Germany. After a few chapters, and in between short catnaps against the tree on this beautiful sunny day in the shade, he heads in the building for class but not before writing a poem outside his Friday class.

REDEMPTION

Night of night no longer dark, at last, it's truly dawn,
my lovely flower, fret it not, yesterday's storms are gone.
Trouble surely departed, at last, it has subsided,
believe in this, and surely this, we be not divided.

He took His time, oh Thy Divine,
and joined us to be found,
my love, my love, my sweet, sweet love,
freed us safe and sound.
It's clear as day my love is not, transiently excited,
and in my arms, my lovely flower,
your love suits me delighted.

A brief short time has passed, and surely I have found,
my sweet darling, I'll fail you not,
that we will have such fun.
My love for you will never stop, nor it un-recited,
and in the end, it is my dream, that we are truly one.

James finishes the poem and starts to head toward class. He wasn't exactly sure whether it was better to arrive in class first or whether he would rather her arrive first because whoever arrived second was going to be pressured as to where to sit in class. James, however, was in a playful mood this day and wanted the challenge of arriving late so he could play a little joke on her. There was a natural feeling between the both of them, which was a fear that this was going to be terribly uncomfortable. Anyways, James goes to class late on purpose to dictate the result of this growing anxiety on his own accord.

The classroom for philosophy on Fridays is huge, so sitting on opposite sides of the room could mean sitting as far as fifty or sixty feet from each other. This room was similar to a typical Ivy League classroom, where the professor is much lower and the audience is rounded into an arch, much like that of a Roman amphitheater. Today, Josie sat in the second row from the back and to the far left of the professor. James, however, walked in the door in back of the room and to the far right of the teacher. This worked out perfect for the plan James had. The reasons being, he wanted to tease Josie to lighten the mood and kick off the day together on a playful note. The problem is James is the only one that knows what's going on, and this might not be all that humorous to her or the professor for that matter. Nevertheless, he comes in and sits down in her row roughly fifty feet away. He puts his left elbow on the table in front of him, puts his head in that hand, and stares at Josie for about five minutes.

He completely disregards the lecture, which is completely out of character, and Josie periodically plays along and pays little attention to the professor as well. James begins to think, what a great sport she is, but James begins to show a little empathy because he's starting to think from her point of view. She could have this fear that he was going to sit there for the entire three hours, and he begins to wise up. James couldn't take it anymore; it was breaking his heart to see a discomfort in her. So he finally ends the stress and immediately grabs his bag and heads to her. Upsetting the teacher was worth it for James just this once, as a smile began to surface permanently upon Josie Weather's face.

Professor King yells to James, "Excuse me, James. Are we interrupting something in your day?"

"No, Professor, I'm so sorry," James says with a straight face. "The air-conditioning was blowing on me."

"Well, I hope you're comfortable now," Professor King sarcastically says.

After he and James exchange a mutual grin of amusement, Professor King returns to the lecture. During this moment, Josie and her friend were just hopelessly laughing, but they stopped as soon as the teacher returned to his teaching. James sits right next to Josie, on the opposite side from her friend. He gives her friend a hello, and she returns with the same. Then he took a deep breath, looked down at the professor, and turned back to Josie. She turned to him. He assured her that he would never do that again and that he had planned it that way but it had broken his heart to continue, and she became happily reassured by this confession. She turns to look at her friend and gives a sigh of relief, as her worst fear was that he was going to remain sitting far away for three hours. She felt that would have been a very uncomfortable start to a much-anticipated day for her.

James reaches over and grabs her hand and says that he was just kidding with her, and that he was sorry. He also reassures her that he had been looking forward to this day and that he thought about her a lot last night. She returned with a happy-go-lucky look on her face, as if he just told her the one single thing she wanted to hear. Nevertheless, they begin to follow the lecture, but they never fail to realize the other is there, and they periodically glance at each other every five minutes. They eventually begin to trade flirtatious grins at each other. James writes a note to her that says,

> Josie, it's been a long time since I looked forward to something like I do to this afternoon with you.

He glances at her to see her reaction, and she was wiping one of her eyes as if she had a tear. James immediately looked back down at the teacher before she could notice he was looking. He could see out of the corner of his eye that she was putting the tissue back in her bag, and when the teacher turned his back to the class, she leaned over to James, and gave him a kiss on the cheek. She squeezed his hand tight and didn't let go the rest of the class. James looks to her and tells her that he never wants to go to bed again without having her phone number. He specifically wanted to hear her say good night to him last night. Josie sends him a little note with nothing but a smiley face on it.

They come to the end of the class, and Josie says good-bye to her girlfriend. James waits for her to put her bag on her shoulder and turn to him. Then he grabs her hand. "You're with me now, beautiful!" James says with authority.

She smiles and says, "Sounds great to me."

Fridays on campus are pretty collegiately festive, with live music, book sales, and fairs, as well as many food stands. It's literally like being at a sold-out afternoon ball game at Yankee Stadium. Columbia football games are on Saturdays at noon, so the campus is pretty rocking from early Friday until early Sunday. Low Plaza, in particular, is quite the place to be on campus when not in class, studying, or sleeping. It has been said by many that Low Plaza is the pinnacle experience in American college life in terms of a social on-campus atmosphere. Low Plaza was designed to specifically give the feel of being at an ancient Greek amphitheater. Students come here in all times of the day to relax on the steps (Low Steps) and study or just nap. It is the quintessential urban beach, if you will. Many students that visit Columbia usually get hooked by the outdoor life, of which no other institution has it beat. In addition, the Manhattan area that the university resides in is another of its great advantages, as students can't find another city in America more desirable to spend their college experience in.

James and Josie are holding hands, walking very patiently, as if there isn't but a worry in the world other than the fear of it ending. As they approach the plaza and get near Low Steps, James has another urge to be outrageous. He steps up onto a park bench, with a crowd of people surrounding, as if he was ready to give a speech. Many people are looking at him in confusion, as he has this jokingly devious grin on his face. He turns to Josie and reaches for her hand. She gives him a funny look, like, "What are you doing?" James insists, and he pulls her up to him. When she gets on the bench, James puts his hands on each side of her cheeks and gives her a long and patient kiss. As the people in the area begin to clap and cheer, Josie begins to melt into his arms, as if James had surprised her romantically again. This was the one single moment when it clicks in Josie's mind that this is it. This is what a girl wonders about her entire life until she gets there. She didn't want to reveal too much of this to James because she didn't want to take the chance of ruining it.

After James had done this to Josie at Low Plaza, she couldn't help but look around and notice all the girls with looks of wonder on their face, as if they doubt somehow that they too will ever be experiencing that. To say the very least, this really made Josie's day, and anything that followed would be just a contribution to an already great day. James grabs her hand again to head over to the steps, and before they sit, he turns to her and embraces Josie, and he says, "I'm going to spoil you bad."

"Don't you ever stop," she reveals while smiling from ear to ear.

"I won't stop," James says. "I'll enjoy forever."

The two of them aren't quite dressed for sunbathing, but they are dressed for the temperature, which is a pleasant seventy-seven degrees. They lean back on the steps and against each other and just take in the festivities, saying very little. They both seem to find it very pleasant to just be experiencing the campus together for the very first time. Each of them trade sweet little nothings now and then, but for the most part, for about an hour and a half, they just seem content at simply being.

During this moment, Josie has a curiosity about the black notebook that James is always writing in on campus. She reaches down at his bag and pulls it out and asks, "What gives with this book, James?"

"It's my poem book," James says while he grabs it out of her hands.

"I want you to read some."

"I will later," James says. "When we get back to my place."

"Oh, please, please, pretty please?"

"Okay. I'll read you one I wrote about my mother. This one is about her years following my father leaving."

"Okay, I'm ready," Josie eagerly declares. "Fire away."

James searches through the pages to find that poem. At that moment, nervousness comes over him, as it isn't the easiest thing in the world for him to reveal his writing to her. For a writer, it's like opening up your soul. He once again states that this poem is about his mother during the years after the divorce. Nevertheless, he begins to read.

HER BIRD

A pierce still felt strong, thorns are a dulling,
solace ahead not long, a season her a mulling.
Sing us this bird a song, subdue his a cunning,
Free her Lord along, and fill us with your loving.

Encroach his disposition, and ambush his agenda.
Sing this bird sing long, so she can jump and dance.
Love my love not wrong, hold here this umbrella,
Sing us just a song, and let this bird romance.

James takes one look at Alma Mater, which is a statue watching over Low Steps. He gives it a salute then stands up and asks Josie if she's ready to go. They arrive back at James's apartment and head upstairs to grab something cold to drink. When they get into the apartment, Josie asks James where the bathroom is. He directs her and asks what she would like to drink, and she says water. Sitting on the couch with two cold waters, he looks at the photo he printed out of her last night and laughs. He's thinking to himself that she's in there inspecting the bathroom like girls probably do. James had a grandfather that was nitpicky about latrines, so she's getting a surprise about now. His grandpa also once told him that keeping a bathroom clean like that would one day win him a prize, and he hadn't been talking about a carnival toy. He was basically saying that this will one day put you in the good graces of a great woman. The only question now is will she confirm the existence of her investigation of the bathroom or will she not mention it? James waits for the answer.

She opens the door to the bathroom and doesn't even take a second step toward the couch before she asks if a maid cleans his place. He rolls on the couch, cracking up. Josie is so confused and asks him what is so funny. James can't even answer her. He's laughing so hard. She can't help but giggle herself as he pulls her on the couch, hugs her, kisses her, and tickles her.

As they settle down, she notices a tennis picture of herself next to her water and turns and asks, "How did this get here, James?" She's looking at him intently with these convicting eyes.

"I don't know. Maybe someone put it there while we were gone," James says playfully.

She's not buying it and says, "Come on, spit it out."

James surrenders and says with a big smile, "Okay, okay. I'm a big fan!"

She smiles and says, "It's okay."

"I had a hell of a time last night without hearing your voice before bed, and I started wandering through the tennis page," he says. "I'm guilty as charged. I slept with that picture on my chest," James reveals with a humorous nature.

"What else are you guilty of seeing, James?" she playfully asks.

"I read some really cool stuff about your career."

"Like what, my dear James?"

"Oh…um…ah…some nice stuff," he babbles, suddenly losing the capacity of his brain functions. "You know, stuff on the website."

She cracks up and says, "Okay, no more interrogation. I'm sorry."

"I forgive you, sweet Josie," he says. "You really let me off the hook there."

"I know, and you didn't deserve it," she says, tickling him in the process.

"My new favorite sport is tennis," he enthusiastically says.

"It better be!"

"This girl has such beautiful legs," he playfully says to her while gazing at the photo of her. "She is beautiful." He held the photo like it's his new blankie.

Josie blushes and leans against him to hide her embarrassment. They kiss for a while and lie down together and close their eyes. James is behind her, and they are facing the same direction, with James's arm around her. They both lie there like they are in heaven and periodically, they open their eyes only to confirm there's no place either of them would rather be. James really likes her a lot, and he wants to establish a comfort zone for her at his place because he spends a lot of time there alone, and he wants to change that just for her. For a while, they whisper hometown stories back and forth, and for the first time, they really learn details about each other. After James begins to pet her hair and lightly scratch her back, she falls asleep, and then he does as well, as they lie there in each other arms. Josie and James remain at the apartment in Morningside Heights, New York. Both of them seem to be completely content with sleeping all afternoon on the couch.

———————

Back in Macomb, Lisa and Ben are going through the routine of getting accustomed to each other's changes from while they were apart this summer. They have a great day in Terre Haute with their friends, and Lisa and Ben also got an opportunity to break away from Amy and Steve that day and really do something on their own. They all rendezvous back at the Terre Haute restaurant that evening and had dinner and went back to Macomb. Ben drops Amy and Steve off at Amy's house, and Ben heads home because his mom invited Lisa over Saturday night for popcorn and movies. Ben's mother picked out one of the movies, and his father picked out the other one. Mr. Wilson chose *The Day After Tomorrow* with Dennis Quaid and Jake Gyllenhaal, and Mrs. Wilson picked out *50 First Dates* with Adam Sandler and Drew Barrymore. Ben and Lisa finally get popcorn and take a seat in the love chair in the family room.

"Have you ever seen these movies?" Lisa asks with a whisper in Ben's ear.

"Nope, can't say that I have with all the reading I have been doing this year."

"We'll soon find out how good they are," Lisa adds.

"Yes, we will, my dear Lisa."

"Have you spoken to James in a while?" she asks.

"Not recently, no," Ben says. "He's been really busy."

"Do you think he is serious about you being his campaign manager someday?" Lisa asks curiously, while she leans back and puts her feet under a blanket.

"Most of the time, when we are talking about it, we are mostly joking around, but as often as it comes up, you have to believe it is something that is on his mind periodically. You have to understand James. There are experiences that James has had in his life, that might make it difficult for him to be in politics without having a brother or a friend at his side," Ben explains to Lisa. "He's not skeptical about us, but he is about strangers."

"Well, I'm praying for you, Ben. I hope you too end up doing great things someday," she says. "You deserve it."

"Me too. I think that would be awesome. Two kids from the sticks of Macomb, Indiana, wouldn't that be something?"

"Sure would, Ben."

They both stop talking and begin to watch the movie. Ben and Lisa are sitting next to each other. She has her legs lying on top of his, and Ben's arm is around her. His parents are on the other side of the family room, with a blanket over them as well, as it is becoming quite a cold evening in Macomb.

Over the remainder of the first month of school, Ben and Lisa continue to see each other every other night or so, as Lisa continues to become a better musician and Ben works to become a better student. Both of which will have much influence on where they'll end up going to college. They had a wonderful time with each other at homecoming, and Amy and Steve, in particular, became closer that evening, so they started double dating together.

After reading Derek Jeter's autobiography, Ben, over the next couple of weeks, reads *The Essential Erasmus* by Desiderius Erasmus, *The Awakening of Intelligence* by Jiddu Krishnamurti, and *The Bait of Satan* by John Bevere. After the first four books, Ben still feels a slight level of resistance, even though there are lights beginning to shine in his head. Nevertheless, Ben is slowly becoming one that can be viewed as well-read but still has much work to do.

Over the next few weeks leading up to November in Macomb, Ben continues to reestablish himself as a better student, as he, in addition to the books he's reading for class, was able to finish four more books from James's pole barn loft. After reading *Death of a Salesman* by Arthur Miller, *The Partnership that Saved the West* by Joseph P. Lash, *The Prince* by Machiavelli, and *Utopia* by Thomas More, Ben began to feel a mild case of the effects James told him he'd get with reading persistently once he took reading seriously. It began to make Ben feel like he wanted to write, so he started to write a journal every day, so he could express what he was going through as he read these books. Reading is enjoyable, but what is most enjoyable about it is that it causes you to write, and it is that writing that literally gives you wings to fly. Writing is the most magical thing in art. There is nothing at all in the arts that allows you to escape quite like it.

For the most part, for the time up until Thanksgiving, Ben continues to reach new heights in school, as some of the grades he gets back from teachers are some of the best scores he's ever seen. Also, he begins to increase his reading volume as the semester goes along and is beginning to enjoy the increased desire to write extensive material. It becomes an enjoyment for all who have experienced the transformation taking place in him, and he begins to have a great admiration for what James meant to him as a friend and even more so as an encouraging influence.

Ben has yet to narrow down a subject of preference, but judging by some of the early reading choices and the fact that James and he had joked for years that Ben would be James's campaign manager one day, he seems to ironically be leaning towards political science. It is still quite early, but the humorous chatter between he and James over the years does seem to be encouraging him to try and press certain subjects into his reading. James had always made it clear to Ben that because his father left him at such a young age, it isn't easy for him to trust people. Trust is a major problem. Consequently, he found it to be of mild importance to start planning his campaign management years in advance. James has just always believed that with his hesitance with people, he had always found it to be mighty important to develop a campaign leader well in advance because that trust between a campaign manager and a politician is of the utmost importance, and with James in particular, that would be a sensitive necessity to say the least.

CHAPTER 8

B ack at James's apartment, Josie and he remain sleeping on the couch after their afternoon at Low Steps following their Friday class. This was their first real planned date, and the night was still very young.

Josie wakes up in James's arms and takes a drink of her water. As she turns back toward him, she glances to notice that he too is just beginning to open his eyes. Both were apparently tired after class, because they had slept for two hours on the couch. The reason being, that they both started their day early on Friday—James at Apple Tree Super Market before his run and her at the gym. She kisses James on the lips and puts her cheek up to his and holds it there, and she whispers, "You have very soft and gentle lips, James." This was music to his ears.

"Yours are sweeter than black grapes, Josie."

"That's nice," she softly says with a smile. "That was a sweet thing to say."

After a few minutes of trading sweet nothings, James and Josie just lie there and stare into each other's eyes for a while. Neither one can think of anything they'd rather be doing. James asks, "Are you hungry?"

"I could eat, or I could wait," she replies. "It's up to you."

"Can I make you something?" She returns her water back to the coffee table in front of her.

"Sure!" she surprisingly responds with a smile. "What do you have in mind?"

"Okay then," James says with joy. "It's a surprise." He leaves her alone on the couch and heads to the kitchen.

James goes to work and continues to talk to her while chopping veggies. She is somewhat curious as to what he is making but also likes surprises as well. He asks, "You like tuna?"

"Sure," she answers. "It's one of my favorites." She grins from a far.

"Red or white onions?"

"Oh, I'll go with red," she says. "I like white as well, but definitely red."

He opened the fridge and rummaged inside. "Green pepper? Cucumbers? Spinach leaf?"

"You're making me hungry. I like all those things," she answers. She turns to lie down on her stomach, her eyes following his every move.

He peers at her over the fridge door. "Feta?"

"Mmm, I love feta." She watches as he turns back to the fridge.

"How about yellow, red, and orange peppers?" he asks.

"Like 'em all."

He closes the fridge with an armful of ingredients, which he places on the counter. Then he grabs the chopping board and starts cutting up peppers with surprising precision. "Dressing? Ranch is pretty decent with tuna."

"I agree," she responds, smiling. She was enjoying seeing this side of James.

"Salt and pepper?"

"Pepper," she says, "are you going to do all the cooking in this relationship?"

"I'd love to."

"Wow!" she says with a look of optimism. "You are going to spoil me."

"I have a dream of my wife coming home from a rough day at the office, and me picking her up at the front door and taking her to a bubble bath." At this point Josie is hung on his every word. "Undressing her myself gently and patiently. Then picking her up and placing her in the tub—"Josie looks at him as if she has died and gone to heaven.

"Oh my," she interrupts. "Did you say—"

"Now let me finish," he insists. "She places a hand over her own mouth as if she can't help herself.

"Oh my gosh! She says. "There's more? Sorry. Continue."

"After I place her in a bubble bath, I hand her a glass of wine and go to the kitchen to finish cooking her dinner. Of course, all the laundry is washed, dried, and folded. The house is completely free of any possible chore or need. After about fifteen minutes pass, I return to the bathroom to add more hot water to the tub. Of course, she greets me with a smile. Once dinner is done and on the table, I reach down and pick her up and dry her off. Then I take her to the bedroom and place her on the edge of the bed and leave and say, 'Dinner is on the table. I'll be waiting,'" James finishes.

"Oh my, I love you. Can't believe you said all of that. You must be an angel?"

"Nope," he bashfully returns. "I'm far from it."

"What planet did you come from, James? At this point she is ready to tie the knot tonight. She's seen and heard enough.

"Huh." He chuckles. "Planet earth."

"I have to tell my mom you said all of this." She says. "But I won't tell her too early." Josie is thinking that she can't wait to tell her mom.

"Well, don't tell your mom right away. I don't want her to think we're taking baths together." He suddenly looks concerned.

"Oh, don't worry. I won't," she reassures him.

"Okay," he demurely puts it.

"What makes me such a special girl that you would place that romantic anticipation in me?" she asks.

"What do you mean, Josie?"

"I'll think of that every time we're together and wonder if I would be so lucky someday," she eloquently puts it. "Lucky, and curious when it will be exactly, that I get to experience this for the first time."

"I'm almost done with dinner," James creatively and auspiciously changes the subject. He's putting vegetables back in the fridge, and wears this look on his face like he just got away with something.

"I noticed that. You changed the subject."

She continues to periodically glance at James while he is preparing her dinner, wondering if it gets any better than this. After three lonely years at Columbia, she is feeling very happy here at this moment. James tells her to turn the television on, and that the US Open semi-finals are tonight. She is in utter amazement that he knows this quite surprising information. She proceeds to tell him that this tournament is in Flushing, just across town. He responds with a smile, as the ever-growing passion of the subject arises within her. It's as if he knew exactly when it would be on, and that being here at this moment was his plan all along after reading last night how important her tennis career was to her. Her interest shifts to the tennis match.

"It just started," Josie says. "I love watching tennis on television."

"I know." Her attention wanders from him as he answers her, she becomes glued to the TV. He has this look on his face as if, he has suddenly lost his conversation with a beautiful woman.

"Don't know much about Kim Clijsters except that she's Belgian," she astutely says. "She's beaten some great players."

"She must be good to be in the semi-finals of the U.S. Open."

"Sure," Josie responds. "This is one of the four grand slam tournaments. You have to be great to make it this far."

James hands her a salad and sits on the floor between her legs with his back to her while she sits above him on the couch. She, for a moment, takes her most concentrated attention off the tennis and notices how colorful and professional-looking her salad is, from a culinary perspective that is. She reaches around and kisses him on the cheek and thanks him for making her something.

"Did you work in a restaurant, James?"

"No, but I cooked dinner for my brother and my grandfather a million times," James confesses. "My grandfather taught me how to cook when I was young." For a moment, James remembers a couple of those moments in the kitchen with his grandpa.

"Does your mom cook?" Josie inquires.

"She's a registered nurse at the local hospital and works afternoons most of the time," he reveals. "She really doesn't have any time to cook." A look temporarily consumes him. "I'm hoping to do well enough to retire her."

"Well, I'm awfully impressed," she says, smiling.

"It's nothing."

"I'd like to see something if this is nothing," she adds. "I'll be the judge of that Mr. modesty."

She smiles and eats the meal he prepared and watches the US Open Woman's Tennis Tournament with her new friend. James suddenly asks, "Do you mind if we stay in?"

"Not at all. I'm happy as we are."

"Okay," James agrees. "I have a couple movies around her somewhere."

Josie reaches down from behind him and puts her lips on his ear, and with her sensuously moist breath tells him she's happy anywhere with him. He gets goose bumps and turns his head to kiss her lips and says, "I feel the same way, Josie."

"Good."

"Do you want to stay here?" he asks.

"Wasn't that what we were just talking about?" Suddenly, Josie is not at all on the same page with James.

"No. I mean stay with me tonight and let me make you breakfast in the morning?" he nervously clarifies. "I mean spend the night."

"Oh! Umm, I'd love to, James." She cautiously says. "Are you sure?"

"I've never been more positive," he enthusiastically expresses. "I'd like to spend more time with you. I won't bite." She pauses for quite a while, unsure of what to say.

"Okay, I'm yours for the night," she says, excited but cautious. Her heart was telling her that she'll be fine, and his demeanor and spirit was also telling her that she trusts him as well.

"Do you have something to wear in your bag?"

"I sure do," she quickly answers. "I have my tennis shorts."

"If you need anything, I have stuff you could wear. It would be big on you, but they have tie strings on them," he offers.

"Okay, thank you." She imagines wearing James's cloths, and has a momentary chuckle on the inside. It was a hilarious image in her mind.

"There's a brand-new, unopened toothbrush in the medicine cabinet. Put your name on it."

"I will, and thank you."

"Don't mention it."

She is pleasantly taken at how sweet and thoughtful he is but cautiously curious as to what spending the night will lead to. It presently consumes her every thought at the moment because there have been more than a couple of moments today where she wanted nothing more than to just jump his bones. She hasn't disregarded completely the possibility that tonight could get so much hotter than what has transpired up to this point, that boundaries of inhabitation could be vulnerable. However, not to be confused with Josie's thoughts on where this night will go, she has never wanted someone in this way before—this is new to her. She's thinking that James is not at all concerned with this because, otherwise, he wouldn't have so easily asked her to sleep over after only knowing each other for just three days. After being pleasantly surprised with everything James has done to this point and how he's approached it, she begins to relax and trust that he wouldn't have a problem doing things with her best interests in mind.

Going back to Wednesday evening, she hadn't planned on going up to James following his prayer at Low Steps, but when she saw how comfortable he was speaking to God in front of people, it caused her to approach him. It's as if, in her mind, God made her do it. When she and her family moved around so much, it was not easy meeting new friends every two years, but her values made it even more difficult meeting boys. She grew up in the church, and everywhere she went, it seemed as though her peers didn't care too much for God. It was quite a lonely experience at times, and tennis really helped channel that energy, and it got her here in one piece. One of the great moments for her when becoming a freshman here was all the faith-based groups you could join on campus. Nevertheless, her experience and faith has led her to James as a virgin. Many times in high school, she was heckled for it, but now as a young woman, she is very much proud of it and wouldn't change a thing. She is tougher for it, and no matter what happens this evening, she is confident things will work out in the long run. It may not always be perfect, but she can tell that not only was it his conservative nature that attracted her, she suspects that it was her same values that attracted him too.

James grabs one of her feet and starts to massage it and plays with her toes. He checks to see if she is ticklish under the foot and confirms that she is, as she started to squirm around like a snake. James asks, "Do you have fingernail polish?"

"Yes," she answers with a strange look on her face. "Why would you ask this?"

A moment passes, then with a humorously devilish look on his face, he looks at her and says, "I want to paint your toenails."

"Say what?" she asks while laughing.

"I want to paint your toenails." She has up and gone from secure in his every step, to think he is off his rocker, tapping him on the head asking if this is James that is still sitting in front of her.

"Okay," she says, amused. "Here you go," handing him a bottle of hot pink nail polish.

James takes her salad bowl to the kitchen and asks if he can get her anything else, and she says no. He returns with a towel, a tub of warm water, and Ivory hand soap. He gets on his knees in front of her and asks her to relax. He is confusingly distracted by how beautifully perfect her legs and feet are, which appropriately match everything else about her. He puts one foot in the warm water and begins to massage it with soapsuds. He then rinses it off and dries it and repeats the same process with the other foot. When he finishes, he grabs the fingernail polish and begins to paint her toenails. She is leaning against the back of the couch and has her foot on his chest and feels like she's being catered to by a pleasure slave. After each toe, he puts his lips up close and blow-dries each one with his breath—not to mention getting in a few kisses of her feet here and there, which is really driving her nuts on the inside. She giggles and chuckles with every move he makes, but deep inside, she is a volcano about to erupt. James is in a trance with regard to how beautifully cute her little toes are and begins to play with them with his lips. She is beginning to breathe a little harder with every touch and kiss. As James continues to paint, she says, "You have really soft lips, James."

"You said this earlier."

"I know, they're really soft."

She is beginning to feel hotter on the inside, with him playing with her feet, but those feelings she is having on the couch are quite new to her. His kissing of her feet really turned her on, and having him paint her toes is quite soothing and gives her goose bumps. She can't get over how cute he truly is for not only wanting to do it, but for going through with it like he has done it a hundred times before. Josie Weathers is beginning to fall in love with James Ryan Roberts. Her spirit is telling her things it has never told her before. She is becoming totally vulnerable to him, and beyond this point, she will have great difficulty resisting a very hot advance by him. She is becoming hopeless to the mercy of his will. As James is finishing the second foot, she closes her eyes and prays silently,

> My Lord, you have been with me my entire life.
> I've felt your strength lift me
> when I was down and your patience when
> I needed to get myself right.
> You have been the great love in my life,
> and I ask that you protect James
> and I tonight, as we come together.
> Give each of us strength,
> to not lose sight of your will for us.
> I pray this in Jesus's name. Amen.

As she opens her eyes, she notices the content and happy look on James's face, and she can't help but feel that her prayer drew some level of grace in his direction. He says, "Done. Hot pink toenails for a very pretty woman."

"I feel like one, James. How could anyone not with this service? My goodness."

"I told you I'd have that effect on you," James said, as she lies there in the partially dark family room, waiting for his next move.

"You did, didn't you, James?"

"Why don't you take your things and get comfortable in the bathroom. There's a clean shower, toothbrush—whatever you need. I'll grab some pillows and blankets, and we'll look for a movie."

"Okay," she says. "Thank you for having me over." She enters the bathroom with her bag.

"I'm so glad you're here tonight, Josie," he says quietly. "There's nothing I'd rather be doing, than hanging out with you tonight."

She turns to look at him from the bathroom, and smiles, "I'm glad to be her too."

James brings pillows and blankets from the closet to keep them warm as the Manhattan temperature drops a little. He sits on the couch and changes the channel a few times and looks for something she might enjoy, so he stops on the movie *Mona Lisa Smile*. James also lit a few candles, turned the lights off, and put two glasses and a bottle of red wine on the table. For a couple more moments, he waits for her to return and is consumed with what she'll possibly be wearing. James is noble for having the best intentions a man can have, but he is a man, and there is no denying sometimes, the overwhelming nature of a woman's beauty.

The suspense begins to consume him, and when he hears the sink turn off and the bathroom light go out, anxiety comes over him. She opens the door and remains standing on the threshold in an S pose, as if she is thinking, *Here I am, my darling, for you to completely ravage me.* James could tell faintly, while she was standing in the doorway, that she had very short shorts on, and by her shape in the dark, he could also tell that these shorts were tight to her skin. His heart started to beat faster and faster, and as she took a couple of steps toward the couch and into the candlelight, he could see what beautiful long legs she had. She must have been six feet tall or almost that, and she certainly had long sexy legs, and those legs were going to be with him tonight. His heart wasn't the only thing experiencing tremors at the moment. His entire body was shaking. Josie approaches him slowly with this look on her face, like she knows she's in control now. James is completely in a trance over her exquisite beauty and shiny golden skin.

Now for the most challenging moment of the night, James is sitting on the couch with his feet on the floor. Josie sits down next to him. She sits down Indian style, and she instantly begins to kiss him all over his face and neck from that position, trying not to press her body against his. She gets to a kneeling position and leans in without her body touching his and kisses him more. They are making out like they have only one day left to live. All the other kissing up to this point was casual; this was steamy. James gets cute and spanks her butt, and she screams, and in the same moment, lies down beside him.

"Your butt is really firm," James says with a goofy look. She was surprised by his spontaneity.

"It is, huh?" she responds. "You like me don't you?" Now she's beginning to get cute with him in response.

"I do."

They lie there on their sides, and stare into each other's eyes while trading kisses. In the candlelight, she can see James's face and the light that is in his eyes, and she begins to say, "You are beautiful, James."

"What?"

"I'm serious." She confesses. "Your eyes are entrancingly unavoidable. I see how women look at you." She's being serious while James is denying it with bashfulness.

"I don't see that stuff."

"Did you see me two Fridays ago walking to class while gazing you down all the way to the door?" she asks. He was shocked by this revelation of hers.

"Oh my gosh! You were looking at me?" James asks. "I stared you down the whole way."

"Yes, I was. Well, anyway, I notice them looking at you. You have that look—with shiny black hair, with beautiful blue eyes— but most engaging is your confidence. That drives women nuts," she informs him passionately. He's dumb founded.

"How'd you know I had blue eyes?" he asks.

"I can tell because I haven't been able to stop staring at them since that Friday last week," she admits.

"Now you're spoiling me, Josie."

"I have to catch up with you James," she says. "You've been spoiling me rotten."

"You have done more than you could imagine, Josie. I have been here for three and a half years. This is the best time I have had to date. In fact, it's the three best days I think I've experienced here at Columbia."

"You're so sweet."

"You've made me feel things I've never felt before," James cautiously reveals. "You make me tremble when we're inches from each other.

"I feel the same," she says as a tear drops from her eye. He wipes it from her cheek and kisses her all over the face.

"Oh, James, I've never met anyone like you. I just pinch myself every minute, thinking I'll wake up from a dream. But I realize it's not a dream."

"Not a dream," James says. "It's your new life."

"I'm a virgin, James." She nervously reveals. "Please don't think I'm weird for saying this out of the blue." A moment of pause, as they ponder the new subject at hand.

A moment of speechlessness came over the two of them, after Josie nervously dribbled those words out. She fears she said too much, but then notices a tear in his eye, and he returns with, "I suspected that you were because I prayed at the beginning of the semester that God would bring me the one. I also asked that he send someone that I would have something in common with, in terms of saving myself for marriage. Two hours later, I saw you walking to class on the first day of school, and I started to have feelings come up within me."

"You're a virgin, James?"

"Yes, Josie."

"Oh my, and I was nervous how sleeping here would go. You must be just as nervous?"

"I'm scared to death," James confesses. The two of them have gone from heckling each other to a state of seriousness.

"We were meant to meet, James. This wasn't an accident. Think of what percentage of twenty-year-old kids today are virgins, and now think of how mysterious our meeting was. We are both the same age too."

"If that doesn't show a nonbeliever the real work of his grace and power, I don't know what will," James says. "He is Lord, and he will do as he sees fit for his faithful."

"This is so exciting, James." Josie is so taken this week by how easy he finds it to speak to God. It almost reminds her of her father's faith in God.

"I know," he adds.

They cuddle together, rubbing noses, and both are grinning from ear to ear as they kiss for a while. As time passes, James asks at about 10:00 p.m. if she would like a glass of wine, and she says yes. They both sit up, and James pours her a glass then he does the same for himself. She acknowledges that the candles were a nice touch. She also thanks him for dinner with a big kiss, that tastes like red wine. They just sit there, leaning against each other for a couple of hours, watching television and periodically kissing. After a while, once both of them feel the buzz of a glass and a half of wine, James asks, "What time do you have to wake up?"

"I don't have to get up early, I just need to go to the gym for two hours and study for a while."

"So you can sleep in?" James asks.

"Yes."

"We're eating fruit in bed in the morning," James tells her. "You have to stay in bed too. No getting dressed until breakfast is over." As James is setting the plans for the morning, Josie is falling deeply for him. She can see how easy it is to be with him. She acknowledges that he has no mannerisms or quirks that make him difficult. To her, this is perfect.

"Okay. Nobody's ever ordered me to stay in bed but sounds fun," Josie playfully adds. "I like it!"

"You're teasing me," James bashfully whimpers.

"I'm just kidding, dear. Don't fret, I can't wait for the morning."

Josie tackles James lightly and hugs him and kisses him all over his neck. She was only playing because it was so cute to her how James had this entire evening planned out, and she couldn't resist.

"Do you want to lie down?" he asks. "Or do you want to stay up?"

"I'm good. It's kind of early," she observes. She's nervous about the bed thing, and doesn't want him to know.

"What time do you usually go to bed?"

"Well, my roommate stays up until 12:00 a lot, but on Fridays and Saturdays, she comes in late. I sometimes sleep through it, and sometimes, I don't. She's on the tennis team, so we do things together."

"I understand," James says. "So it can get frustrating sometimes?"

"At times, but I'm not complaining," she says. "School is flying by, the next thing you know, it will be over, and we'll miss these people forever." Josie is pretty tight with a couple of her homies.

"Well, if there's ever a time you'd rather be somewhere else, I don't care what time it is, you get your butt over here. Okay?" James tells her, bringing a smile to her face.

"You're on, and thank you. Aren't you a bit nervous that I might rather be here every time?" she asks with a giggle.

"Not at all, I would rather you be here than not here."

"Wow! Thank you."

"My pleasure."

At about midnight, Josie dozes off in James's arms. He gets up and picks her up like he's carrying her through the door on their honeymoon. She opens her eyes again in amazement and wraps her arms tight around his neck and leans her head against his shoulder. He gets to the bed and lays her down on one side and puts the covers over her. She looks at him like she's waiting for prince charming to give her instructions, and he says, "I'll be back in one second."

"I'll be waiting," she says sensuously.

James locks the door, turns the lights out, but leaves one candle lit, so she can see her way to the bathroom in the dark. He reenters the bedroom and takes his jeans off, which was something she had to see inconspicuously out of the corner of her eye, as he was facing the other direction. Her bottom lip drops about three inches when she notices his muscular upper legs. She pretends to not be watching but can't help but notice he's wearing white sports briefs—the ones that look like tight shorts. He then puts a pair of shorts on. She was watching his every move and swallowed when she saw how fit he is. She hasn't experienced a moment as sexy as that in her entire life, and the hungry lion is beginning to come out of her.

James rolls over to her and gets his body touching hers while she's on her side. He puts his free hand on her side and stares into her eyes for a moment then begins to kiss her. He stops and whispers to her, "Hello."

"Hi," she replies happily.

"You're going to share tonight with your girlfriends, and they're going to talk, please keep us genuine," James seriously asks. "It's none of their business. All it turns into is rumors and gossip." Josie seemed to be impressed with his suggestion, impressed with how mature it was.

"What do you mean, James?"

"I mean, no matter what happens tonight, I'm looking out for what is best for us," James clarifies. "I'm not saying that we should have a secret relationship, I'm just saying that people don't need to know what goes on between us."

"That's why I picked you, James. I knew you were different, and I couldn't let you get away."

"And now here we are," James expresses contentedly.

"Yes, we are James, and there's no place I'd rather be."

He kisses her and reaches his hand around her back, and she pulls him closer toward her. James lies on her partially for a time, and as feelings start to erupt inside of him, he pulls back and lays his head down on the pillow. She lunges slowly toward him and puts her leg over his body. She kisses him as she places her hand on his chest. They trade moments like this back and forth for an hour or so, and each time, it tapers to a better judgment. It has to be agonizing to them to be in this position and continue to resist. They are just two passionate people that just want to let go of the inhibitions that seem to be chained up inside of them. There is nothing that either of them would rather do in the entire world right now than rip each other's clothes off and make passionate love until morning.

Josie places her head on James's chest and her hand on his side and just stares in awe of his body. He has one arm wrapped around her, and his free hand massages her head. He runs his fingers through her hair and around her ear. He kisses her head and seems to be realizing that she is about ready to fall asleep, so he lies there and lets things be. He is very pleased with where things have gone since Wednesday night, and he closes his eyes with a smile on his face.

Each one of them periodically wakes, only to realize they are together and fall back asleep with smiles on their faces. At 8:00 in the morning, they are together like two spoons, with James sleeping behind her. She's lying on one of his arms, and his other hand is on her stomach. When he wakes and realizes where his hand is, a smile comes to his face. Meanwhile, she has her eyes closed but is every bit awake, intensely waiting to see what happens. It is driving both of them mad. As James begins to take his hand away, she grabs it and returns it to the same spot. She keeps his hand there as if to say that this is where his hand has always belonged.

James helplessly begins to move his hand all over, dragging it on her hip and running his fingers across her smooth upper leg. He has an intense case of curiosity about this most beautiful goddess lying in his bed. He loves her body and can't seem to stop investigating it like a spaceship exploring a new planet. He is mesmerized by how soft every inch of her is, and she turns and lunges toward him and sensuously whispers into his ear with a wet, warm breath.

"You're driving me absolutely crazy, James."

"Do you want me to go make you breakfast, Josie?" This is not at all what she was thinking of, as she is a million miles away from the thought of anything except his sexy body.

"No. I want your hands to touch me everywhere, but…" she trails off.

"Just lay here with me for a moment," he asks. Bringing a content smile to her face.

"Okay, darling," she says with a smile.

James pulls her to him, and she lays her head on his shoulder and places her hand on his chest. They both close their eyes, feeling each other's heartbeat and taking in each other's presence. It was a rocky road this morning, but the time wasn't right, and they both frustratingly knew it.

James starts to say, "I want you so badly. We'll have to temper this a little next time, or at least most of the time. This will take a lot of discipline if we do this every week."

"It's okay, James, because it was the right thing. I trust you."

"Are you ready for breakfast?" James asks.

"Yes."

"I'll be right back, Josie. Don't you go away."

"I won't, I'm just going to the bathroom," she says. "I'll be back."

He gets up and leaves her to herself for the moment.

James heads to the kitchen to pile up some fruit for breakfast and then returns to bed and sees Josie waiting patiently for him. They look at each other while eating strawberries, oranges, and bananas, and mutually breathe a sigh of relief that they didn't throw anything away this morning. They lean back against the headboard and eat while they play with their legs tangled. He can't help but notice her sexy, smooth legs on his, and she can't help but feel his sexy, hairy legs on hers. He says, "Your feet are so cute with pink nail polish."

"You painting them, was so sexy," she says. "I'm never cleaning them off. I wonder how long it will last."

Josie and James finish breakfast and have one more small bout of kissing and bodily exploration but nothing like earlier, as they're both re-strengthened by their earlier display of discipline. James has one last thing to say in bed before she gets dressed. "Josie, I know this is early, and we just started to get to know each other, but I believe in the feeling I have right away. I believe you know right away, and the rest is just experiencing each other's differences for better or worse. If this feels right to you, I ask that you not allow the forces of nature to encourage you to take your time. I guess what I'm trying to say is, I don't believe in slow. I don't believe financial, political, cultural, social, or any other thing that could get in our way. I just ask that if you feel this is right, then trust it. Don't let anything change your feeling but me. One other thing, don't ever limit yourself because you don't want to crowd me. I've been waiting my entire life for you, and I don't want anything but you sitting right beside me as often as I can get you to. Here's one of my keys to the apartment. I want you to know that you are welcome any time, even when I'm not here. You are welcome to stay here, study here, or sleep here whenever you want. You don't need my approval."

"Wow, James. I do feel good about this, and it feels right so early to me too, so I will trust it." She was quite impressed again with his ability to articulate his thoughts and feelings.

"I'll be here studying all day and night, so when you're done today, feel free to come back. The shower is yours, my room is yours, and my kitchen is yours. Everything is yours."

"Okay, I will," she joyfully says. "Thank you again."

"My little brother is expecting me to call him at 10:00 p.m., so I have to stay in tonight as well. I would love to see you though."

"You will see me tonight, James," she says. "Trust me."

She gives him a huge kiss, and he could tell that some of what he said caused her to tear up, so he wipes her salty tears with his lips and kisses her. Josie gets dressed and puts her shoes on and heads out the door.

"Good-bye, James." She heads down the steps.

"Bye, darling." He waves and has a look on his face that is half happy, and half sad that their visit has ended.

"I promise you'll see me tonight," Josie assures him. "Don't worry."

"Okay, can't wait," James says with relief. The look of concern left his face and began getting excited over getting to see her again that night.

James watches her head back to her apartment building, and as she is getting farther and farther away, he's talking to himself, saying, "There she goes. There goes my girl. There goes my future wife. I wonder if she feels the same."

CHAPTER 9

A week passes, with James and Josie seeing each other just about every day. That weekend in late September was Josie's first tournament of her senior year, and she was absolutely dominant like she had never been. The coach was quoted as saying she was a different player. The tournament took place in Philadelphia, so it was a long weekend for James with not seeing her, but he sent her off with a pretty emotional pep talk, and she responded by becoming a ferocious competitor. James had been working with her on some things at the outdoor courts, not anything of a technical nature but strictly psychological. James has been a huge fan of tennis his entire life, as Steffi Graf is one of his all-time favorite athletes. So he knows full well that tennis, more than any sport, demands the competitive spirit of a lion for one to survive.

If there's any advice James can provide to an athlete that would be a substantial breakthrough in their performance, it's regarding the neglected focus and discipline of today's athlete. Not that Josie wasn't focused or disciplined, but it is much neglected in today's coaching. Nevertheless, the things they've been working on have made a substantial difference in just one week. He's not teaching her to play tennis, but he's trying to incorporate the determination and focus that made so many so great. That is what made Steffi Graf the best player in the history of tennis. She has won the most Grand Slams in the history of tennis, and she did it in a condensed period of time and in the toughest era in the history of women's tennis.

When Josie returned to campus on Monday, she couldn't wait to see James, and instead of going home, she went straight to him at his place. His door was open, so she walks right in and calls for him, and as she gets to the top step, he's there to greet her with a hug.

"James, I missed you so much." She buries her face in his neck, and didn't move.

"I missed you too," he says with laughter. "It was lonely without you." She was expressionless, all she cared about was not letting go.

"I didn't think it would suck being away, but once it got to Saturday night, I really started to picture what you were doing. I couldn't stop thinking about you," she reveals. "I agree, it was lonely."

"I did the same. How did you do?" he asks.

"Oh my gosh! James, I was incredible. You should have been there. I never felt in control of my game like that, and I played one of the best players in the Ivy League, which made it even more special."

"Oh, I'm so proud of you," James adds. "I knew you had it in you." There's a pride that is on her face now when speaking of her own tennis game…a pride that was missing before. James would call it the psychological effects of having command with something.

"It was unbelievable with the things you helped me with, but the thing that made me feel so invincible was the security provided by your love. It gave me so much strength," Josie reveals in amazement. "What have you been doing, James?"

James responds with, "Fortunately, I had lots of research and a meeting with Model Congress and Apostolos Campus Ministry. I had my Bible study with them tonight at 7:30 p.m. Also went to Church on Sunday. I tried to stay busy because I could tell on

Saturday that sitting in a chair was agonizingly difficult because I couldn't stop thinking of you as well."

"I wanna go to church with you," she says. "I want to go everywhere with you." She does not want to leave him again like that.

"You're very welcome whenever you want."

"Can I come Sunday?" she asks.

"It's a date, Josie!"

They dance slowly in place within each other's arms for quite a while, and all he can feel is her heart pounding like crazy and her face buried in his neck. He had been listening to music before she came up, so you could faintly hear, ironically, "Lucky Man" by The Verve in the background. She didn't seem like she wanted to let go anytime soon. This told James everything he needed to know about how she felt and whether or not she feels the same about him as he does about her. She really missed him, and James doesn't know it, but she's tearing up because she is spending the happiest moment of her life. She has just disposed of a great women's tennis player from Penn, in straight sets, like that player wasn't even there, and instead of boasting like a hyena, she's speechless in love instead. This is the first moment that James had thoughts that she might not be opposed to being married, even though her career would have her all over the world. It crossed his mind before, but it didn't stick because as soon as he thought about her having a schedule everywhere but New York, he assumed she'd be opposed. However, he would be fine with it as long as their hearts are together, and that they are one no matter where they are. Besides, he can already see the difficulties in saving himself for their wedding night for a long period of time, and it just isn't going to happen. So if they would endure two careers far apart, then there is no reason to wait for marriage.

For the next few hours, they just lie there in bed together saying very little. Once in a while they would whisper sensitive conversation back in forth, but for the most part, they are recovering from the shock of being apart. Later in the evening, Josie starts to speak in a curious tone, "James, when you see yourself over the next five years, what do you picture?"

"I see getting a job and finishing school in the evening."

"You mean, the degree you're getting now?" Josie asks.

"Yeah, it's going to take three or four years to finish and I'm not waiting that long for a career. Besides, I'm getting signals from Secretary Purcell, like he is going to have a job interview for me soon."

"A job where?" Josie asks with curiosity. "Wow! That would be a pretty good job, knowing it was from a member of the President's cabinet." Amazing she thinks.

"He said here in Lower Manhattan with the State Department at the United Nations (UN) building downtown." James wonders what that job interview would be like.

"Wow! That would be incredible to have your resume start with the US State Department," Josie says in amazement. "I'm quite impressed."

"I'm pretty wild about it as well."

"What do you see as far as a family goes?" Josie asks. She's inconspicuously sizing him up.

"I want a family. There's nothing I want more in life. I can't do what I want to do without a family," James reveals. "I've never had a normal family atmosphere at dinner time, and into the evening on a school night, or a work night. I dream of it every day."

"What do you mean?" she asks.

"I just have plans, and they include a partnership with someone. They include children, maybe not necessarily right away, but being married is something I want immediately in my life."

Josie kind of hit a speechless moment, so maybe she heard all she needed to hear. It sure seemed like her spirit was lifted by this piece of information from him. Maybe she too is wondering what his thoughts are on a partial, long distance-marriage. Of course, both of them are well aware that financial success would increase the opportunities with which they could see each other more. With traveling being so expensive, it would allow them to be together at some of her tennis tournaments. It would also allow her to fly home when she isn't playing for three or four days.

"Why did you want to know about the next five years, Josie?"

"I don't know. Just curious, like a woman is about things."

"Can I ask you something?" James asks.

"Sure, ask away."

"What do you see for five years following graduation?" James is creeping his way into the inconspicuous inquiries now.

Josie says, "I see myself playing professional tennis. I see myself being married, and having kids at some point. I'd have no problems having kids once my career was established enough for me to miss a season here and there and still not have to start over when I returned."

"Sounds like my answer, Josie."

After James said that, she grinned really hard and smashed her nose against his and looked straight into his eyes. She had this look like she approved of what he said. She must have taken the "sounds like my answer" comment to mean that they both seem to want the same things. They talked about this tonight, as if each have had the same conversations with other people in the past, but neither of them know that each of them have never talked about these things with anyone before.

They have been slowly getting to know each other over the first few weeks of the semester, but being away from each other all weekend really sparked up curiosities about the future. Both of them had lots of time to think about what it is like being away from each other, but the thing that sparked Josie feelings is the security of marriage. She loved the idea that even if they were thousands of miles apart, he would still be hers no matter what.

Because they got such a late start on this Monday night, with her getting in so late, they just got ready for bed.

"Did you miss me, James?" She asks. "I mean, really miss?" Playfully her mood.

"I have to say, I have never missed someone in my life like I missed you this weekend. It was quite eerie to say the least."

"You're so sweet, James. That's what I missed most."

"You're going to fall asleep at my place again tonight."

"Yes, I am." She says. "Is that okay?"

"It's so okay that I would rather you stay here." The two of them are growing more and more comfortable. The thing about two people that are on the same page personality wise, they can expedite their relationship without months and months of misunderstandings.

"Really?" Josie asks with surprise.

"Yes. I am positive, Josie. When I'm out and about, I daydream about you being here when I return." James is enjoying himself while entertaining Josie with his sweet nothings.

"Wow. I dream about you too," she says with a yawn. "Except of course, I day dream about you lying in bed in your shorts." Risqué, is the look that has appeared on her face. "Don't ask for details."

They lie against each other, and both of them instantly fall asleep in each other's arms. During the course of the night, each of them wakes up to either go to the bathroom or grab a drink of water, only to stop for a moment upon returning to bed to smile and watch the other sleeping peacefully. Once each of them lay back down, it was difficult to fall back asleep each time because it became ever so entertaining to lie there and watch their lover sleep next to them. There is something quite warm—even though it is kind of creepy—to lie there and watch a passionate love sleep. Listening to the whisper of their breathing is extremely satisfying. It's only creepy when the love is not equally mutual. That's only spoken from experience, as it is quite annoying to be watched by someone who is more into you than you are them.

Nevertheless, morning arrives with the sun shining in on them lying in each other's arms like two spoons, with her behind him. Periodically, due to the warm evening in New York, a few articles of clothing had been shed here and there during the course of the night but nothing inappropriate for these two, at least not after already spending the night together four or five times. That first time she spent the night was a learning experience for both of them because neither had ever had their abstinence challenged so strongly. However, as they spend more and more time together, they both have become stronger, and because each knows the other shares the same conviction, they aren't scared of losing each other over it. It is quite an accomplishment, especially in this world today, with all the influences to fornicate freely wherever and with whomever you please. Fortunately for these two, they ended up at a university that welcomes and provides the hospitality of a conservative lifestyle.

With Josie's father being an army chief of chaplains (two-star general), this particular subject was their family's number one priority for their daughter being away at school. They didn't want Josie being in a crazy atmosphere. They wanted her to be comfortable with whom she is, and Columbia was at the top of her father's list of colleges they visited.

"Good morning, darling," she greets him. "You look handsome in the morning." With a wide smile, her face two inches away from his as he opens his eyes.

"Hello, beautiful," he says with a smile. "You're my morning flower."

"You have anything today besides research?"

"One thing. I'm meeting a brother from Apostolos Ministry at 3:00 p.m. He's been struggling with something and needs my help."

"Okay, can I swing by after class at 8:00 p.m.?" she asks.

"I'll be waiting for you with dinner on the table at 8:00."

"What's for dinner, James?"

"It's a surprise," he says with a grin. "It's my favorite dish."

She says, "Can't wait. I love surprises."

"I know." James is perceptively aware of this fact. "I pay attention."

James and Josie get cleaned up and head out the door together like two people already pretending to be married, well except for the things that must wait of course, until they are one in marriage.

James grabs her for a hug and says, "Are you busy Friday after class?" He loves hanging out with her now after that class.

"No, because I have my workout and practice in the morning," she says. "I am free that entire day after class." Josie was thinking even if she were busy, how could she turn down a date with this guy?

"We have tickets to see *Annie* on Broadway."

"Oh my gosh! James, how did you do that?" Josie asks in a completely hysterical state. "I'm speechless."

"I knew you'd be fired up," he says. "It's a great show, and we have to go."

"Fired up? I'm beside myself!"

"Senator Purcell had to cancel because of something that came up, and he and his wife are not coming to New York this weekend. So they wanted us to have their tickets," James reveals.

"Wow, you're important, James. I can't believe this." She gives him a big hug.

"Tell me about it," he says. "It sure feels weird getting all this treatment from such important people." After being in Macomb, Indiana his entire life, and serving and fending for himself, he sure is getting used to this treatment from the Purcell family. Josie's not having a problem with it either.

"Do not dare say that, James. You help me with my tennis, and I'm helping you with this one. Don't for one second think that you don't deserve this. God has provided this opportunity for you. He is laying the foundation for a stage that will hold your podium. This is bigger than both of us, so don't. I'm not letting you," she says in a scolding tone.

"Wow! Did that just come out of your mouth?"

"I care about you. I'm sorry for sounding so bossy," she bashfully says.

"No, I loved it," he says. "You answered my question from last night."

"What question?"

"The one about why I need to be married," he says. "You remember?"

"Oh," she says, short and sweet.

"A man's weaknesses are always balanced by the strengths of his better half," he says. "I see it all the time in politics."

"You want to be in politics, James?"

A few moments pass, with James looking off into the clouds while she is waiting for him to answer her question. When he looks at her, this feeling of trust and conviction comes over him, and he realizes what Josie means to him. He says, "Yes, very much so. It's been a dream of mine to be a politician ever since I can remember,"

"That's great, James. Now I see what you mean in terms of the family thing."

She came to the realization that kids don't grow up dreaming to be senators or secretaries of Homeland Security, so she allowed the subject to dissolve on its own. Even though she was quite proud of this noble ambition, she didn't want him to have to reveal details of how high he was shooting because those are tall mountains to climb. Only one person gets to live at the White House every four years, so she was fully aware of the sensitive nature that might come with revealing that dream. She got the picture though. Furthermore, another level of pride for him came over her now that she had squeezed this from him. It was different now, trying to figure out all these peculiar mysteries about him. Now, having an idea of where he's going and why these important men keep popping up, she understands because it all fits with his dreams.

Nevertheless, they are about to part ways until eight, Tuesday night, and she says, "What time is the show on Friday, James?"

"7:00 p.m. And we are going to dinner at 4:30 at Gennaro Ristorante." She has heard about this very restaurant, and can't wait until Friday.

"I love Italian," Josie reveals. "It's my very favorite."

"Good," James says with a mysterious smile. He is making homemade red sauce for tonight, but he's keeping that a surprise. "Don't be late for dinner tonight."

"I can't wait until Friday, James."

"Me too, we'll talk about it tonight." James says as he kisses her good-bye.

"Bye, darling." She walks away with that pep in her step, the one that she gets from him.

James responds with, "See you tonight, my beautiful."

When James goes to pick Josie up on Friday night at her apartment, he's dressed very nicely—black dress pants, a white shirt, and a blue sport coat. She will feel mighty important tonight, as James has this aura of prominence about him. It's quite impressive for one as young as he is. However, all his control would be short-lived when she comes to the door, he just about drops dead on the spot, because she's gone from being an athlete, to an elegant lady and made the transition quite impressively. It was an uncanny shift from the bouncy-step athlete with the ponytail flopping around, to a lady of graceful elegance. Josie is wearing a black sleeveless sarong dress. It is cut just above the knee, and she is wearing four-inch black stiletto heels with an ankle strap. Probably the most impressive aspect of her transformation was the ability to go from tennis shoes to stilettos and do it with this level of gracefulness.

James is mesmerized by how beautifully long her legs are in those heels and how she has become this catwalk supermodel all in one night, and he can't seem to gather his wits. He finally gathers himself enough to realize he brought her a short-stemmed rose and hands it to her. She returns with a slow, wet, sensuous kiss for payment and then puts her arm through his, and they begin walking to their ride. She glances over at him and realizes that he has regained the poise that he had before she scrambled his tower with that appearance. She smiles because it was the cutest thing she had ever seen. Seeing a man with total control have his brain waves scrambled so easily by a black dress was quite the entertainment for her.

"I got us a cab," James says. "It's just over here." The two of them look so amazing and are turning heads in Morningside Heights.

"You didn't have to. We could have taken the bus."

"My girl isn't riding on a bus looking like you look tonight." He's very protective of her, and rightfully so, she looks like an angel.

She was quite taken by his protective nature regarding her comfort this evening. They get to Gennaro Ristorante at a perfect time, with very little wait. It is quite difficult for a young couple to be in an establishment with such a distinguished clientele and still hold on to the confidence of a couple that belongs. James and Josie were doing this very thing this evening, and it is the most impressive thing about this night. James has always felt confident wherever he has been, and apparently, Josie claims a similar attribute because they are working the scene tonight. They finally get their table, and James does the gentlemanly thing of pushing her chair in for her. A woman never lets gestures like that go unnoticed, as they make up the subtle details of their dreams. Most men are unaware of such things, but there are a few who really want to know what makes a woman feel special, and James is one of those rare finds.

He asks her what she wants for dinner and inquires of any details that might be needed, and he orders her entire dinner for her. She didn't have to say a word to the waiter, which was pretty impressive for a young man to know. But little did she know,

James's grandfather taught him way more than anyone would think, as he himself was a charmer. She is witnessing all of this and still asking herself, *Where did this guy come from?* Even after a few weeks, he never seizes to amaze her. They stay for a few minutes after dinner to finish their wine, and then they head out. James called a taxi about twenty minutes before they were done, and as soon as they get outside, they are able to get right into their ride.

"Will we be there too early?" Josie asks.

"No, they suggest getting there forty-five minutes early, and by the time we get through this traffic, we'll be lucky to be there thirty minutes early."

She squeezes his arm and puts her head on his shoulder and says, "You are so amazing, James. I don't want this night to ever end."

"Here we are," James says as they arrive at their destination. "Broadway!" Both get out and look around for a moment, excited to be there.

Watching them make their way through the theater as a young couple was impressive, as they give off this vibe like they've been there before, no matter where they are. She holds on to his arm the entire way. She is confident as a woman following his lead. It sends chills down a woman's spine when they find a man that makes all the decisions and does all the leading. They finally get to their seats and sit down. Josie brought a matching black evening wrap to put over her shoulders. She crosses her leg toward James and leans close to him as they trade whispered sweet things for the thirty-minute wait.

She turns and puts her lips to his and kisses him and says, "Thank you, James." She smiles as every girl knows this is a dream of theirs, to see Annie on Broadway, and with an amazing man.

"You're welcome, gorgeous."

"You really know how to make me feel special, and I can't wait to tell my mom about this. She's going to cry as I am about to," Josie says, overcome with emotion. "This is a dream."

He puts his arm around her and places his hand on her head and kisses her all over her forehead and her ears. It draws a giggle from her. She looks at him and smiles as he says to her, "We're going to be okay, partner."

"You called me your partner," Josie says with enthusiasm.

"Yes I did," he responds. "You are more than a partner." Josie drops a tear from the eye, and James wipes it with his handkerchief.

"You referred to your future wife as a partner when we were talking on Monday," Josie says with a grin. "Does this mean what I think?"

James says, "I did, didn't I?"

"Yes, you did, James."

"Hmmm," he ponders. "I guess I did." He's beginning to become slap happy about the subject.

"Does that mean that I'm your wife?" Josie playfully asks. "Wouldn't that be great? You and I raising kids in New York?" The idea of this brought excitement to her demeanor just before the show starts.

"When you're in Europe playing at a tennis tournament, I'll be Mr. Mom like the movie. Ha-ha," James says with a laugh.

"Would you do that?" Josie asks with a cautious curiosity.

"Hell yes, I would. You know those front baby carriers? Where your child can hang in front of you while you're pushing another kid in a stroller?" James asks her.

"Yes, that is an adorable image."

"I had a dream the other night that you had to leave New York for Wimbledon, and days later, I brought the kids there for your match," James reveals with confidence, like this is going to happen someday. She was shocked again. He never seizes to amaze her.

Of all of the previous moments over the past few weeks that blew Josie away and are firmly embedded in her memory, this one that just came out of James's mouth went directly to the top of the list. If she wasn't completely and utterly overwhelmed before this moment, she is now. A date with the love of her life in formal attire, a five-star restaurant, a Broadway musical, and now a vision of her future children being nurtured by their father. She has this feeling like, *Is this guy for real?*

"The show is going to start soon," he says.

"I'm really enjoying myself tonight, James. You've really outdone yourself this time."

As the show begins, Josie grabs his hand and becomes a spectator. James looks at her out of the corner of his eyes and sees this incredible amount of excitement in her face. She's totally tuned into the show. It gives James a great feeling of warmth and satisfaction to have made her feel this good. He was previously overwhelmed by her incredible beauty, but now that he sees her in a dress and all done up, he has a constant pounding in his heart. He is still trying to get over the idea that she is his, and now that he sees her tonight, he's even more amazed. Once they get deep into the show and James has a moment where he can whisper something to her, he says, "If you have to go to the bathroom when the curtain goes down, I recommend that you move quickly because the women's bathroom line, I've heard, gets pretty long."

Josie returns with, "Okay James." He was looking ahead, and making sure that his woman wasn't inconvenience in any way.

"I'll be waiting outside the bathroom for you. What do you want to drink?"

"I'll have whatever you have," she says.

"Are you sure?" James asks. "Coffee, tea, soda?"

She says, "Positive, I'll have what you're sipping on."

As they return their attention to the show, James begins to think what a wonderful feeling it was to not only have her but to also have the comfortable feeling you have when you're with your best friend. They both have plenty of friends, but it's been more than three years since James had someone he could talk to like he could when talking to Ben back in Macomb, Indiana. There are a couple of people in Apostolos Campus Ministry that James is pretty tight with, and there's a friend at Model Congress, but nothing close to Ben—until now. Josie has healed a lot of things that had become overdue in James's life at Columbia. For three weeks, he has been different in his endeavors on campus. She has done something to him that has made him better than ever.

As soon as the intermission curtain started to drop, she took off like a shot out of a cannon, and it gave James a little chuckle. When she got to where she was going to turn and go up the steps, she looks back at him with a laugh. It seems as though she was making a joke over how bad she had to go to the bathroom. When she comes out of the bathroom, she sees that he got a coffee for them to share.

James says, "I've heard that people are really weird about eating during the show, so I was kind of nervous about getting more than just coffee."

"You're so cute, my sweetie." She raps her arms around his and lays her head on his shoulder.

James giggles as she teases him and says, "You ready to head back?"

"Let's go." They head back to their seat with her arm wrapped around his. She is the most beautiful woman in New York on this night.

After the show, they get into a taxi and head back to Morningside Heights. When they get there, they decide to have an ice cream before going home. So they find a nice, not-so-crazy place where they can eat outside. They both get hot fudge sundaes, as they are both quite fond of chocolate. James puts the two chairs close together on one side of the table facing the street. This isn't the first ice cream they've had together, but it is the first one they've had while out as a couple.

"I had a great time tonight, James. Thank you." Graciously appreciative of everything that they have been through. She thanks God every second for this new life of hers.

James responds with, "You're welcome, and I had fun too."

"I've never been on a date like this, James."

"Neither have I."

"You haven't?" Josie asks, surprised. "Not even back home in Indiana?"

James says, "No." Positively certain he is. "Not even close."

"I find that difficult to believe, as you look so natural in such high places," Josie says. "You're a heartbreaker then, because every woman that caught a glimpse of you tonight is feeling pain right now." Josie knows more about how much of a hot item he is.

"I wasn't always like this. You know, you have something to do with it." James reveals.

"What do you mean? she asks.

"It's not hard to be confident in places like that when you have the most beautiful woman in the city wrapped around your arm." This made Josie feel good.

Josie suddenly became speechless with what James just said. When she looks up, James could tell with how wet her eyes are, that what he said touched her deeply. He puts his hand gently under her chin and reached in to her and kisses her. They finish their ice cream, and James walks Josie home to her apartment.

Josie asks, "Are you walking me to my place?"

"Yes. Is that where you want to go?" Josie's not in much of a hurry for the night to end. She doesn't care what time she goes to bed, so long as she gets to see him longer this evening.

"I want to see you more tonight. Can you wait for me to change?" she asks.

"Absolutely."

They get to Josie's place, and she invites him up and informs him that her roommate isn't home. They pass a few girls on the way up, and one of them says, "Damn, Josie girl, look what you all and went up and got yo-self."

James and Josie start cracking up over what her neighbor said. They get inside her room, and James looks around and takes it in and says, "So this is where my girl stays?"

"This is it. Most of the time, I stay at my boyfriend's place," Josie playfully says.

"Are you changing here or at my place?" James is wondering because this might be difficult to do with there being no place to go except in the hallway, so he begins to improvise.

"It doesn't matter."

James says, "Show me what you're going to wear over my place." James has things running through his mind that only he knows. He has this mood about him as if he's sizing something up.

She shows James what she's going to wear as she's folding the clothes and stacking them on the table. James turns around and walks to the door very slowly, without her thinking something is up. He gets to the door, and he closes it. And as soon as it closed, she looked at him like she was curious why he needed the door shut. Her roommate left a dim lamp on over on the other side of the apartment, so James switches off the light that lit up Josie's side of the room. You could still see well, but it was dim, as if just a couple of candles were lit. He gets to her while she is still wearing her dress and heels. The only thing she had taken off was the evening wrap that kept her shoulders warm this evening. James gets on his knees in front of her while she is still standing, and he slowly puts his hands gently on her hips, moves her to the bed, and sits her down. She asks what he's doing, and he instantly puts his index finger over his lips to tell her to shush and trust him.

James reaches down to unbuckle the ankle straps on her heels, and then he takes one shoe off at a time, very slowly and patiently, while periodically making eye contact with her. Once her heels are off, he gently runs his hands up and down her lower legs, drawing an increased breathing pattern from her instantly. He moves his body closer and closer until he is between her legs, and he reaches around her lower back and pulls her close to him. He gently places his hands on the outside of her upper legs and takes his hands and runs them underneath her dress to the outside of her legs. He continues to move her dress further and further up her leg until it can't go any further, completely exposing every inch of her long legs. He slowly looks up at her and realizes that she is in a trance. James looks back down to her bare upper legs and is amazed at her beauty. She puts her one hand on his shoulder and the other on his head and slowly massages the hair around his ears, as if she approves at the moment.

When James begins to kiss her legs, she really begins to breathe harder. She simultaneously strokes his hair and massages his shoulders. James asks her to lift up, so he can get her dress completely out from under her, and she cooperates without hesitation, which really got his heart pounding, especially with her panties becoming completely exposed. When he was rubbing her back earlier, he could tell that she didn't have a bra on, with the shoulder straps to the dress being so small. This fact is the one thing that is causing hesitation in him. However, he proceeds, and the only reason he does is because he loves her, and she trusts him. Nevertheless, he reaches for the shoulder straps on her dress and begins to lift it in order to take it off. Josie lifts her arms straight up, so he can remove her dress completely, and James sets it to the side, completely exposing her entire beauty except for her light blue panties.

James looks right into her beautiful eyes and turns to reach for the shirt she had folded.

"You are so beautiful, Josie. I mean your body is like the most perfect thing I've ever seen." He is so hot for her right now, and she is at the mercy of his discretion.

"Thank you, James. You're so sweet."

He takes the T-shirt, and he puts it over her head while guiding each hand in one at a time. And then pulls it down over her beautiful breasts. Then he grabs the shorts that she set aside. He places her feet in one at a time and pulls them all the way up to her panties. She looks at him with a grin because she notices the hypnotic nature with which he is expressing regarding her beauty. Finally, she lifts up her butt, so he can pull her shorts all the way on. She proceeds to get dressed while James takes a deep breath, like he doesn't know how much more he can take of these hormonal stop signs.

While Josie's getting dressed, she whispers to James, "That was the hottest and sweetest moment we've had since that first Saturday morning a couple weeks ago."

James returns with, "I'm sorry. It's my own fault." He enjoyed himself, but knows that he's flirting with danger.

"No, James, you were in control," she confesses. "I trust you."

"Do you still want to come over?"

"There's no place I'd rather be than with you, James, so yes."

"Okay, but bring your stuff for tomorrow too, so you can get ready at my place. You can shower as well." At this point school and tennis have taken a backseat to love.

Josie responds with excitement, "Okay, I will." She has this look of contentment on her face, like she has already met her future husband.

"Bring everything," James says with a smile. "Stay the weekend."

Josie grabs her bag, and they head back to James's apartment. When they get there, it's already midnight, so they instantly get ready for bed.

CHAPTER 10

When they return to James apartment, he lights a couple of candles while she relaxes on the couch. Then he goes to his bedroom to change and get something from the closet. When he returns to her sitting down, he puts something behind the couch that will be within reach for him while sitting.

James sits close. Josie is sitting on the couch Indian style, and he leans back, holding her hand. They are both just taking in the late night in the candlelit room—one candle lit in the bathroom as well as one on the television set. The TV is off. Instead, the CD player is on, playing "Mr. Bojangles" by Neil Diamond. James has a wide-ranging taste in music. Nevertheless, they both just meditate on the ambience of the room while looking deep into each other's eyes, reminiscing about presently being in the midst of their best night ever together. After a while passes, Josie says in a soft whisper, "Can I say something?"

James returns with, "Sure, what's up?"

"Don't think I'm weird, I just want to get something off my chest, and I don't want you to say anything. I just want you to hear me out, James. I'm at the point now, where the fear of saying or doing too much is no longer going to dictate whether I say what's on my mind or whether I do what is in my heart. For a week or so, I have had this terrible fear of scaring you away, but after spending last weekend without you, I can't take it anymore. I love you, James. I really love you. I didn't want to ruin tonight so that is why I waited until now to tell you. For three years, all I saw ahead of me was graduation and my professional tennis career, but all I can see now is you, and I needed you to know this."

James kisses her lips and says, "I love you too."

She wraps her arms around him, and they hug and hold each other for a while. Josie is silently crying happy tears on his shoulder. After a moment passes and after a few sniffles from Josie's nose, James gets right in her face and rubs her nose with his, and their foreheads just lean against each other's. They stay like that for a while—with him holding her hand up against his chest and "Hello" by Neil Diamond playing in the background. James begins to whisper the words to the song.

"I love this song," Josie says. "There are a million romantic songs in music history, but there's something about this song. I can't quite put my finger on it."

"Me too." There's a special place in James's heart for good music. "Why are you crying?"

Josie answers with, "I'm happy."

James wipes the tears from her face with his lips and begins to kiss her all over her face. She has her hair up in a ponytail, so he's able to kiss her ears as well. James asks her if she wants anything, but she wants to finish what she was saying before. So, she continues, "Maybe I shouldn't."

James says, "Shouldn't what?" He looks into her eyes, wearing a look of slight confusion.

"I don't know," she says with a confused state of indecisiveness. Maybe—"

James reassures her with, "Don't worry, Josie. Everything will be okay."

"How do you know what it's about?" she asks.

"I can take a guess, and tell me if I'm wrong."

Josie returns with, "Okay."

"I was going to wait, but now I can't wait." He puts his finger over his lips as he did earlier, and says, "Bear with me sweetheart."

James reaches behind himself and grabs something and then stands up, not allowing her to see that he has anything in his hand. Josie tried to ask what it is that he is doing, but before she could get out a syllable, he puts his index finger over her lips again, as if to say hush. So she remains sitting Indian style on the couch with her arms in her lap, impatiently waiting for his further instruction. All the while, James is peculiarly standing in front of her. He begins to talk, "Don't say a word until I am done, please."

Josie responds in a bashful whisper, "Okay." She sits up straight with an attentive look of excitement. Wanting to get what she had off her chest, but is willing to indulge James for a moment.

James begins, "When I left Indiana three and a half years ago to come to New York for school, I had no idea what to expect. I was unaware of how it would go, but I was positive of two things. One, that I was going to get the education that I dreamed of, and two, I was coming here to find the woman that is in all of my dreams. Those are the two instructions my grandfather had for me the day he passed away. His words exactly while gasping were, 'Find her!' I've been here for almost four years, and for the very first time, a month ago, I asked God to send someone into my life. He sent you Josie. I know now that you are who I want to spend the rest of my life with. Whatever it is that I don't know about you yet or anything that we haven't experienced together yet, I look forward to enjoying them with you for the very first time. But those things aren't what tells someone whether someone is perfect for them or not. Those are just subtle details. Besides, all those things, I am told, are much sweeter experiencing under exclusive circumstances and not on casual dates. I was going to wait and do this downtown in a couple weeks, but I need to do it now because I can't wait any longer."

James drops to one knee and grabs her hand, and instantly, when he does this, a tear comes streaming down the side of Josie's face. James begins to say, "Josie, we have spent a few weeks together, and I have been wild about you for even longer than that. Even though it is a short time, I think both of us have experienced something that is way bigger than a few weeks. Waiting until tonight is no indication of when I knew you were the one. I knew this three weeks ago when we were walking back from Tom's Restaurant together."

James takes his other hand and places a shiny diamond ring on her ring finger, all the while tears are gushing down both sides of her face. He looks into her eyes and softly says, "Will you marry me, Josie?"

She had been nodding her head up and down as if to say yes even before he could get a word out in that last question. Once she gathers herself enough, she says, "Yes, I will marry you, James."

She hugs him and kisses him all over. She is crying and laughing at the same time, and James half-jokingly says, "So what were you trying to say earlier?"

Josie answers, cracking up, "Never mind. This covers it completely."

While she was answering that question, James was chuckling the entire time as if to say he knew the entire time what it is that she was trying to say. James reveals to her that he too has been afraid of scaring her away for the last couple of weeks, but he just knew that it was the right time. When she came home Monday night from her out-of-town tournament and she asked those peculiar questions about the future and marriage, he had begun to think that she too was ready. Tonight, when she was having a hard time spitting out what she wanted to say, he knew instantly that tonight was the night to propose.

"I'm so happy, James." She needs a towel, before she soaks her t-shirt.

"You think you can live with me?" He asks. "Forever?"

"Yes, my dear. This ring is beautiful. Where'd you get it?"

"My mother gave it to me," he reveals. "The last things she did or said when she was leaving to head back to Indiana was giving me that ring. She said 'Find the one, and don't let her get away.'"

"You didn't let me get away," Josie adds playfully, a huge smile on her face. "It happened the way your mother suggested." He smiles with pride, as he thinks of his mother and grandfather for a brief moment.

"I was going to wait two weeks, but this week really made me want to do it sooner."

"I'm so happy you did it," she says while on cloud nine. The smile on her face keeps getting wider and wider. Her cheeks are going to burst.

"Josie, I also want you to know that this will not affect your career in tennis, nor will a busy tennis career keep me from wanting kids. I can wait a few years for you to establish yourself in pro tennis. The important thing is that we'll be together." At the moment James has never been more proud in his life, than he is sitting there with Josie, while staring at her shiny ring.

Josie is speechless with happiness. James sits next to her on the couch, and she leans against him and gazes at her shiny diamond ring with an irremovable smile on her face. Both are happy that the anxiety is over and that they will be husband and wife. The only thing left to discuss now is when to tie the knot. James asks, "What kind of wedding did you see for yourself?"

"I'm not going to lie. I had a dream of the wedding every girl dreams of, but there's no reason we can't do what we want later."

James responds with concern, "You mean get married later?"

"Oh no, I mean we could have our big reception later, after our lives aren't so busy, and we are both in our careers. I want to marry you tonight and don't want to wait. We'll have a reception and honeymoon in a year or so when we have time. We can get married downtown as soon as you're ready, and we'll invite ten people to dinner to celebrate after." She was singing music to his ears, as if it was his voice in her head. He loved the idea.

James breathes a sigh of relief, as part of the reason he wanted to expedite this process of engagement was due in part by the fact that he wants to make love to her and can't wait any longer. The more and more he falls in deep love with her, the more difficult it becomes to resist his physical attraction to her. And tonight had been the most difficult, with her sitting on the edge of her bed while wearing only her panties. Just the thought of it now causes the purr of a lion inside of him. It has become quite difficult for her as well, as she just wants to move to the next stage in their relationship. She asks, "James, do you have any reason to wait?"

"No, I want to marry you yesterday." For weeks it has been difficult to keep himself from letting go with her, but he didn't want to betray his faith in the Lord. Now he doesn't have to. He and Josie will be married shortly.

Josie reveals, "I do too, James. We'll get moving on it right away." She leans into him, and closes her eyes.

"Okay. We can get married at the courthouse, and next year, we'll do the church and reception." She opens her eyes for a moment to look up into his eyes.

"Sounds great, James."

She stands up and grabs his hand and walks him into the bedroom. They stand in front of each other at the side of the bed, looking passionately into each other's eyes. She lifts her T-shirt up over her own head and removes it completely. She is completely bare everywhere except her shorts. Then she grabs his T-shirt and lifts it up over his head and off, presses her bare body up against his warm chest, and hugs him. She begins to kiss him all over his neck and shoulders while he rubs the small of her back. Now both of them have nothing on but their shorts. She rubs her hands up and down his chest and stomach, while completely exploring his entire body.

This is an intimacy that they haven't shared yet, and it begins to drive Josie absolutely nuts. She pulls him on to the bed, as each of them inch their way to the pillows. And they both just lay next to each other, trading kisses for a while. James is doing his best to show a responsible restraint, but when she reaches around behind him and grabs his butt with both hands and presses him against her, he could tell that she wanted him, and he stops. She asks him if he's okay, and he says yes, and she returns with, "I love you, James."

James remains in a speechless state, and he looks at her eyes. And then he looks down at her beautiful body wearing only her tight shorts and then returns to her baby blue eyes. It's so difficult for him to not be overrun by every single thought of how ripe she is to be plucked. As soon as he realized that it was carnal desire trying to talk him into deflowering her, he stopped. His gaze returns to her lips, and he lies down next to her and says in a faint whisper, "I love you, Josie, but I can't just yet. There isn't anything I want more in the world right now than to make love to you all night, but my wife is going to appropriately wear white on her wedding night."

Josie responds with, "I love you too, James, and I trust your decision." Although she wanted him like she never has before. He showed amazing discipline.

"We have our whole lives to make love to each other, but we only have one chance to get this right."

"You're right, James. I was getting lost in your body, and I was forgetting what is important. I was losing the reality of the will that God has for us, as well as the celebration He has planned for our wedding night."

"I wanted the same as well," he says. "That night is going to be amazing between the three of us." He's referring to God's presence in the bedroom on their wedding night.

James reaches over to grab her T-shirt, and he proceeds to put her shirt back on her. Then he puts his shirt on. She was watching him the entire time, and she presently has a deep admiration come over her for how he has handled things in their relationship. She thinks for one moment of how proud her parents will be for her picking someone like James. They are going to love him instantly when they finally get to meet him.

James rolls her onto her side, pointing her away from him, and he puts his arm around her and pulls her tight to him. She holds his hand in front of her while they cuddle in a spoon position. James is thinking, before he falls asleep, that this beautiful goddess lying in his bed will be his property forever. She is going to be his wife soon, and he will then be able to release every single bit of desire that is harbored within him. Now instead of proposing to her on the sweetest day in two weeks, he'll now be able to marry her and make love to her by then.

They wake at 9:00 on Saturday morning with him on his back and she with her head on his arm and her hand on his chest. A short time passes with both of them just lying still, enjoying getting to wake up next to each other once again.

"I had never been to a Broadway show, but it has always been at the top of my bucket list—ever since I started school here. I can't believe you actually got the tickets to *Annie*. That is like every woman's dream to see that show—and in a Broadway theatre, wow! Thank you so much, James. I had the best night of my life last night."

James responds with, "I enjoyed it too, especially the end of the night."

"Oh my gosh, yes! That was the icing on the cake to say the least."

"Do you have to do anything outside today?" James asks as he realizes rain was pouring down.

"No, everything's inside. It's a great day for a couple to stay in and cook dinner together," she enthusiastically says.

"It's a date," he says. "I'll be back this afternoon for dinner."

They continue to lay there in bed and listen to the sound of the rain hitting the ledge outside. All these two seem to be interested in today is tangling legs and the sound of each other's breathing.

"Was it hard cooking that dinner on Tuesday?" she curiously asks.

"No, because it was fun." It's a passion of his dating way back to the mentoring of his grandfather. The spirit of his grandfather remains alive in much that James does, and cooking is one of them.

"How do you make that red sauce?" she asks. "It was so good."

James explains, "I use crushed tomatoes and a little less tomato paste than most people do and red wine. I cook it with ground veal and bulk Italian sausage. First, I sautéed garlic, mushrooms, and onions in olive oil then I brown the veal in it. I cook the sausage separately while I add the veal and vegetables to the sauce. I don't put the sausage in until later, but I do get it in there for taste. I'll put a couple bay leaves in the sauce when it simmers at the end, and I boil my paste when the sauce is fifteen minutes away. I left out many details, but that is basically it in a nutshell."

Josie says, "Wow, where'd you learn to do that?" She's impressed once again, to realize that she will be living with a saucier chef soon.

"I'm a self-taught chef, my dear."

"What are we cooking today?" she asks. "I want to help this time." She demands that he teach her the art of his kitchen skills.

"I haven't decided yet, Josie. Maybe we can go to the market together for the first time?"

"I'd love that."

"Have you ever had lamb chops?" he asks. "It's one of my specialties." He looks at her and smiles as she has this look of hunger on her face.

She says, "I don't remember ever having lamb chops."

"I haven't cooked that in a while. We'll come up with something tonight."

"Hmmm, you're making me hungry," she reveals.

"Do you like steak, Josie?"

"Yes, I do. My family would always do steaks on a grill after work on Fridays."

"I know what we're having next Friday," James says with a playful tone. "Steaks."

"What?" she asks. James chuckles at her for a moment.

"We'll have steaks that night." He says. "It will remind you of home."

"Oh, you're so sweet, my dear James. You already remind me of home every day."

They both get up, and James goes to the kitchen to make her scrambled eggs and toast. She takes her bag into the bathroom, so she can take a shower. Thirty minutes later, she's dressed and comes to the table to eat. She walks over to kiss him and says, "A girl can get used to this kind of treatment."

"I love you, Josie. I'm going to do this every morning for you." She looks up at the ceiling and thanks the heavens for sending her an angel.

"I can't wait to marry you," she says. "I've already seen enough to know, that I will be the luckiest wife on planet earth someday. You have redefined the book on a woman's expectation. "I love you."

"Me too, Josie." He returns to the skillet to fry up some breakfast.

After breakfast together, James gives Josie a note. Though they are in the electronic communications era, they still find it comforting to trade paper notes back and forth and read them later when they are apart. Nevertheless, they head in their separate directions for the day—him to research and her to tennis. He said he'd be back at the apartment at 3:00 to pick her up for the market, and if she is done before him, she is welcome at his place, which is now hers too. It crosses her mind, as she's walking to the tennis complex, that she will be living there soon, and she better talk to her roommate about it because she won't be living with her anymore. She calls her mother while standing in the rain in front of the tennis complex, and her mother answers.

"Hi, mom!"

"Hello, sweetheart. How is everything?"

"Everything is great! Josie says. "I have something to tell you."

"What is it, dear?"

"I first have to ask you not to think I've gone off my rocker, but it's about James, who I've been telling to you about for the past two weeks." Her mom begins to think that she is going to reveal bad news to her.

"What is it, dear?" her mom asks again.

"I love him, and he loves me."

"That's great, honey, and I'm so happy for you," her mother says. "Is that it?"

"That's not it."

Her mother asks, "What is it?"

"We're getting married." Josie got choked up before she could get the final word out.

"Oh my God, Josie! I'm getting on a plane," her mother says frantically.

"No, no, no, it's not a good time, mom." Hoping her mother doesn't take offense. "I'm just so busy with midterm exams and project deadlines.

"Are you sure he's the one?" her mom asks.

"Mother, I've never been more positive about anything in my life. He is such a gentleman, and he loves me, and he's a virgin too, and we both want to be together."

"I'm so happy for you, Josie."

"Thanks, mom, I have to run, but I'll call you tonight, and we'll talk more about it."

"Don't forget to call me Josie. I want to hear all about it."

"I will, mom. Good-bye." She hangs up and wipes her eyes, as it was emotional telling her mom.

After Josie gets off the phone, she steps into the door and pulls out the note James gave her and begins to read,

Dear Josie,

Oh my….how sweet it is to share a love with God. I was blind as a bat for about twenty-one years of my life and can see so much better with you in my life. I have a greater appreciation than I ever have before about what God meant when he created Adam and Eve in the Garden of Eden. Not only do I believe that our marriage will be blessed because of the love we have for God, but all of the children that grow up under our roof will be as well. Every single day that has passed has been a progressive escalation of the many feelings that I have for you, and they get stronger and stronger every day. Not only do I recognize again and again that God was the orchestration of our finding each other, but I have a greater understanding now of why he did bring us together and why He is the one driving this vessel.

I thank you so much for your part in keeping the lust of the flesh out of our love affair at the beginning. I will spend the rest of our life in the bedroom, making up for that show of discipline to you. We have something that is so special and rare, Josie, that I don't think you and I have even scratched the surface of that which God has entirely in store for us. I look forward to spending the rest of my life with you and growing old together.

Every moment that you came close to me yesterday, my heart started beating faster and faster out of my chest. There is nothing at all in the world, other than the Father filling my heart with His love of course, quite like a woman causing my heart to have that similar kind of reaction. Nobody on this planet knows what it is like to love you like I do—especially you. And I feel like the luckiest person who has ever lived to know this. God didn't just send a beautiful, kind, and passionate woman to fill the emptiness in my heart, He sent me the very best that he had available—he sent me you. For that, not only do I owe it to Him to honor the wishes that He has for us, but I owe Him for the amazing gifts that he has blessed us with along the path of our relationship. He has presented me with the greatest gift He has ever given me in the history of my life, and that is you, my lovely, beautiful, understanding, graceful, intelligent, talented, gentle, adorable, and precious flower.

I owe Him my life, but I really owe Him my very best effort for what He has presented me with, in you.

All of my love,
James Ryan Roberts

James returns at home right about 3:00 p.m. and Josie was sitting on the couch, talking to her mother. She immediately tells her mom that she'd talk to her on Sunday, gets off the phone, runs to her man, and hugs him.

"How was your day, James?"

"My brain is fried," he says. "I read too much." He feels like a vegetable, and needs to sit still.

"We can hang. There's no rush. I grabbed lunch at 11:00 a.m. anyway. Why don't you make something small, and you can take a nap, and we'll go later."

"Nope, I'll shower and change, and I'll be good as new, once I sit still for a few moments," James says confidently. "I'll be good as new."

Josie with a burst of happiness says, "Okay, sweetie." She couldn't wait for him to get home.

James and Josie spend the rest of the day shopping at the market and cooking their very first dinner together. Over the next week or so, they go through the necessary hoops to acquire the appropriate documents in order to get married. Later next year, when they have the time to do it in a church, they will. James was able to get a spiritual leader that he had met in the Apostolos Campus Ministry when he was a freshman, and he is going to informally consecrate them together in the university chapel the day of their marriage. James really wanted to do this in his church because of his faith in Christ, but he is also aware, through his and Josie's obedience, that they will be fine with this process going forward. In James's opinion—no offense to the ecclesiastical establishment in the world—Christ is in their hearts. And no matter how they do this, Christ will be with them both, and they will be one through the blessing of their heavenly Father.

Josie and James both tried their hardest to keep everyone from coming. They assured them that they would have a ceremony sometime after her graduation. For now, they just wanted something inconspicuous and fast, with two witnesses. However, that idea would be short-lived; her mother insisted on coming, and James's mother, Charlotte, felt the same. They wanted to see their babies get married. They did, however, get one commitment from their parents. They made them promise that they would go home immediately after they are married because they are going away for a couple of days after the ceremony. However, their parents did get to come a couple of days earlier, so James was able to get to know Josie's parents. As well, Charlotte was able to get to know how sweet Josie is. Once both parents spent a couple of days with them, they came to a clear understand as of why this thing materialized so quickly.

It wasn't a problem for James and Josie having to sleep in their own beds those last couple of nights because they had decided for her not to sleep over anymore after that last night. They both thought it would be more appropriate that they not do that again until their wedding night simply because the devil would be pulling out all the stops, if you will, the closer and closer they got to that night. Nevertheless, all prewedding festivities are over, and Josie dominated in another tennis tournament—this time having an article written about her in the New York Times athletic section. James was all up-to-date on his studies and prepared to be gone for a couple of days. Josie's family arrived in the morning, which was two days before the wedding, and they are staying at a hotel on the other side of town. Her parents are going to visit friends in Rochester that they haven't seen in years, so they didn't mind being on the outskirts of the city. Charlotte arrived a few hours later and was staying close enough to walk back and forth to Morningside Heights. James and his mom would have a couple of opportunities between a mother and son, when they went to breakfast both mornings, and on the day of Josie's tournament, they were able to have lunch together as well.

After spending much time with James, her parents fell in love with him instantly and were very impressed with him in fact. And as Josie tells her mom almost everything, they didn't verbalize it but were very pleased that she is still a virgin. As a young man, you couldn't accomplish anything more admirable to impress your fiancée's parents, than to preserve the sacred innocence of their daughter. Furthermore, they believed in their daughter but were quite curious on the way to New York about what could have possibly had her go and grow up so fast since the last time they saw her. Needless to say, they already loved their son-in-law as if he was one of their own. Her father, especially, was quite taken by his faith, and they really had a lot to talk about. Her father had given her a check earlier in a wedding gift envelope that she hasn't mentioned to James yet, because she doesn't want to bum him out. She knows he would want to give it back, so she is taking it as part of what she contributes to their combined newlywed finances. It wasn't so much the check that she thought James wouldn't want, but it was the amount. Because her father gave her a check for $20,000—it had been saved up for her future wedding—and since that isn't happening until much later, he thought she and James should have it now.

Nevertheless, moments before they enter the courthouse on this early afternoon on Friday, October 14, 2005, James and his mother exchange their hugs and kisses because he won't see her again once he leaves the building, as she has a flight at 5:00 p.m. that day. Josie and her parents do the same, as they'll be leaving for Rochester after the wedding. Emotions are running at a peak, and nobody has even entered the courthouse yet.

Without further ado, they enter. It is a very small wedding, which is the way they wanted it. Josie's friend, Allie, and James's friend from church, John, stand in as their witnesses. Off to the side are Charlotte and Josie's mother and father. James is wearing a black suit, and Josie is all done up in a white dress that was handed down from her mother. It's no knock on anyone in today's society, but it's difficult not to be proud of her, as she is truly wearing white appropriately. You can just hear the angels dancing and singing in heaven with her standing up there.

Everyone is in their place, and the ceremony begins. James and Josie have these looks on their face like they're experiencing the best day of their lives—one that was in every dream each of them had ever had in their lives. Now they get to live it, and fittingly so, for two children of God who are trying to do some good in this world. The ceremony concludes, and Josie has become Josie Roberts all in just a few moments. She looks as if she is the happiest person in the world.

There wasn't a woman present with a dry eye the moment James and Josie turn to greet those that came. They spend a few moments thanking everyone for coming, and James has a special emotional moment with his mother. After they separate, James and Josie Roberts head out to the front of the courthouse for a couple of pictures, but they can't wait to get into the limousine that is waiting for them. After Josie looks at their driver, she turns and looks at James and has a goofy moment where she is hinting at wanting to get into that darn car already and go to the hotel. They had decided against a dinner after the service, and they indicated to everyone that they wanted to start their honeymoon immediately after leaving the courthouse. Only James and she can truly appreciate what that's all about. They just planned on being alone in the hotel room all afternoon and evening and decided to have a late night breakfast for room service. Who can blame them after the restraint they showed these last few weeks?

They get into the limo and wave to all as they drive away. James indicates to the driver that they are headed for the Shoreham Hotel, as they have a suite booked for the weekend. After heading down the road, Josie and James make out in the back of the limo, and she puts her head against his and says, "Let's crack open that champagne, my dear."

"You got it my love," he says.

Josie says with a playful impatience, "I can't wait to get to the room." She is as eager as James has ever witnessed her.

James, chuckling, returns with, "I've been waiting a month for this. "Tell me about it. Who has time for dinner at a moment like this?"

Before the wedding ceremony, James had already received the key for the room, and he also dropped their suitcases off there as well. So they have absolutely nothing at all to do until they check out on Monday. They both enter the hotel and head straight for the elevator, and they hold hands the entire way up. When they get to the room, James opens the door and turns around and picks Josie up and carries her into the room. He kicks the door shut behind him, and sets her down. They stand there for a moment, kissing. Then James asks if she wants a drink, and she says in a little while. James picks her up again and takes her to bed.

The lights are dimmed perfectly for the occasion, and James lights a couple of candles by the bed. Then they begin to undress each other—one article of clothing at a time. Josie looks at James and says, "I love you, James."

"I love you too, my angel."

The remainder of this night is between them and God. There were angels in Heaven dancing and singing in that hotel suite on this evening. The spiritual discipline they showed in saving themselves for this night was being celebrated and rewarded by many. It was a discipline that many people today don't find important enough to fit into their premarital agenda. Everyone wants to be husband and wife years before the marriage; and we as people wonder why our divorce rate is so high, why domestic violence is so prevalent, and why children have all kinds of disorders and learning disabilities. Lives that are free from these bad things are blessed for a reason, they submit to the authority of God's law, and in return, they receive his fruits.

Josie Weathers and James Ryan Roberts, all in the blink of an eye, have become Mr. and Mrs. James Ryan Roberts. They have become one, and individually, will contribute to a platform that will one day materialize into a stage of prominence for conservative politics for years to come. They each will contribute strengths to the cause, and together, along with the connections James has in Washington, they will expedite a political career that will allow James to be one of the youngest success stories in the history of politics. Moreover, it will give Washington something that it has been missing since early in the twentieth century—a young and conservative Teddy Roosevelt–like Republican.

CHAPTER 11

A s Lisa and Ben's senior year at Crenshaw came to a close in the spring of 2006, nothing substantial materialized for Ben in terms of a local university. However, Lisa would commute to Indiana University for her freshman year, and after Ben aced a year at the local junior college, he was accepted to Indiana for Lisa's sophomore year. They were finally together in college, and Indiana University is one of the finest music schools in America. As well, it has one of the best political science programs in the country. Ben finished strong at Crenshaw but spent a lot of time improving his academic aptitude outside of school, which in the long run, benefited him greatly. Had he spent all of his time on schoolwork, he might not have been able to pull off a junior college freshman year like he did. Not to mention the fact that he took difficult classes in junior college, due in large part to how much he read on his own, which also enhanced his Indiana University application.

Back in New York, Secretary Joe Purcell of Homeland Security had an interview set up with James at the United Nations Headquarters Building. This interview wasn't exactly pertaining to the State Department, Homeland Security, or the United Nations. Secretary Purcell's old roommate from Harvard was in the Central Intelligence Agency (CIA), and he was a deputy director of a department specializing in international intelligence in the Middle East and Northern Africa. This office has been keeping a file on James for quite some time—ever since the secretary pushed to get him in. Their interest wasn't just because of his performance with the curriculum at Columbia but more so because of his choice in curriculum as well.

James used all of his electives in his undergraduate studies on Arabic language courses as well as Persian (Farsi) language classes—Persian being the predominant language of Iran. James had studied Arabic in high school and always planned on Middle East studies once he arrived in college. However, Crenshaw High School in Macomb didn't offer those languages, so James taught himself, and every chance he got to speak to an Arabic person, he did so. His grandfather had told him not too long before he died that Iran was going to develop into a problem for the United States someday and studying Arabic and Persian would go a long way in helping James succeed in a world that is growing increasingly Muslim in terms of international conflict.

Even though James wasn't exactly sure what his plan was going to be upon the completion of his PhD in a couple of years, he went to the interview anyways just to see where he was at and also to honor the help he was receiving from Secretary Purcell. James was expecting to take an elevator up to a specific floor and head to a specific office at the United Nations Headquarters, but little did James know, that he'd be escorted to the basement of the building to meet up with his interviewer. That was quite an unusual turn of events as it was unfolding, but James went along, even though it was peculiarly secretive. The weirdest moment during the events was when the elevator reached the basement floor; the door opened, and the person escorting James said, "Good day, sir," as if James could handle it from here.

James takes two steps out of the elevator, only to notice how dark the basement was, and a couple of seconds later, he could see and hear a man lighting a cigar from about fifty feet away. So he walks over to him and introduces himself, "Good day, sir. I'm James Roberts."

"Nice to meet you, James. I'm Steve Lampley of the CIA."

"Nice to meet you, Steve."

"My pleasure. I went to college with Joe Purcell," Lampley says. "He assured me you were a patriotic American." This interview for a brief moment was quite eerie. It seemed as if Steve was being awfully quiet, even though the two of them were alone in that basement.

"That I am, sir."

"Well, I head up a department at Langley that specializes in intelligence in the Middle East and Northern Africa. As you know, these regions are increasingly troublesome in international affairs, and we are looking to fill up our department with America's best. Does that sound like something you'd be interested in?"

"Absolutely sir, as you know, my interest lies in Arabic and Persian studies. I chose them for the same reasons you are illustrating

"From what I know about you, James, and what I've seen so far, you seem like a guy I can count on as my right hand someday—someone the secretary and I can trust."

"I am, sir. And serving my country honorably is at the top of my list of priorities. I have a couple years left here at Columbia, but other than that, I would love to gain the experience through intelligence." James is beginning to wonder if this interview is regarding a job right now, or if this is something they are thinking of after school is over in two years.

"Your file says you're well-trained in self-defense?" Lampley asks. "Good, because not all of our work takes place in an office."

"I studied aikido karate with my grandfather for about ten years."

"Good. We'll want to put you through extensive training, and you haven't had any military training, so you'd be okay with this?"

Curious over the training Steve mentioned, James ponders what it might be like.

"I'm fine with that, sir," James answers. "I do a lot of running, so at least I have a lot of wind.

"It was great to meet you, James, and you and I will be in touch in due time." Lampley begins to walk away as he shakes James's hand.

"Thank you, sir," James says with enthusiasm. "I look forward to it." He shakes Steve's hand, and nods to him.

"Good-bye, James."

"Have a good one."

James had a double take for a moment as Lampley disappears into the elevator. For the moment, he is just in awe of what just transpired between him and Secretary Joe Purcell's roommate from Harvard. He always pictured his first interview being in an office and getting an insignificant job that started out small, maybe a administrative position in an office full of people— so many people that nobody would possibly miss him had he disappeared into oblivion. However, this was something entirely different from what he imagined. To be honest, the conversations Jack and Ben had the day before school in 2005 about Washington waiting for James to graduate were a little more along the lines of what had happened here. James was a little more modest in his anticipation of what to expect, so it all makes sense for him to be surprised with this type of interview.

James finally makes it into the elevator and heads back up to ground level. He's jokingly thinking on his way up that the basement he was just standing in was probably sniffed out by dogs looking for counterintelligence surveillance or leaks in security. When he gets back outside to the beautiful late spring weather, he realizes how nice it will be that he had a job interview and how nice that will feel this evening around Josie, who is already beginning to look like this family's breadwinner, especially with all the money tournaments she has lined up in the early stages of her young pro tennis career. James will have to get used to this mighty quick because that looks as if that will be the situation for a couple of years—her establishing her career and him finishing his PhD at Columbia University. He wants to work, but it has to be conducive to his research for it to work. The last thing James wants to do this late in the ball game is to make a decision that will prolong his schooling. He has dreamed about this for too long and wants to finish it as soon as possible. Furthermore, with the money that Josie is about to bring home from tennis, he will have no worries soon with finding time for work.

On Valentine's Day of 2006, James and Josie returned to Broadway for a show and then went to dinner on the Hudson River. Their table was right next to a wall of glass, and they could look out and have a beautiful view of the river. James got her a card, and instead of giving it to her earlier, he decided to wait until after the show so she could relax and read it while waiting for dinner.

> The rare love that you and I share,
> can't be outdone by words nor compare.
> After seasons upon seasons of storms;
> of being lost at sea and alone,
> my vessel has found its port
> and can say that it's finally home.
> Having you on this day, as entirely mine,
> has truly been nothing short of divine.
> Thank you, Josie, for being you
> and for being my valentine.

> Love,
> James.

Josie's senior season came to a close, and she not only won collegiate player of the year in woman's tennis, but she was also the captain of the Ivy League Champion Columbia Lions. She also graduated with a degree in sociology. James was so proud of her that he threw her a surprise celebration at Amsterdam's and invited the woman's tennis team, as well as all the friends they have accumulated over the years. It was more than just a celebration for many because with her professional tennis career beginning, Josie was quickly going to be very busy going out of town from one weekend to the next. It was a concept James couldn't get off of his mind. He was dreading the fact already that she was going to be away for two weeks at a time. However, this is what they talked about, and both of them will have to be strong and trust each other's love, because it will have to carry them through in this challenging time.

Just a short week following the surprise party at Amsterdam's, Josie began her pro career at the Hastings Direct Championships in England. This tournament, unfortunately, was on grass, which Josie purposely scheduled because she wanted an early crash course on the surface. If she was going to be able to succeed in tennis, she needed experience playing on grass. Otherwise, she would never be able to remain consistent enough to maintain a high ranking, and if anyone knows tennis, they know that playing low-ranked players to start a tournament is an advantage. Players that are ranked around no. 50 might get an early freebie versus a low-ranking player, but they go right into the winner's bracket which usually means top fifty players. So it is a major advantage to be ranked high.

Josie didn't light the world on fire in England, but if you consider she has never played a tournament on grass, she did pretty well, getting knocked out in the quarter finals. She brought home very little money, but the overseas grass experience was what she was looking for.

A little over a week later, she won her first tournament at the Western & Southern Financial Group Masters and Women's Open in Cincinnati, Ohio. It was only a $28,000 tournament, but a win is a win—not to mention, it will pay the rent someday. It was a return back to a hard surface. And since James drove to the event, the good luck charm she had in the stands gave her much needed strength. The two of them had a chance to drive back to New York together and stay the night at a hotel halfway through the trip. Josie was able to stay in Morningside Heights for just a couple of days then it was off to San Diego for the largest money tournament of her young career. Also, because it was a $196,000 event, all the best players in the world would be there. This was the first big test for her in terms of preparation for a grand-slam event like the US Open. The Acura Classic in San Diego would make Josie more money as a semifinalist than she made winning the Cincinnati tournament. Losing in the semis of a big tournament was no small feat. In fact, you could make the case that it was the best finish yet because that finish caused her ranking to climb more than anything she had done to date.

A week later, at the Rogers Cup in Montreal, James had another opportunity to meet up with her at the tournament. The two of them had the chance to go out on the town before he had to rush back to New York for research. She lost in the semifinals again, but like San Diego, it was another big-money tournament, and some of the high-ranking girls are starting to get the idea that this Josie Weathers-Roberts is for real. When she would return to New York for the US Open in Flushing, she and James would be living financially comfortable for the first time as adults, and that was a relaxing thought, considering all the penny-pinching they did to get their education. James will be able to fly to her tournaments now, and she will be able to fly home more often in between events. Her early success on the tour has made their life comfortable a lot earlier than they had envisioned. But the events that will unfold over the next couple of weeks at the US Open will change their lives more than anything since they were married.

The US Open in Flushing, New York, was so close to home in Morningside Heights that James was able to spend the entire tournament at the complex. The big-money tournaments she has recently played in were only about $200,000 events. The US Open is a $1.7 million tournament, and one of the four grand-slam events in woman's tennis, along with the French Open, the Australian Open, and the big one—Wimbledon. Anyway, this was a big one also, and Josie ends up finishing in second place to the no. 1 player in the world. Not only has this put her on the map nationally, but it will put her on the cover of every sports magazine in the country. The climb she has made in such a short period of time from being ranked in obscurity, has been one of the most monumental feats in the history of women's tennis. This second place finish in Flushing placed about $900,000 in her and James's bank account, so the days of managing a budget have come to an end in terms of a priority in this family.

James and Josie both could have never imagined this would turn out like this so quickly, but it has, and Josie is absolutely exhausted. Consequently, she decided to skip the next tournament in two weeks and take a month off and enjoy her and James's wedding reception and honeymoon in Hawaii. They were going to do something simple like Niagara Falls for a honeymoon, but in lieu of the financial events that have unfolded this summer, they changed their plans to Hawaii. When they finally arrive back at the apartment in Morningside Heights that Saturday night, all they did for about two hours is just silently lay in each other's arms. Neither one of them could hardly find the desire to muster anything else. Eventually, they would get up and cook dinner together and watch movies all night.

James and Josie, rather than have their wedding reception in New York or back home, decided to do it in a city that was convenient for everyone. So they found a city that worked for those that live in Macomb, Indiana, and Virginia Beach. That city was Columbus, Ohio. This way, nobody has to drive halfway across the country. To make traveling easy for their closest friends on campus, they rent a van that leaves the night before the reception. So they can get their friends there cheaply, and their friends can drive the van back to New York and turn it in while the newlyweds head for Hawaii.

The reception was beautiful, and James had a close pastor friend offer up an opportunity for them to renew their wedding vows at the beginning of the night. It was the first time in a while that James had a chance to see Ben and Lisa. Also, seeing Mr. Johnson from the old theater in downtown Macomb was quite a treat for him as well. Mr. Johnson had been able to grab a ride with Charlotte and Jack. It wasn't a huge wedding, but all the important people to both the bride and the groom attended the event, and it turned out to be a blessed night. Ben and James had many opportunities to reminisce about old times and ponder the future for both of them. With Ben being a few years behind in school, it will take some time to catch up and get into the workforce. However, one day, their time will come in politics, and they'll both be ready for it. Later in the evening, they have one last cigar outside the hall before the reception comes to a close.

"When are you planning on getting into politics, James?"

"Oh, not for years, and it could wind up being ten or fifteen years depending on how things go," James says. "It will be a while."

"Oh, that's good. That gives me some time to get my act together and get where I need to be."

"Sure, this thing is going to take time. I may even go on a mission after I get my PhD. I've always wanted to do that and don't want to do it during my career," James reveals. "If I wait, and do it later, it will never happen.

"Yeah, it would be great to do that before the chips start to fall in your career. Once you get that head of steam going downhill, it would be tough to disappear for two years without dismantling all that you accomplish early in politics," Ben says.

"When did you go and get so articulate?" James asks with a chuckle. "You sound different."

"Oh, I wouldn't say that, James." Ben is becoming bashful with regard to the due compliments that James is throwing his way.

"Everyone denies the improvement they have made because they don't realize the change that has come up within them. They still see themselves as who they were. But you have made a miraculous change, Ben."

"I feel better about myself," Ben reveals. "I have so much more to write about."

"You should. How many books did you read from the loft?"

"Like a hundred."

"Wow! That's amazing. I told you it would turn on lights in your head," James said with confidence.

"You did say that. I used to have a lot of trouble writing papers for school. Now it's really easy," Ben reveals.

"That's because you have words bouncing around in that imagination of yours," James says. "Writing is magic." Ben is sporting this aura of confidence that he never had before.

"You have said that before many times, and I didn't know exactly what you meant, but lately, I have been thinking about those exact words. It has been quite a ride having all of this stuff to write about outside of school," Ben reveals.

"You should write a book, Ben. People would love to read about your story."

"It has crossed my mind before because sometimes, I get to writing, and I just can't stop," Ben says. "The pen just takes off and never slows down."

"Well, it's been a pleasure seeing you tonight, Ben."

"You too, James. Have fun in Hawaii with Josie. She's such a sweetheart. You did yourself some good picking her." James looks over at Josie from across the room. She was talking to Charlotte, but periodically kept glancing at James while he was talking to Ben. They make eye contact, she blows a kiss, and he lips syncs, "I love you."

"Thank you, Ben. You go off to school and get your degree, and do the very best you can. We'll be together again soon, I promise." This brought a smile to Ben. He never got too out of hand with the dreaming of being in politics, but since speaking to James on this night, his ambition is going to the next level.

James and Ben hug each other for a moment, as Josie can see from over where she is sitting with her parents and Charlotte. She can tell that Ben is a big part of James's life, and she had that feeling from the beginning of the night. As Ben and James separate, they say their good-byes and walk away. Josie and James greet everyone at the door as each guest exits the hall. The DJ was the last to leave, so he still had a slow dance playing. Josie and James have this last dance before they leave for the night, and James says to her, "So much has happened to us in one year. What a ride!"

"You could say that again, James."

"I dreamed of a woman like you, Josie, but I had no idea I deserved someone as special as you. You have truly been an angel." James kisses her.

"That's sweet, and I still pinch myself in the morning, waking up next to you, wondering if I'm dreaming as well," Josie says. "I wondered if this was all in my imagination." Fortunately for both of them, she isn't dreaming, nor is she imagining their life together.

"Well, let's head out, my darling," James says. "We have a big day tomorrow."

"I can't believe I'm going to Hawaii with you," Josie says with laughter. I'm going to lay on the beach all day and drink margaritas.

"I know. Isn't it awesome?" James asks. "It's been a paradise only in my imagination, now I'm getting to go there."

"Absolutely!" Josie adds. "I want hot sand, and cool sheets, in an air conditioning room." Apparently, Josie has being alone with James in the room on her mind.

They leave the hall and head for the hotel, as they have a flight for Hawaii in the morning. They didn't want to be flying after a party, so they will get to have a second wedding night at the hotel a year after the first one. When they arrive at the hotel room, just like a year before, James lifts Josie into his arms and takes her into the room. He places her on the edge of the bed and says not to move. He lights a couple of candles and pours two glasses of champagne before returning to her in bed. He sits next to her on the edge of the bed and hands her a glass. They both take a sip, and James puts the two glasses on the nightstand. He begins to slowly undress her, one article of clothing at a time. After she has been completely separated from all articles of clothing, she begins to take off his shirt, one button at a time. The rest of the details of the evening will have to unfold by the individual imagination that is imagining it. For James and Josie, the passion and romance doesn't seem to have faded one bit. In fact, it has gone to another level entirely.

When they return from Hawaii, it is fitting that James has to immediately get back to his research because Josie has to get ready to depart for Stuttgart, Germany, for the Porsche Tennis Grand Prix. For the next six weeks, Josie is busy with finishing the season strong. There is a natural off-season in tennis that takes place during the holidays from Thanksgiving until New Year's. That will give James and Josie an opportunity to catch up on time apart. But not before Josie wins two small tournaments, as well as finishing in the quarterfinals of another. Her ranking to finish her first season is going to be respectable, and she will start the 2007 season, after the New Year, as a household name in women's tennis. It's not every year that a young superstar comes along this quickly. It only happens maybe once every twenty years.

Because Josie and James wound up staying close to home for their first holidays together last season, they take a trip to Virginia Beach to spend Thanksgiving weekend with her folks. They would spend Christmas in Macomb, Indiana, and James would have an opportunity, for the first time, to take her around Macomb and show her off. They lucked out with the weather being mild that deep into December because he wanted to take Josie down to the stream that runs through the back of the Wilson property, and it is much better experiencing that in not-so-bad weather. After she saw that for the first time, she wanted to buy a house on the other side of the stream. It didn't take her long to fall in love with that ambience.

They went back to Manhattan for New Year's. James heads back to researching full-time, and Josie gets ready for the start of her first full season (2007) on the women's tour. This year, she'll be attending all four grand slams, as last season she was only able to play in one of them (US Open). The Australian Open was going to be real early in this 2007 season, with it being played in mid-January. Meanwhile, Josie did well at her first ever appearance down under at the Australian Open. She finished with a heartbreakingly close loss to the third-ranked player in the world at the semifinals in mid-January. In the time that passed between the end of January and the French Open in May, she won two smaller tournaments in the United States, as well as finishing high in a couple of other events. Moreover, when she approached the French Open in early summer 2007, she was ranked number eleven in the world, which was unheard of if you consider where she was ranked one year ago after graduation.

The French Open was on a clay surface, which Josie wasn't all that experienced with in tournament play, but she played a lot of tennis on clay in her life, so it didn't take her long to get the feel back. Once again, the big lights always seem to raise Josie's game to another level, which is the mark of a ferocious competitor. She finished with a loss in the quarter finals, but for the first tournament on clay, she held her own, and many of her peers, who knew she never competed on clay, were stunned at the high finish. Even when Josie loses, she somehow gains the respect of her fellow tennis pros.

There wasn't much time in between the French Open and Wimbledon, so Josie returned to Morningside Heights for a little over a week before she had to get to England. To make the long story short, Wimbledon 2007 would be a lifetime of experiences for more reasons than one. Furthermore, she miraculously—considering all her inexperience on grass—made it all the way to the finals on Saturday night. Unfortunately, she lost in a close match with the no. 1 seed in the tournament, but this performance really put Josie Weathers-Roberts on the international stage as the greatest young player to come along in tennis since Steffi Graf. Those were some pretty high praises from international tennis analysts, especially with all the great young players the history of tennis has produced. To compare her to the best ever, was downright amazing for this point in her career, and she'd only been on the tour for a single year. As great of an experience as this was, it had to compete with something else that came up that weekend—something that would challenge for the most memorable of moments in her and James's young marriage.

After a couple of days of post-Wimbledon press conferences, interviews, and photo shoots, Josie was able to return to New York and be greeted by James at the airport. This time, she had paparazzi to deal with, as she has become America's darling daughter overnight. After they got into the car and were able to get a few miles down the road, Josie asked James to find a park or a nice place to stop and take a breather. Ironically, they were just about to pass a college with outdoor tennis courts, so James immediately turns onto the exit. They both get out of the car and walk over to a picnic table near the tennis courts, and they hug. Josie pulls a few inches away from him and says, "This would not have been how I drew it up in my memory in terms of places to tell you this, but I had to tell you as soon as I saw you. The paparazzi distracted me from that plan."

"What is it, Josie?" James asks with a slight concern. "Tell me, sweetheart."

"It's nothing to worry about, darling. I'm going to tell you some good news."

"I know. I watched the entire tournament on television. You were amazing. We already talked about this on the phone. What is it?" James asks again.

Josie says, "James, I'm pregnant with your baby." James instantly went into a trance. "Are you okay, honey?"

James couldn't say anything. Before she got a word out after the word *pregnant*, he dropped to his knees and tears poured out of his eyes. She drops to her knees and hugs him and says, "Oh, darling James, isn't this so amazing?"

Nodding his head up and down, he chokes out, "Yes, hopelessly amazing." It's an emotional moment.

"Are you okay, James?"

"Yes. I'm just overwhelmed by God's continuous blessing on us. He is really pouring it on," James reveals. "My cup runs over."

"I know. It's so great. Let's pray," Josie suggests.

They both hold each other's hands while kneeling in front of each other. This time, Josie is the one to lead in prayer, considering how shook up James is.

"Dear heavenly Father, thank you for
all the blessings you have
poured out on James and me since we met.
Thank you for the
blessing of a baby within my womb. Protect our child
while it grows inside of me. Bless this child to be
everything that it can be,
and guide him or her to stay firm on the path to serve
you in your Will. Thank you so much for sending your

son into the world and dying for our sins, so that we can
speak directly to you and have a relationship
with you. Bless James and I to make the
best decisions possible
so that we may grow closer to you in our
quest as servants of your
will for us. I pray all these things in the name of
our Lord and Savior, Jesus Christ. Amen.

"That was nice, Josie. Thank you," James says. "I needed that."

James and Josie get back into the car and head home for a weekend of gentle and silent bliss. She is absolutely exhausted with tennis, paparazzi, media—you name it. She wants to enter that apartment and shut the door and order delivery food for a week.

After taking just a little over a year for her ranking to climb all the way to number seven in the world, it was evident that time off was coming. However, Josie wanted to condense that time off to as little as possible—that way, her ranking won't fade while she is pregnant. She would already get two months of off time during the winter break, so she'd played a small tournament in mid-July and played one more tournament in late September. She took time off during the rest of the season from October until the end of November, and at the start of the season in January, she had to skip the Australian open and a few tournaments in leading up to late March.

James and Josie had a baby boy on March 7, 2008. They named him Michael after James's late war hero grandfather. They enjoyed being parents for the remainder of March, but Josie returned to her tennis career at a small tournament on March 29, and surprisingly, after all the time off in October and November, managed to remain highly ranked at number seventeen. She would have enough small tournaments in April and early May to get ready for the French Open in mid-May. By the time the French Open did approach and with Josie being busy again with tennis, James was the one that was losing all the sleep late at night with the Mr. Mom duties. Josie's mother came to New York and stayed with James at their new condo in Manhattan and gave James some much-needed relief to finish his PhD thesis. However, as soon as she went back to Virginia Beach, it was back to the graveyard-shift daddy duty for James.

Josie returned home with her first ever grand-slam title at the French Open, and showed the world that she not only was going to be compared to a young Steffi Graf, she was also showing the court surface versatility that Graf also showed early in her career. Being able to play on grass, clay, and hard surfaces is very difficult for any player. Anyway, Josie was able to return home to New York, and she decided to give James a break and skip the tournaments leading up to Wimbledon, giving her a couple of weeks to be Michael's mom.

As Wimbledon week of 2008 approached, the memories of a second-place finish in 2007 started taking up much of Josie's attention span. It was six days before she had to get on a plane and head for England. As the week went along, it became increasingly more and more difficult for James to conceal the secret surprise he had planned for Josie. While she was preparing for Wimbledon that week, all she could think of is that runner-up finish the year before. She wanted to win this year's Wimbledon so bad she could taste it. If James had been revealing any signals at all that he was planning a surprise, she didn't pick up on it with how anxious she was about Wimbledon. It wasn't just the fact that she lost in the finals last year, but it was also the many highly ranked players she had to beat along the way to get to that final, all the while doing so from such a low ranking.

James had been planning this surprise of showing up at Wimbledon with her son, Michael, for some time. The plan was to show up while she's warming up for her first match, and his thought is that, hopefully, it will give her a burst of adrenaline along with a calming effect as well. He has always had a calming effect on her, so that is something the surprise is sure to produce. The fact that they make such a great team, then and now, sparks memories with James about his grandfather's explanation of the importance of finding such a great spouse. As the years pass with him gone, his grandfather's great wisdom never seizes to unravel.

James and Michael show up early in the day while Josie is warming up. They had a little help on the inside that made it possible for them to arrive late and still get so close to the action. He showed up with Michael hanging in front of him on a front baby carrier. They entered the venue, and as soon as Josie sees them, she started crying. She sprinted to the crowd and leaped into the stands. Josie's security was the least of her worries when she saw her hubby carrying her little man. It was an emotional moment for her, as she was missing them terribly. She has a look of pride on her face, as if her two men have arrived. However, she does have to return to the court to prepare for her first match of the tournament. James is catching a little admiration from the surrounding spectators for his rendition of Mr. Mom. He takes it all in and gets a kick out of it. Josie is back on the court and turns around and makes eye contact with James one more time. She blows him a kiss.

After what seemed like weeks, James and Michael watch Josie win the 2008 Wimbledon Woman's Title. She now had two grand slams under her belt, and she was beginning to approach a number 1 ranking going into the US Open in June 2008. It is two years removed from the end of her senior season at Columbia, and she has already established herself as the best young player in the world of tennis. James is extremely proud of her accomplishments on the women's tour. She has already brought their marriage not only national exposure but international exposure as well. She's been on the cover of every sports magazine in the world and every nonmedia publication in America. She never had an interview with anyone without illustrating how much James means to her success, so she is already getting his name out there. Both of them have become America's darling young couple.

James arrived with his son, Michael, back at the hotel at Wimbledon a few hours after Josie had won the championship. She would be a couple of hours behind them, as she had a post-Wimbledon press conference as well as an interview with Mary Joe Fernandez, a woman's tennis analyst. James was able to put Michael down in the travel bed for a nap just before Josie arrived at the hotel. He and Josie didn't whisper any special plans to each other after her win. They just planned on being a family and ordering room service for the remainder of the evening at Wimbledon. Josie arrives and knocks on the door of the suite, and James answers. He picks her up and carries her to the couch as if they were just married.

James is lying next to her, staring deeply into her baby blue eyes. At that moment, both of them feel like it's the first time they have been together in forever. They feel like teenagers again. He slowly puts his lips to hers and gives her a long slow kiss. He moves closer to her, and she wraps her legs around him like a snake preparing to squeeze her prey. After about an hour of romantic entanglement, they close their eyes and fall asleep.

After a while, they open their eyes at the same time Michael wakes from his nap. Josie gets up and goes to the bedroom to hold her boy. She picks him up and sits down in the chair next to the nightstand and feeds him a bottle. For a mother that has been gone for a couple of weeks, she is catching up with her baby boy. She just simply sits there with him for a while and just enjoys being together with her little guy. She hasn't been together much with him this week, and with Wimbledon on her mind the whole time, this was a nice visit to say the least. When Josie and James wake with Michael the next morning at Wimbledon, they feel truly like a family for the first time in weeks. They get on a plane and head home to the condo in New York.

After arriving back at the condo, James went back out to the drugstore to grab some necessities that they didn't think to grab on the way home. When Josie and Michael got into the condo, there was an envelope with her name on it leaning against the fruit bowl on the kitchen table. She opens it and reads what looks like her husband's writing, and it dawns on her that he must have written this before he and Michael left for Wimbledon.

Dear Josie,   July 4, 2008

I decided that since you were not here in New York to celebrate the 4th of July with Michael and me, that we would draw you into our celebration through this correspondence. We are presently praying for your success at Wimbledon, but since you are reading this after Wimbledon, I want to congratulate you on your effort and determination to be a champion. You truly are the hero of this family, Josie.

We have been so busy over the last couple of years that you and I have had very few moments to slow life down to a speed that would allow for us to articulate to each other the verbal intimacies that we so frequently shared in our earlier days. Just in case you haven't heard from me in a while the specific ways in which you mean so much to me and the ways in which you still drive me as wild as you did the first day we met in September 2005, I want to refresh your memory.

The confidence that you displayed and the way in which you carried yourself, as well as the leadership that is so obviously within you, pales in comparison to any woman I have ever encountered in my lifetime. When I first saw you that day in 2005, sitting in the first row of our Friday classroom in your senior year, I knew that you were someone special. It's funny how we get that feeling about people we don't know, but it speaks volumes about the silent nature of a person, their expressions, and the way in which they move. I knew beyond a shadow of a doubt, more than anything I have ever been positive of in my life, that I wanted to get to know you as soon as possible. Thank goodness our Father in Heaven felt the same way about us, and it was so amazing how He so quickly did bring us together. I am forever grateful to Him for sending me you.

The way that you are with our son is so amazing to watch. The most beautiful thing I have ever witnessed in my life in addition to your immense beauty was the first time you put your face together with Michael's face and snuggled with him. The smiles that you and he both made when you did that were the two most beautiful smiles I have ever seen—ever. There is nothing like the beauty of a mother with her son.

Oh, my Josie, it's hardly possible to even remember anymore the feeling I had each day before I met you. Not a day goes by where I don't at least for one moment still have the thought to pinch myself and make sure that I'm not dreaming. You have brought me so much joy and happiness, my sweet darling, that I truly feel like I am the luckiest person who ever lived. Not just the luckiest because I get to be loved by you, but lucky because I must be the only person who has ever lived, that knows how truly amazing it is to love you as deeply as you allow me to.

I can't wait to get you into my arms again, and I will not let you go for hours. You are the love of my life, and I miss you very much.

Your forever loving husband,
James

The morning after writing the note, Michael and James got on a plane and headed for England. The two of them were attempting to arrive at Josie's tournament without her knowing. They were so excited to surprise her at the stadium, and she was quite shocked to say the least.

Wimbledon in 2008 marked a number of milestones throughout James's world. His PhD was finished, and Josie was a worldwide superstar woman's tennis player with a Wimbledon Championship under her belt. Jack was drafted by the Detroit Tigers in the tenth round of the Major League Baseball draft that took place on June fifth of 2008. Consequently, Jack would be heading east for the short-season New York–Penn League that summer and would be closer to James in New York as he starts his professional baseball career. Ben was now a sophomore political science major at Indiana University. It was quite demanding keeping up with that high of a level of curriculum at first, but he is blossoming into a great student. Lisa was a year ahead of him at the university, but because Ben took a heavy load in the two summer semesters, he has caught up to her in credit hours for graduation, so they'll graduate together. It's already been almost three years since Ben began reading books from the loft, and already, he is showing signs of exceptional academic talent. As he and James plan on doing great things in the future, Ben was doing his part to make sure those dreams were to become realities. Not until just recently has Ben Wilson started to think about law school at the end of his undergraduate degree. Nevertheless, 2008 proved to be the year of milestones in James's life, as well for all those who are close to him.

Because of Josie's busy tennis career and how pressed for time James was with his PhD thesis, James decided not to volunteer for the 2008 Republican presidential campaign. He had received valuable experience in the 2004 reelect campaign, but this time around, it just wasn't feasible for him. Besides, things were beginning to look not so great on the surface in Washington in terms of the unity of the Republican Party. The Grand Old Party (GOP) in America was heading for a split, and the likelihood of a Democratic win this fall was becoming more and more probable. It is ironic that James came to New York with the mission of giving long-term hope to conservative politics because the Republican Party was about to head through six years of bad times. In lieu of these developments with the GOP, it is quite ironic that Ben just wrote a twelve-page essay at Indiana University on the subject of wedge politics. That is when a political party or group of people from a campaign, devise a plan to create a split in the political party that they are campaigning against. The idea is to break the opponent down into smaller parts, which is ironically exactly what is going on with the modern Republican Party in Washington. They are being broken down by the Democratic establishment through lies and deception. America will get wise to it though, but it will take some time. The GOP will be back.

James had mentioned to Josie that it was a good time to see about the job interview he had previously with Steve Lampley from the CIA. The reason being, the secretary was going to be leaving the President's cabinet if a Democratic president was to replace Bush. Secretary Joe Purcell was a young politician and would run for Senate after his departure from Homeland Security. And he would get it, so now Senator John Purcell has his son, Joe, in the Senate with him.

Josie's tennis career is greatly enhancing the popularity of her husband, as she has developed a couple of nice friends in the world of tennis media. She is truly putting James on the map, and that will help greatly one day when he enters politics. Not only are Senator John Purcell and Secretary Joseph Purcell helping him, but he has a superstar tennis player for a wife, which is a huge advantage in politics. However, it will, in the end, ultimately come down to the perception of the American people, and so far, James is already high on many people's darling list.

James has always believed that he would not be able to accomplish his dreams alone. His grandfather mentioned it before that he will need much help to truly be successful achieving a goal as lofty as the White House someday. From what Josie has brought to the partnership early on through tennis, she is building the platform where the political career of her husband, James Ryan Roberts, will one day spring from.

———

Back at the condo in New York on Tuesday evening following Wimbledon 2008, James and Josie are just hanging out on the couch and eating snacks after Michael finally fell asleep in his bedroom. They haven't had many times like this with how busy her tennis career has been and with James finishing his PhD. Many married couples after about three years of marriage start to grow apart from each other. However, James and Josie are as in love as they were the night they met at Low Steps before the September 11 tribute in 2005. The time they spend apart has not weakened the relationship one bit as it was feared that it would. On the contrary, it has worked in the opposite way and caused them to long for each other even more, and when they do finally see each other after two weeks apart, it's as if they fall in love all over again.

Josie decided to take a much-needed break after Wimbledon, and take some time and celebrate James's getting his PhD. James had mentioned that he wanted to head to Connecticut and see Jack play in the NY–Penn league. The season started in early June, but there are still a couple of weeks left, so they'll get to hang out and see him play. The question will not be whether or not they will get to see him play baseball. The greater concern is this: will the media leave James and Josie alone long enough to enjoy themselves with Jack? They won't find out until they get there, but the best thing they can do is try to look like normal people and hope the sunglasses and hats will help disguise them as ordinary pedestrians.

"Do you think we'll have trouble with paparazzi in Connecticut?" James asks.

"There's no telling. The best thing we can do is not look like the Roberts family, just for a couple days at least," Josie suggests. "Lets buy a couple of big sombreros."

James mentions, "We can keep to the parts of the ballpark that are not populated." These ball parks that Jack will be playing in, do have many areas down the left field and right field lines, where people can have a little more privacy at the game. They aren't good seats for viewing the game, but that is precisely why they are less populated. Anyways, there will be spots to sit for them to maintain their concealed identities,

"Sounds like a plan, James."

The next morning, they gather up some things and take Michael to see his Uncle Jack play professional baseball. The Wednesday morning that they left was a monumental day. James received a letter in the mail from a publishing company saying that they were going to publish the manuscript he had sent them while Josie was leaving for Wimbledon. James was so excited, and Josie was surprised because she had no idea he had anything else that was finished other than the PhD thesis.

This particular book that James wrote was mostly written back in Macomb before he graduated from high school. The book is called *Raphael's Commission*. It is about the competitiveness that transpired between Michelangelo and Raphael during the Italian Renaissance. It was a completed book before James ever attended Columbia, but there were some things he wanted to fix in it, and he found very little time to work on it with school being so demanding. Nevertheless, he finally got some time to revise it and mailed it out just about three weeks prior to publishing.

"Oh, I'm so proud of you, James," Josie says. "You never cease to amaze me."

"Thank you, sweetheart. I was just as shocked."

"I'm not shocked, my dear James. You are very talented."

"The funny thing is I wrote it years ago when I was a teenager, but just didn't feel that it was finished."

"Well, they must have really liked it," Josie says.

"I worked so hard on that book. It was quite difficult to accomplish it without going to Italy, but lucky for me, I was able to get it finished."

"That calls for a celebration tonight," Josie suggests. "Where do we go?"

"What do you have in mind, my beautiful flower?" Josie is staring into space, trying to come up with a good idea to throw a party.

"It will be my secret, James." She has this devious look on her face, as if she knows the whole plan.

"Hmmm, sounds mysterious," James says. "Will I be invited?"

"To give you a hint, I shall give you your prize after we get Michael to sleep this evening," Josie reveals, while James is quite taken by what she just said about after putting Michael to bed. He has this smile that stretches from ear to ear. She giggles.

"Okay, I'm on the same page now. Can't wait!" James says with a big smile. "Really can't wait to see this surprise tonight."

James didn't have time to contact the publishing company right away, but when they arrived in Connecticut, he was able to get them on the phone. They must have been trying to call while they were in Wimbledon and just couldn't get through. Once he did talk to them, they wanted him to come back to New York to set up a meeting with him and his literary agent, Calvin. James was able to tell them that he'd be back on Friday, but he didn't want to reveal why—he just wanted to spend a couple of days with his brother, Jack.

The next couple of days were about nothing but baseball, going out to eat, and taking care of Michael. Jack was so happy from the visit; he didn't think he was going to see James for a while. However, they were able to spend a lot of time together. On Thursday night, James and Jack went down to the local dive bar and really got caught up while Josie stayed with Michael in the room. James strolled in that night at 1:00 a.m. and when he finally got to bed, he found that Josie had another planned surprise. She woke as soon as he got underneath the white sheets. It wasn't until that moment that James realized she wasn't wearing very much, and she rolled over and attacked him like a reptile seizing her kill.

When they left on Friday morning to head back to New York, James and Josie hugged Jack good-bye. Jack was only eighteen years old and had never even been away from home. James noticed a level of sadness in his demeanor as they were leaving, but Jack is a tough kid, and James knows it. James told him to call him on his cell phone anytime day or night. Now that Jack has a phone, he can keep in touch with his brother regularly.

James walks into the publishing company on Friday afternoon and was met in the lobby by his agent.

"Congratulations, James! First ones are always the sweetest ones," Calvin said. You look great."

"Thank you, Calvin," James says. "I appreciate that. I was shocked."

"Well, apparently, they weren't," his agent, Calvin, says. "They loved the manuscript."

This would be a moment of pride for James because of how financially supportive his wife has been so far in their young marriage. Josie could tell that it was starting to weigh on James that he wasn't working, but this more than made up for it. It may not produce money right away, but James can now be considered a writer, and that was an honorable profession. This endeavor has sparked up curiosity in James whether or not his other three pieces of literature might be good enough to be published as well. This one was a little easier to get prepared for publishing, but the three other pieces may take some work. At any rate, that will be his immediate concern—to get those other books he wrote as a teenager, ready for a publisher to look at. He and his agent walk into the publisher's office.

A few hours later, James was back in Morningside Heights for a celebration at Amsterdam's that Josie orchestrated. He had thrown her parties before, and it was time for her to return the favor. James had a friend at the party named Tony, who asked him, "What is the book about, James?"

"I wrote about the Italian High Renaissance architect and painter, Raphael."

"Why'd you choose him to write about?" Tony asked. "What did he do?"

"Actually, I wrote this book when I was sixteen years old."

"Wow!" Tony says with a surprise.

"I was always fascinated with the threesome of Michelangelo, Leonardo Da Vinci, and Raphael, all being considered the three greatest artists. Yet not much is said with regard to Raphael, and I wanted to do something about that," James confesses. "He's just as great a painter as the others are, and I think he should be revered as much." James is so passionate about art.

"That's interesting, James. Can you tell me more?"

"I have always thought that the competitive spirit that Michelangelo and Raphael shared between them was more significant than history shows. With that said, I don't believe Raphael received his due credit with regard to modern popularity and significance."

"I never heard of him," Tony confesses. "Who is he?"

"Most people haven't. That is why I wrote about him."

"Well, I look forward to reading it, James."

"Thank you, Tony. The thing that inspired me the most about writing the book was that Michelangelo at times was envious of Raphael, and if that existed between them, then Raphael must have been as great, or greater than his modern popularity indicates."

"Makes sense to me, James. Anyway, congratulations." James is pleased with his kindness and interest. He has always liked Anthony's humility.

"Thanks again," James says with pride.

After a week of training for Josie in preparation for her upcoming tournament, James goes back to working on his other three books. The first one he chose from them was the one that he has the least work to do. It is a fictional novel about the mentoring of a grandson via the wisdom of his grandfather. It was inspired by the relationship he had with his grandfather, Michael. Needless to say, it was probably the most enjoyable piece of literature James has ever written to date, simply because of the closeness that he and his grandfather shared. It originally started off as a personal journal, so Jack could grow up reading about his grandfather. However, after proofreading what he had, James came to the conclusion that it might be good enough to turn into a book. So he was inspired to turn it into a novel.

CHAPTER 12

Former Secretary Joseph Purcell contacted James, and wondered if he'd meet up with Steve Lampley of the CIA again for a second interview. James agreed, but not without him thinking it was odd having so much time in between interviews. One must assume that Steve Lampley was on the same page with James originally regarding him wanting to finish his PhD before committing to an agency. Nevertheless, this time, James would meet him in Langley, Virginia. Once that interview was over with, James would be an employee of the United States government. His first job would be working for the Central Intelligence Agency (CIA) as a Middle East research analyst. His duties at first would be reading Arabic and Persian media publications and books and simply writing reports regarding anything that would be detrimental to the national security of the United States of America.

When Josie returned from an out-of-town tournament, they celebrated privately together, as James didn't want anyone to know where he was going to be working. They had to head to Virginia and look for a temporary place until they could sell the New York condo. The governmental and political resume has begun for James Ryan Roberts. The CIA will give him valuable experience in foreign affairs, especially in an important region such as the Middle East. That area, especially Iran, is becoming ever so central to world conflict, and it's only going to increase for years to come. Those Persian language lessons are certainly beginning to pay off for James, and the US government is greatly appreciative of his expertise on the very subject.

At dawn, just before the earth's rotation reveals the sun on the horizon to the east, the sky is decorated with a rainbow of colors. James sits on his favorite park bench near the Hudson River and finds it a magnificent sight to see the sun come up in New York. James just happened to be visiting Columbia this weekend. An old friend from Apostolos Campus Ministry was getting married in Manhattan, and he would have to go stag, with Josie busy at home with Michael and preparing for a tournament. Over the last six years, James had spent many mornings at dawn, sitting with the whistling birds which frolicked in the wet grass. Much of his hard decision making came at this very park bench on campus, as James finds it to be the most tranquil spot in New York, especially at dawn.

Even though James's undergraduate degree was important to his education and to his acceptance into graduate school, he had already been more prepared intellectually than most high school graduates were. The second he arrived in 2002, right out of high school, he had truly been ready to go straight to PhD. However, the bachelor's degree was a necessary three-year formality that couldn't be avoided. In addition, the book publishing was also a major academic accomplishment, even though he had written it as a teenager. With that said, James has about as impressive of an education that any twenty-four-year-old could possibly have— and from Columbia University.

When considering dreams that are as high-reaching as James has in politics, nothing could have been more impactful to his future success than that which transpired in September 2005. That is when he met Josie at Low Steps on that Wednesday evening—the night before the 9/11 tribute speech—when she made the first move and came up to him. That was the single greatest thing that happened in his life that would give him the best possible chance to reach the White House one day. Every great person or organization, no matter what or where they come from, needs the support and stability for the rate of their success to be optimum. The strength that comes from that stability and support needs leverage to lean on—that is, if it's going to remain standing strong through adversity. The most important thing for all of this to come to fruition is the foundation upon which it truly stands. Therefore, an organization or an individual is only as strong as the foundation with which it can position itself upon, and James and Josie as a couple have truly built one with their marriage that is truly unparalleled in America.

Josie's success in tennis and sports media, as well as the character which she shows in everything that she does, has created a public image for James that is unmatched by anything that any young politician could have ever dreamed of. This will eventually shave years off of the journey to his ultimate goal, and that is to be president of the United States one day—something that normally takes a man until he's in his fifties or sixties. He could now be a threat to break Teddy Roosevelt's record of being the youngest ever president-elect. At twenty-four years old, James will have about eighteen years to reach that long-standing record of Roosevelt's.

From all that James had learned from his grandfather and all that has taken place in New York over the last six years, James is perfectly positioned to win the hearts and minds of the American people someday soon. Josie has done a masterful job in expediting that possibility with her worldwide popularity through women's tennis. Grandfather Michael was so right about lofty goals like James needing a marriage partnership such as he has found to provide the stability and complementary attributes that are greatly needed to create one dynamic institution of marriage, for the challenges of Washington DC. That is important in a realm where it isn't what you know, it's who you know, and it's not what you can do, but it's what you have. Grandpa Michael was the mentor that got this ship sailing years ago, and with what he did in Vietnam, he really provided the opportunity, but James and Josie are really the engine that is bringing this opportunity alive and turning it into success.

James leans back on the park bench next to the Hudson River, crosses his legs, puts his hands behind his head, and ponders. He reaches back into his mind and thinks of all that has happened in the last six years, and then he gets a little choked up when he thinks of the single greatest moment that truly provided the possibility of a career in Washington someday. That moment was what his grandfather did on that day in Vietnam while hanging from a helicopter holding the senator's life in his hand. Without the courage and heroism of his grandfather on that day, which caused Senator John Purcell to be indebted to him for life, James couldn't have gotten this far and this fast. James would have been a success story no matter what, but certainly not President, not without the Senator's help. However, with the influence of Senator John Purcell and Senator Joseph Purcell, James found himself at Columbia University with this wonderful opportunity, that ultimately, was provided for, by his grandfather's heroism in the war. However, the impact that the senators have made to get James to this point is only the beginning.

James dreams of his future while sitting with the wildlife that surrounds him on the park bench. He has no idea what lies ahead beyond the CIA. At the moment, he can't possibly imagine that the Purcell family could somehow continue to provide opportunity after opportunity. However, little does he know, the biggest impacts that those two congressional connections have made to this point, pales in comparison to that which lies ahead. When that happens, James will take his largest step in terms of leapfrogging the formalities that presidents have to go through in order to someday reach the White House.

James arrives at the condo after the wedding, and Josie greets him in the kitchen for a late night ice cream snack. He's wearing a black tuxedo, and she is wearing pink shorts and a white tee shirt, and she's hopping around their home on a Saturday night in cute little slippers. They sit on the couch with a couple of candles lit on the hearth and discuss the near future.

"So what is the plan in terms of a working commute?" At the presents moment, he's too exhausted to think about work.

"I'm going to do the ninety-minute drive to Langley every day," James says. "For now."

"Are you sure you will be able to do that every single day, James?" With a slight concern for how long that will last before he becomes tired of driving three hours a day.

"It's only temporary, Josie."

"Yeah, but three hours of driving every day?"

"When you're out of town and your parents have Michael, I'll get a hotel room close to Langley on those weeks."

"That makes sense, but I just don't want to see you get burned out," Josie says. He grabs her gently by the head and pulls her close to him, and kisses her next to her ear, and whispers.

"I'll be okay. I wanted the drive from the condo to Virginia Beach to be short. That way, it's convenient for your parents, with them helping with Michael and all."

"That's sweet of you, James. My parents would greatly appreciate that, but it's unnecessary."

"It's no big deal," he says. "Let's discuss it when it becomes a problem." For now, she rests on the issue.

"Well, you better speak up if it starts to become a chore to commute that far."

"I will, darling."

Josie falls asleep leaning against his shoulder, and he continues to finish his ice cream. When he's done, he picks her up and takes her to the bedroom. Once he tucks her in, he returns to the family room, and blows out the candles that are on the fireplace.

He heads out the back French doors, and sits on a chair on the patio and lights up a cigar. He leans back in the chair, folds his legs, and starts to think of everything that is unfolding in his life and career. After about a minute of scrambling from one thing to the next in his head, it instantly comes to him, of what is most important in his life. His faith.

Heavenly Father, thank you for all the opportunities
that you have most generously provided me. Thank
you for sending your son into this world to die for my
sins so that I can speak directly to you. I praise you for
all the good, and I praise you for all that I didn't
understand that was important for me to learn from.
You are an amazing God, and I could not have made it
without you. Bless my wife, Josie, and my son, Michael.
Protect them from the evil of this world, my Lord.
Lay your hand on me, Father, and guide me
in the direction
that you want me to go in. Don't let me make choices,
my Lord, based on where I want to go, but allow the
Holy Spirit to council
me to make decisions that are best for your will.
Instill in me a pure heart, my Father—one that
can love my neighbors
unconditionally. Love is very complicated,
my Lord, and I
don't truly think that people really understand.
Please bless
me with a love to show them, my Lord,
and one that would be
unavoidable for them. Allow me to be
your lamp of grace in this
world, my Father. I ask these things in the name of
my Lord and Savior, Jesus Christ. Amen.

The first thing that came to James's mind after praying was the fact that he has always wanted to go on a mission overseas.

When he discussed missions with Ben at his and Josie's wedding reception in Columbus, he too agreed that doing the mission early would be most beneficial to his career. That is because, if he waited until later, it might become more complicated if it runs into a young political career. However, James suddenly gets a thought into his head, that he can do something in ministry in the Virginia area instead of going overseas. Other thoughts that are saying that God would have planted him overseas had He wanted him overseas. That he is here for a reason, and he should not think for a second that his being here is not God's doing. So at the moment, the mission is no longer an idea, and the best thing to do is join a local church and get involved in a community. Besides, Josie would not be in favor of both of them being out of the country, especially when considering Michael.

James returns to prayer and begins to ask for a blessing that would enhance both his and Ben Wilson's career.

> Oh, heavenly Father. Give me this blessing
> upon my career and guide me to a community
> in Virginia that needs a servant of your good
> word and grace. Grant me the strength and
> discipline to carry on that task with righteousness.
> Allow for my career with the CIA to prosper in
> a direction that will expedite my opportunity
> in Washington DC someday. Thank you so much
> for sending a friend like Ben Wilson into my life years
> ago. I ask that you place your hand on Ben and
> Lisa and give them a blessing so that they can
> prosper in a way that would allow for Ben to
> meet up with me in politics someday. Bless us so
> that we may be the best that we can be as a team
> so that we can prosper in our first campaign together.
> I'm fully aware of the difficulty and rarity that is
> involved in the chances of someone making it that far
> in politics, but I also know how great you are and that
> you can do anything. Scripture promises that

"greater is he that is in you, than he that is in the world"
(1John 4:4 KJV).
So grant me this promise of your
strength, my Lord, and bless my career, my
most gracious Lord. I ask these things in
Jesus's name. Amen.

After Ben graduates with a political science degree, he immediately heads to law school. He and Lisa marry, and Lisa begins her career as a musician while she supports Ben through law school. Ben spends three years in law school, and when he finishes, he takes a job in New York, working on a political campaign. Ben wants to be an attorney, but there will be time for that. He wanted to get valuable experience learning the ins and outs of a political campaign first. Lisa decided to go into journalism, even though she will continue to do music on the side, and New York is a great place for a journalism career. Once this happens, James heads back to New York as well and gets Senator Joseph Purcell to get him into the State Department. With the valuable intelligence experience he received in the CIA as a part of their Middle East outfit, he is perfectly suited for experience in foreign policy. He'll be very beneficial to the State Department with his Arabic and Persian language skills, not to mention, his intelligence experience.

This would be the last job James would have before he runs for his first political position. Ben is currently gaining great campaign experience in politics, and soon, he and James will be working together in their quest to build a better America as they start their long and arduous journey to the White House. Almost ten years after James graduated from high school in Macomb, Indiana, he is beginning to ripen for his first position in politics. After years of conservative politics being in trouble, the horizon begins to brighten on the side of the right wing. Many in Washington are starting to see the optimism surrounding James Ryan Roberts as America's next great right-wing hope—a right hope.

EPILOGUE

Almost a decade later, James ponders the events that have happened since graduating from high school and losing his grandfather, almost twenty years ago. The first campaign for James and Ben was less than successful, but they gained valuable experience. One of the reasons it was a longshot from the start, was that they were competing with an incumbent Democrat that had been reelected mayor of New York City several times. James wanted to be mayor, but understood that a crash and burn experience was something that was most definitely needed, in order to gain the strength to get to the next level. Several New York publications believed that the campaign was won and lost on a story that the incumbent democrat based his entire campaign on. Their strategy worked, and James was blindsided by the publicity. James had written things in the past about his thoughts on women's liberation, but much of the meaning in which he was writing in, was taken completely out of context by his opponents in the election, and boy, did they run with it. It all started with a liberal news station, which searched with a fine tooth brush, to dig up anything dirty on James. Needless to say, they found absolutely nothing, and in fact, they purposely chose to take his writing totally out of context in order to fabricate dirt on him. It was totally characteristic of liberal tactics, to smear a conservative opponent.

James wasn't exactly disappointed with losing the election, because he is in politics for the long haul. However, he was disappointed with how big the story of him got, of his previously written philosophy on women's liberation. Josie defended him ferociously from her podium in women's tennis. She never passed up an opportunity. Also, she would let go of wise cracks once in a while, that would appropriately poke fun at the feminine left in America, who to tell you the truth, were the specific group that gave wings to this fabrication of lies about James's feelings on women in the first place. What really caused this story to go away finally in the minds of New Yorkers, was Ben's wife, Lisa, who wrote an article that was published by the *New York Times*. In the article she set the record straight with James's specific feelings about his writing, and it spread like wild flowers, and she also spent a lot of the article praising women of Christ, and how nothing pleases God more than a woman that gives her heart to the Lord. It was very powerful, and got rid of the dirt that the New York Mayor fabricated during the election. In fact, in the wake of her article, there was a simultaneous scandal involving the newly elected incumbent mayor. There were photos found of him at a college dormitory party, and the photo showed the mayor smoking marijuana. It was an opportunity for "team James" to bury liberals in New York, but they chose to take the high road, by not stooping to the level of liberal tactics. So, silence was there tactic. A great writer in Washington D.C. once said, "When your opponent is committing suicide, get out of the way" (Charles Krauthammer).

Josie and Lisa together, not only made this story of James go away, but it brought to light how great the four of them are together as a team. This would eventually help James's career, and it would have the opposite effect on women that most people would think. His numbers on women voters were surprisingly high the next time around, so Lisa and Josie were having a great impact.

This was the first time in James's career, that he would put on display, the very conservative values that he possesses, and it would also be the first time for him to see what running for office would be like. It was great experience for Ben, who was beginning to show signs of great leadership in politics, and James knew it. James was starting to notice that asset that Ben was going to have on the next election.

Senator Joe Purcell didn't waste any time getting James back into the saddle, as he got him a job back at the State Department, but this time, he'd be working right beside the Secretary of State. The Middle East was becoming a big problem to America, and James would provide the Secretary with not just a trusted interpreter, but an experience source of Intel on this region of the world.

A couple years later, James got a job at the White House, working as an Intelligence consultant on the Middle Eastern affairs. Word was traveling fast in Washington, of the impressive nature of James, and this time, he made it all the way to the top. James was gaining great experience in very high political places, but he was also being very conscientious about not losing touch with his ultimate goal. He was getting antsy again about running for office.

Senator John Purcell was retiring from the United States Senate, and at his retirement party, he gave an emotional speech. Everyone was there. James, Ben, Josie and Lisa sat at their own table, and the rest of the room was filled with Senator Purcell's family, friends, and colleagues in Washington. His son, Senator Joe Purcell was the host of the evening. James felt more like he was representing his grandfather on this night, more so than representing himself. However, that wasn't the case coming from the perspective of the Purcell family. To them, this retirement party represented old school on the way out, and the future of conservative politics was on the way in, and the Senator made that clear at the end of the night in his speech. James was in his mid to late-thirties, which was an unprecedented age in terms of modern politics, for anyone to be billed America's future, and only be as old as he, was quite an impressive accomplishment for the young man. It was a proud moment for James…a moment his Grandfather Michael would have loved to have seen.

During Senator Purcell's speech that night, he discussed many things in his career, from relationships he built over the years, to the many policies that he worked on in the past. He was proud to have served his country a second time, from the United States Senate. When he spoke of the Vietnam War, his voice got a little quiet, and his speech became a little choked up. It was hard for him over the years to not become emotional on the job when policy was involving military veterans.

Towards the end of his speech, he concluded with an emotional testimony of his friendship with Major Michael Stapleton of the United States Army. When he looks back now, and thinks of the beginning of their experience together in Vietnam, it's easy to see now, how much of an impact that relationship had on so many lives. The Senator wipes his eye, and pauses for a moment while revealing his conclusion. At the end of his talk of the war, he speaks of the Major saving his life, and how he wanted to return the favor somehow.

"I was sure on that day back in Vietnam that I wasn't going to make it home alive," the senator says. "Had I not met Captain Michael Stapleton, I wouldn't be standing here talking to you, I'd be dead." He spoke of how difficult Major Stapleton was with regard to his cooperation about letting him pay back his debt that the Senator felt he owed him. He ends with a short word.

"There's a young man in this room, and many of you who know me well, know exactly who I'm referring to." James and Josie grab each other's hand and smile with pride, as Ben and Lisa both look at them as if they are one strong team. "At first, it started out as a debt." The Senator stated. "However, it quickly turned into this realization that James was the most promising young man he had seen in Washington in forty years. It was no longer a debt, but it became a duty to the American people, to pave the way for a better future of leadership in Washington D.C." The Senator sheds a tear of pride, while he points a finger toward James, and ends his speech. There's your future, America, sitting right over there." John Purcell says. "Thank you very much, and have a great evening." He leaves the stage, and walks directly towards James and Josie's table, only stopping for passing handshakes along the way.

He and James hug, and share a personal word. "You've always been like a son to me, James, your grandfather would be proud." The Senator hugs Josie as well, and has a brief exchange of laughter with her. "Take care of America's future, Josie." The Senator turned back towards James. "You have not surprised me one bit, James, as I have always known that you had greatness in your bloodline. If you ever need anything, I will always be there, as will my son Joe."

"Thank you Senator, My grandfather would have loved to be here tonight." James drops a tear into a napkin, while Josie puts her arms around him.

"I know he would, son." John Purcell says while he walks away.

The Senator returned to his wife, and sat down to have a drink. Then, the night returned to what it was intended for, a celebration of Senator Purcell's career. This was fine with James, as he was beginning to get a little uncomfortable with the unnecessary attention. It's not that he's not cool with the exposure, but he doesn't like it out of respect for the Senator, as it is his night of honor. However, it was the Senators intention to praise James in front of all of his Republican colleagues.

James and Josie dance the night away with Ben and Lisa Wilson. For once, the four of them have a chance to celebrate the beginning of great years together.

Two years later, James would run for the United States Senate, and he would win by a large margin. He was now the Senator of the state of New York. Being a junior senator is somewhat difficult for every politician, but James still managed to ruffle the feathers of his Democratic opponents on the other side of the floor.

Josie took a leave of absence from the game of tennis, and seriously considered retirement, but for now, she hangs up the sneakers. Her career was magnificent even if she doesn't return. She was the first women's tennis player, to complete the grand slam in a single year. She won the French Open, Wimbledon, Australian Open, and the U.S. Open all in the same calendar year, which hadn't been done since 1988, when Steffi Graf did it. Josie became the best women's tennis player of her era. However, for now, she wants to be with her son, and enjoy her marriage to her loving husband, James. Her dreams are his dreams now, as a women's place is with her husband.

James would do great things as a young Senator from New York, though it is customary for junior senators to be quiet early in their career, James couldn't help himself, and developed a reputation as a very intelligent and persuasive advocate against the status quo. He'd been in Washington long enough, to know what needs to be changed, and he was on his way to making it happen. Democrats couldn't stand him, but he was excellent at blocking it out, and developed a reputation for a willingness to spread bipartisanship throughout the Senate. Before he arrived, the Senate was not bipartisan at all, as it was turned upside down by the divisive Democratic president that replaced Bush. Nevertheless, James was already becoming well noticed as the next star in D.C.

He would run for New York Senator one more time with Ben, and after that, was asked to be the running mate of the next U.S. President. This was his first big shot, to go from the senate floor, to Pennsylvania Avenue as the Vice President of the United States of America. James would gain valuable experience in that office, and after that, then it was him and Ben's time, at the next republican primaries. A little under twenty years since arriving at Columbia University, James was now on the doorstep to realizing his dream, of putting America back on the course for greatness.